A CURIOUS PROPOSAL

Freda Michel

FAWCETT COVENTRY • NEW YORK

"Tell me, do you believe in fairies, Miss Northwood?"

"Fairies, Mr. Penrose?"

"Yes, ma'am. If a fairy were to descend in our midst at this very moment and grant you a wish, may I ask what that wish would be? -er- other than wedding your lost beau, of course."

He sat regarding her closely, stroking his clean-shaven chin as she weighed the question.

"I think I should like most of all to be borne away out of London, as far away as possible," she replied at length. "Somewhere remote where I might find solitude and peace."

"Would Northumberland be far enough, mistress? Way up north on the Scottish Border?"

"It would indeed, sir. Pray why do you ask?"

"Come to me two weeks hence and I will lay before you a most interesting proposal," said Mr. Penrose.

Also by Freda Michel:

SUBTERFUGE   23609 $1.75

A
Curious
Proposal

One

"I-I'm sorry, Francesca, but it would appear I can't wed you after all," stammered the fashionable spark in primrose cut-velvet and gold lace, his anxious brown eyes deviating about London's St James's Park like a distraught butterfly, in a concerted effort to evade the disconcerting gaze of the handsome young female before him, who was struggling to recover her sense of speech.

"You *what*?" she ejaculated at length in a nervous reaction for she had heard well enough.

"Dammit, Fran! How many times must I say it?" vituperated Lord Tristram Fortescue, testily. "I can't marry you—I simply can't! I'm sorry, but there it is and an end on't. I hope you'll understand and not create a scene."

It is a sad but irrefutable fact that nothing in the world is guaranteed to create a scene quite as much as exhorting a female *not* to, which my lord here discovered to his further mortification.

"Not create a scene!" exploded she, her exquisite features growing as red as the lustrous curls peeking from beneath the lappets of her starched linen mob cap. "What

7

do you expect me to do? Simply curtsy out of your life with a polite 'as you wish, my lord' and forget you exist?"

"Sh-Sh, Fran! Everyone's looking—"

"Tristram, you can't be serious! You can't mean it!" she besought him wildly, seizing his huge gold-buttoned cuff to restrain him, for he seemed about to abscond at any moment, and heedless of the curious glances being cast their way by the simpering fashionable ladies with their simpering fashionable beaux parading close by along The Mall. "It's a trick, a wager—be honest, Tristram! I'll forgive you for frightening me so, I promise, only please tell me it's all a horrid ruse?"

How he was to assure her that it was *not* a horrid ruse was something Lord Tristram could not bear to contemplate. He could not even look upon her stricken heart-shaped face, the expression of which pained him more than the anguish in her voice.

"I-It's true, Fran . . . it harrows me, but I'm afraid we can never marry."

"Why? Why?" came her pitiful cry, tears now perilously near. "You vowed undying love for me! You even proposed—"

"It was a long time ago," he tried to vindicate himself, shuffling from foot to foot in acute discomfort. "We were both very young—too young to know what we were about."

"You didn't think so at the time."

"Fran," he pleaded in desperation. "Six years ago I was but a callow youth. I was but eighteen."

"So was I!" she retaliated bitterly. "We would have been already wed, my lord, but if you recall you preferred to wait until you came back from the Grand Tour."

"But by then your parents had departed this life—"

"And I was reduced to the dire straits of earning my living. Is that what you mean?" she parried tartly, suddenly conscious how conspicuously her employer's cast-off gown of blue quilted damask was contrasting with the bevy of finery sauntering behind.

"No—er—n-no, I mean, your straitened circumstances would not be of the slightest consequence, Francesca, but

8

for the fact that they're no more straitened than mine since *my* sire kicked up his heels and Bernard became Marquess, for my brother ain't nearly so sympathetic to my cause."

"Marriage cause?"

"No—er—gaming cause."

"Oh Tristram! You haven't lost *again*?"

My lord had the grace to look shamefaced. "Everything, plague on't."

"So that's it!" she seethed angrily.

"I'm sorry, Fran," he reiterated once more, placatingly. "I know I shouldn't but the green baize beckons me like Selwyn to a hanging. I thought it an excellent way to improve my fortune."

"It never occurred to you, I suppose, that you might lose as you have done every time before, and thus ruin our entire future?"

His fair head shook forlornly as he stubbed a divot with the toe of one gold buckled shoe.

"I now have the unenviable choice of a commission in the army or marrying the Lady Georgina Hesketh—and you know I'm not a fighting man, Fran—er—which seems to leave only . . . Georgina."

"And do you choose her solely because she happens to be an heiress?"

"Of course, Fran! What other reason? Damme, you can't imagine I *love* the female!"

She flung him a look of unmitigated scorn. "You'd rather suffer wedlock with her than me, merely to live in luxury and pay homage to your green baize every night?"

Lord Tristram seemed just as appalled that she should doubt it. "Egad, what choice do I have?"

"If you truly loved me, Tristram, wealth and position would be wholly immaterial," she declared passionately, her tone now supplicating. "You now have no fortune yet I love you no less. We could still find happiness if you're willing to try. Let us run away together, now, this very moment! We have enough money to rent a cottage and an acre of land. Oh Tristram, think how wonderful it would be!"

This, Tristram was striving his level best to do though the strange hue and distortion of his personable countenance as he fidgeted with the feathered fringe adorning his modish cocked hat would seem to indicate he was not achieving much success.

"We would live happily ever after, together forever!" she rhapsodised, visualizing the domestic scene as the cultivated laughter and affectation of the tawdry pretentious world around them faded into obscurity—perhaps a little too obscure for her swain's peace of mind. "I should sew, bake and feed the livestock—maybe even learn to weave," she giggled excitedly, "while you tilled the land—"

A peculiar asphyxiated sound curtailed her pastoral soliloquy, drawing her starry gaze from the azure heavens to his lordship's face which had graduated from ashen to a sickly green.

"Y-You can't mean . . . w-work, Fran? That I should actually soil my hands like some cloddish yokel?"

Francesca could not resist a chuckle at his incredulous expression and she hugged him impulsively.

"Don't worry, Tristram, you'd grow accustomed to it and eventually even enjoy it. After all, who would have thought ten years ago that I'd be earning my own living? La, my dear parents would writhe in their graves if they knew. It is surprising what one can do when necessity demands."

Tristram was not surprised. He was downright flabbergasted that she should entertain the notion and writhed in sympathy with the deceased Sir Robert and Lady Northwood.

"No, Fran, I-I couldn't, really," he mouthed in abject horror, backing steathily away from her, step by hesitant step. "You don't understand, I've never done so before. I couldn't possibly sacrifice all this . . ." He gestured round the drones of society swarming up and down The Mall. "I could never live anywhere but London. Ecod, I'd wilt and die like a flower out o' sunlight."

"But don't you love me, Tristram?" she besought him

tearfully, clinging frantically to his arm as her cherished hopes began to crumble before her eyes.

"Yes! Yes! Of course I do, Fran, and always shall! But hang me, we must be practical," he remonstrated, endeavouring to extricate his velvet sleeve from her feverish grasp. "No reason why we shouldn't still be friends, sweetheart, but you surely see that I'd only be a burden to you." Here, he finally liberated his bruised arm and began his retreat in earnest, further and further until he was obliged to shout to make himself heard. "So there's nought else for it but for me to sacrifice my happiness with the woman I love and shackle myself to Georgina ... Good ... bye ... Francesca."

Before she could voice any further protest he had rounded on his fashionable red heels and vanished amidst the throng of courtiers, macaronis, dukes and duchesses, lords and ladies, all clad in a blaze of silks, satins and brocades of every hue, priceless gems, frizzed toupees, lace fripperies and hooped petticoats, and who tittered behind masks and gaily printed fans to conceal their identities and decaying teeth as they responded with fatuous laughter to the droll wit of their equally droll companions.

It was then that Francesca realised with a pang of despair that it was nevertheless the world to which Lord Tristram Fortescue belonged. How could she hope to compete with such? Oh how naive she had been to believe that love alone would be enough for their marriage and happiness to thrive upon—enough for herself, perhaps, but evidently not for Lord Tristram who was, after all, brother of the Marquess of Wrixborough and who had been accustomed to having his expensive tastes indulged accordingly. And no matter how she battled to convince herself that Tristram still loved her in his own way and her scheme had been admirable in every respect, she was forced to concede eventually that such a marriage would have been doomed from the outset with the constant lure of the great metropolis hanging inexorably over their heads.

Francesca stood stricken for some considerable time,

staring with unseeing eyes at the beautiful people until tears began to descend one by one, two by two, and the scene became a colourful blur as if she were staring at a rainbow through a heavy shower; and to hide her shame and bitter mortification she stumbled blindly away across the open parkland where she collapsed on a wooden bench in a deserted spot and cried as if her heart would break. To think the afternoon had begun so well. She had been so full of elation upon this the half-day holiday her employer was pleased to grant once each month; she had run in eager haste all the way from Clarges Street, her feet scarcely touching the cobbles until she was quite out of breath and her heart was beating wildly, not solely because of her running but in anticipation of seeing Tristram, *her* Tristram, the man she loved with all her being.

How long she cried she neither knew nor cared. Her whole world along with all her cherished longings had crashed about her ears in ruins and time now seemed meaningless. Nothing mattered any more for without her beloved lord she had no future, no life, no choice but to remain in bondage to the Baroness Brindley for the rest of her days. At this ghastly prospect Francesca snatched off her frilled cap into which—as she had forgotten her pocket-handkerchief—she cried harder than ever.

This, it must be said, was somewhat alien to Miss Northwood's cheerful well-ordered disposition. Moreover, as companion to one of society's most fastidious matrons she was obliged to maintain a sense of decorum at all times and to school her emotions accordingly, even in adversity's darkest hour. But the recent blow was too much, even for Miss Northwood who was too distraught at that moment to pay the slightest heed to what her employer would say when she anon returned to Clarges Street with red swollen face and eyes to match. One must not assume that Lady Brindley was not one of the most considerate employers a girl could have, indeed she was; but it was not to be compared with having one's own home and children, and a life of wedded bliss with the man one loved.

Something else Miss Northwood did not heed was the fact that she was no longer alone.

"Good gracious me! My dear child, what on earth can have overset you so?" exclaimed a mature masculine voice of a sudden. "Surely at your tender age the world is not such a terrible place?"

Up bobbed her head with a start and at the unexpected sight of an elderly gentleman in austere clerical garb of black frock coat, large brimmed round hat, gaiters and white Holland stock she flushed with embarrassment and made haste to dry her eyes and tidy her appearance as best she might.

"I-I crave your pardon, sir. I was not aware that anyone was passing. Pray forgive my momentary weakness."

"And an educated female, to boot! By Jove, ma'am, the tribulation must be of some magnitude to reduce such an one to these lamentable depths. May I venture to ask if I might be of assistance? Indeed," he hurriedly appended, "you are under no obligation whatsoever to satisfy the curiosity of an old man. However, you do seem in need of a sympathetic ear which, I am told, I am rather adept at giving."

Francesca readily accepted the offer and poured out her tale of woe.

"It is but a moment, honoured sir, since the man I love . . . sp-spurned me in favour of another of . . . b-better fortune," she stammered brokenly, her eyes downcast upon the damp cap which was now twisted out of all semblance of such. "I had hoped to wed him in the not far distant future."

"I see," accorded the gentleman, a wealth of understanding in the two simple words. "And you feel there is no hope of a reconciliation?"

She shook her head and sniffed wretchedly.

The gentleman pursed his lips, pensively. "Alas, a tragic situation and no mistake."

"Indeed I should have been able to leave my position as companion to a certain venerable lady but now I shall be obliged to stay—and when she forsakes the world I shall be utterly destitute!" she babbled forth in one breath to end on a note of complete abandonment.

"Nay, nay, child," commiserated he, bestowing a paternal pat upon her bowed shoulder. "You are now being a trifle melancholic and rushing out to greet trouble before it has entered in the gate, as my good lady would say. Come, dry your tears and honour me with a smile."

Francesca sat up, wondering why she was confiding so much to this total stranger, and moreover, why he was condescending to listen for her lamentations were anything but edifying, and did her best to fulfil his request. It was as she turned her face full upon him and presented her pathetic smile that the gentleman fell uncommonly quiet. In fact, so long did he remain thus that she began to suspect he had lost interest in her plight which would certainly not have surprised her. Neither would she have been particularly sorry for, although she appreciated he was merely trying to be kind, she had a great yearning for solitude.

But on the contrary the gentleman's interest in the distressed girl was waxing by the second as he pondered whether or not he might be of even greater assistance— greater than she could possibly imagine for, although the girl herself might have been disinclined to believe it, it had not been her convulsive weeping which had first attracted his attention but her striking red hair glinting in the sun like burnished copper, and he had ventured nearer to take a more detailed inspection.

As if coming to a decision he doffed his flat black hat from his bushy white wig—both as affected by the learned and medical professions—apparently anxious to make himself known of a sudden.

"I beg you will forgive my presumption, child, but you seem to be of good breeding," he probed with trepidation generously laced with curiosity, hoping she might deign to disclose her name, and evidently not in vain.

"I am Francesca Northwood, only daughter of—"

"Not Sir Robert Northwood of Leicestershire, perchance?" he completed to her astonishment.

"The same, sir," she accorded eagerly. "You knew my father?"

"Alas no, ma'am. I merely knew of him through the offices of my profession—er—perhaps you would permit me to introduce myself, Miss Northwood," he went on, bobbing forward in a kind of bow. "I am Mr Josiah Penrose of Penrose, Speke and Bull, attorneys-at-law of Lincoln's Inn."

Francesca was duly impressed and rose to respond with a demure curtsy, then resumed.

"My father died all of five years ago, and my dear mamma shortly afterwards."

"Poor child. And you are all alone in the world?" Mr Penrose sounded incongruously hopeful.

"I am, sir."

"With no surviving relative?" he pressed her, striving to quell his enthusiasm.

"None, Mr Penrose. My employer was a close friend of my mamma and she kindly took me up as companion for I was not only bereft of parents, but fortune."

"Excellent! Er—I mean, how tragic! How terribly, terribly tragic!"

How strange, thought Miss Northwood somewhat indifferently, being too conscious of her shattered heart to pay much attention to the gentleman and his peculiar mannerisms as she sat gazing mutely into space, rapt in anguish while the lawyer's small button-bright eyes absorbed every detail of her face, form and apparel from glorious red mane to multi-darned slippers which matched to perfection her multi-darned stockings. Apparently he was not discouraged by what he saw for as he continued his eagerness mounted visibly. "I wish most earnestly, Miss Northwood, that I might be of some help but I'm afraid I am not very adept at mending broken hearts."

She returned a wan smile at his attempt to humour her.

"However," he went on with even greater fervour, "I might be able to—" He broke off suddenly, viewed her through narrowed eyes then asked a rather odd question. "Tell me, do you believe in fairies, Miss Northwood?"

"Fairies, Mr Penrose?"

"Yes, ma'am. If a fairy were to descend in our midst at this very moment and grant you a wish, may I ask what that wish would be?—er—other than wedding your lost beau, of course."

15

He sat regarding her closely, stroking his clean shaven chin as she weighed the question.

"I think I should like most of all to be borne away out of London, as far away as possible," she replied at length. "Somewhere remote where I might find solitude and peace."

"Would Northumberland be far enough, mistress? Way up north on the Scottish Border?"

It was now Francesca's turn to regard Mr Penrose closely, a look of reappraisal, as if trying to establish if he were henchman of God or devil.

"It would indeed, sir. Such a spot would be ideally suited to my need. Pray why do you ask?"

To the lawyer's satisfaction the young lady's curiosity was now nicely on the simmer and he desired nothing more at present as he delved deeply into one capacious pocket of his frock coat to retrieve a small card which he proffered to her.

"Here is the name and direction of my chambers, ma'am. Should you be of the same heart and mind two weeks hence perhaps you would be good enough to call, when I shall hopefully be able to lay a most interesting proposition before you. Of course I hasten to point out that you will be under no obligation whatsoever to accept it. However, I shall be extremely surprised if you do not." He rose to his feet and gave a jerky bow rather like a puppet. "Good day to you, Miss Northwood. I look forward to furthering our acquaintance in due course."

He certainly seemed very confident in the assumption.

"Good day, Mr Penrose," replied she puzzled, watching him as he clapped hat to wig and sauntered off, smiling to himself with the utmost complacency.

Two

Miss Northwood returned to Clarges Street in a state of considerable bewilderment for her entire life had been turned upside down during her brief sojourn in the park. Indeed, which was the greater, her unhappiness at losing her dearest Tristram or her amazement at Mr Penrose and the prospect of his mysterious proposition, would be difficult to estimate. Even so, she did feel it incumbent upon her to enlighten Lady Brindley concerning the former lest her ladyship be on the alert for a replacement companion. She did so to find my lady most sympathetic. In fact, so sympathetic and understanding was she that Francesca felt sorely tempted to relate the whole, including the meeting with Mr Penrose but considered it wiser to hold her peace for the time being as it was more than possible that the proposition, whatever it was, would prove abortive.

Therefore, the strange little attorney in black was relegated to second place in Francesca's mind in deference to Lord Tristram over whom she languished and wept throughout the ensuring days and whom she might have tried to win back from the arms of the Lady Georgina but for a surfeit of Northwood pride. Not until the evening preceding her appointment with Mr Penrose did she finally decide to put Lord Tristram and her broken betrothal behind her, and see what the lawyer had to propose. After all, it would do no harm to listen to the man for he had stated quite emphatically that she should be under no obligation, besides which, a desolate spot like Northumberland sounded very, very, tempting.

Thus was Francesca drawn to the austere chambers of Penrose, Speke and Bull, situated in Old Buildings, Lincoln's Inn, and which she deemed very aptly named. However, upon arrival she would not have been in the least surprised to find no such firm of lawyers in existence for her unusual meeting with Mr Penrose, which now seemed an age ago, had somehow faded into the realm of fantasy, and the image of the incongruous lawyer with his allusion to fairies and wishes had assumed the ethereal quality of a fairy god-father.

But here was no fantasy as she discovered upon ascending the dilapidated stairs to the second floor where sure enough she spied a door with gleaming brass nameplate designating Josiah Penrose, Ezra Speke and Obadiah Bull, attorneys-at-law, established in the Year of Grace, 1746. As the door was invitingly ajar Francesca peered inside to behold a modest office wherein a scribe in sober garb sat scratching urgently with a quill in a large tome. The furnishings were scant and drab as befitting the dignity of the law, and above the empty blackened fireplace—which seemed as if it had never embraced a blazing log in its life—hung a ponderous oak-framed portrait of a most formidable-looking gentleman.

The scribe, a thin young man of about her own age, leapt to attend her and Francesca requested of him to see Mr Penrose, stating that she was expected. She was politely invited to be seated on a somewhat hard unwelcoming wooden settle while the young man absented himself, presumably to seek Mr Penrose. As she waited she idly contemplated the portrait opposite, wondering which of

Mr Penrose's remaining partners it might be. She had finally decided upon the redoubtable-sounding Obadiah Bull when the door swung open and in gushed Mr Penrose himself, rubbing his hands—in satisfaction for it was not a cold day—and beaming most bcatifically, his florid blue eyes dancing over his spectacles.

"Ah, Miss Northwood, ma'am! How exceeding delighted I am that you have condescended to grace my humble office," he enthused with a series of obsequious bows as if she were at the very least a countess. "I feel you will not regret the time and inconvenience to your person. If you would be good enough to sit here, ma'am," he added, ushering her into a more comfortable chair close by his desk.

Miss Northwood was not a little taken aback by such a fervent reception which seemed to imply that she was about to do Mr Penrose a service instead of the other way about. With a further bow he seated himself behind his desk most of which was obscured by a veritable mountain of documents and papers, while his visitor sat upon the edge of her chair, viewing him with an air of expectancy.

"I presume, Miss Northwood, by the very fact of your being here that you are prepared to listen to and, hopefully, consider the proposition I mentioned two weeks ago?"

He paused, peering questioningly over his spectacles.

"I am, sir."

"Good," he approved, then went on. "I am acting on behalf of a client, ma'am, a very rich client on whose authority I shall duly make the proposal."

"What kind of proposal, Mr Penrose?" she urged tentatively, her interest fired along with his.

"That, I shall disclose in due course. However, permit me to say first of all that upon returning from my propitious stroll in St James's Park I wrote to my client divulging all that was necessary concerning your good self and I am delighted to report, ma'am, that my assistant returned but yesterday forenoon with the most encouraging news." His voice shook with excitement. "Indeed, mistress, my client is so well pleased with all he has been told that he would have you depart hence to Northumberland without delay! Er—however," his enthusiasm waned visibly, you have yet to approve his proposition, have you not?"

"Would it be alternative employment of some sort?"

"In a way of speaking . . . in a way of—hum—speaking."

The lawyer's uncertainty on such an important issue threw his listener into some confusion for her ingenuity, keen as it was, did not extend to the medium of mind-reading; and she was, as yet, quite unable to perceive his meaning which he still did not elect to clarify but instead proceeded to sift through the sheaves of papers on his desk while she schooled her impatience.

"Before revealing the intimate details of such," he resumed, finally running the errant document to earth and placing it before him, "I trust you will voice no objection to affirming or denying as the case may be, one or two relevant facts about your good self, as my source of information might be at fault, you appreciate?"

Francesca nodded, gulping down her chagrin.

"No doubt you will bear with me, ma'am, if I tend to repeat myself as a deal of my information comes from your own lips. Er—let me see," he murmured consulting the document, "you are the only child of Sir Robert and Lady Northwood, deceased, of Uppingham in Leicestershire, and due to impecunious circumstances find yourself in the employ of the Baroness Brindley, resident at present in Clarges Street, Westminster. You have been employed thus as companion for the past—hum—four years, prior to which you received an exemplary education under private tutors and later at Dame Rawlinson's Finishing School where you distinguished yourself in petit-point, singing, sketching and horsemanship. You are four and twenty years of age, of unmarried status, and—er—have never done anything—hum—anything—er—untoward."

"Untoward?" prompted she, perplexed.

20

The lawyer reddened considerably, unable to voice in lucid terms exactly what was stated on the agenda.

"Er—defiled God's law, ma'am,"—cough—"a law of a moral nature," was the best he could overture.

"I am still in full possession of my honour, sir, if that is what you are asking," she responded calmly enough.

He smiled his gratitude, heaved a sigh of relief, cleared his throat rather loudly and put aside the document.

"The facts are accurate, Miss Northwood?"

"Quite accurate, Mr Penrose."

The moment of truth was fully come. The lawyer discarded his spectacles and laid them alongside the document with due deliberation, ready to embark upon the most vital stage of the proceedings. He sat awhile in solemn meditation, tapping the tips of his knotted fingers together as if this simple act helped quell the tension within him.

"My client is a most distinguished personage, ma'am, most distinguished," he saw fit to impress upon her. "He is a viscount, no less, of long outstanding lineage, lord of an imposing estate in Northumberland, covering some twenty-three thousand acres. Should you deign to accept my lord's proposition, Miss Northwood, you would be established for life and guaranteed never to want for anything, with your own carriage, town house second to none in Grosvenor Street, and regiment of servants to do your bidding. The doors of society would be flung wide and—"

"Pardon me, Mr Penrose, but in exchange for what?" she broke in to query suspiciously, for it all sounded too good to be true.

"If I might crave your indulgence a moment longer, ma'am, while I divulge the contents of his lordship's proposition as set down in his own impeccable hand."

Suddenly the term proposition assumed an ominous meaning, a meaning all too familiar to Miss Northwood and for which she cherished little enthusiasm. Yes, she had received such proposals from wealthy landowners before—even aristocrats—proposals which did nothing but generate a sickening disgust in the pit of her stomach.

And having placed her interpretation upon the lawyer's words, she rose indignantly to her feet.

"You may save your breath, sir!" she enunciated hotly, smarting at the gentleman's effrontery in presuming her to be a female descended beneath all moral principle. "I am only too painfully aware of the precise nature of such a proposal and I suggest your noble client presents it to a female of fewer scruples. Destitute I may be, but not so desperate as to fling my reputation to the winds and offer myself as diversion to the highest bidder, viscount or no! Good day, sir!"

"Miss Northwood!" the lawyer's shocked voice arrested her progress to the door. "Ma'am, I vow you gravely misunderstand. I swear on oath that nothing is further from my client's intent. Please, may I prevail upon you to sit down again and allow me to at least explain the intricacies? Afterwards, should you still wish to leave then you will be quite at liberty so to do."

Francesca turned to view Mr Penrose with extreme caution, preferring to remain standing where she was in preparation to take immediate flight but equally prepared to hear him out.

"I hasten to inform you, ma'am, that it is all perfectly respectable or I should not have approached you nor had any part in it. My lord stipulates most categorically that the lady must above all considerations be of good birth and unblemished character. Indeed, Miss Northwood, he would offer you the highest honour a man can bestow upon a woman. He would offer you—marriage."

Francesca stood rooted to the spot, gaping at Josiah Penrose as if he had sprouted another nose before re-seating herself with some alacrity lest her trembling limbs should precipitate her upon the polished floor.

"M-Marriage, Mr P-Penrose?" she mouthed, when able. "Did you say marriage? With me?"

"With you, ma'am."

"Forgive me, sir," besought she, bewildered, and like to be for some time to come. "I've never received a proposal of marriage from a peer of the realm before."

It invariably required a surprise of some magnitude to stagger Miss Francesca Northwood for throughout her twenty-four years she had been subjected to a wide variety of shocks but none as great as this, and so she was ready to own herself well and truly staggered.

"But why me? Who is this viscount? I'm sure I don't know any sufficiently well to—"

"You do not know him at all, ma'am. In fact you and he are, I believe, utter strangers. He is Clarence Edward James Montague Fennistone, ninth Viscount Kleine. The estate forementioned is his country seat, Kleine Castle, and is situated in the remotest part of Northumberland amidst the Cheviots. A truly desolate spot, I grant you, but of a rugged grandeur and rare beauty."

"It all sounds so overwhelming, Mr Penrose," breathed she in awe. "Such a man must surely cherish very high expectations of a wife, expectations I, in my humble capacity, would be unable to fulfil."

"On the contrary, ma'am, my honoured client does not want a wife—er—not in the full literal sense." He threw her a dubious glance, wondering how she would interpret this. "He—ahem—would make you his wife for one reason only—to beget him an heir."

"I see. And when his heir has been begot shall I be discarded like an out-moded waistcoat, sir?" she challenged shrewdly.

"Indeed not, mistress!" asserverated the lawyer strongly. "My client is a gentleman and plans to draw up a contract. You will remain his wife—though of course in name only—throughout the term of your natural lives, with all the advantages the illustrious status of a viscountess entails. You will, in truth, lack for nought, ma'am."

"Is this his only stipulation?" she probed sceptically.

"It is, ma'am, apart from one or two of a minor order, as follows." He paused to take up a second document and replace his spectacles upon the end of his thin pinched nostrils. "If I might quote his precise words . . . 'to be of good birth, of robust health, and some degree of intelligence with no peculiarities or irritating mannerisms'—er—I presume you do not happen to—"

"Not that I'm aware, sir," she forestalled him.

"Hum, where was I—ah, yes, 'bereft of all encumbrances—'"

"Human?"

"I believe so—'of a civil disposition and prepared to endure a life of solitude and domestication.' Does this meet with your approbation, ma'am?"

"Is that all?"

"Yes. Would you be prepared to suffer these conditions?"

"To be a viscountess, Mr Penrose, I'd willingly suffer the rack," she rallied him good-humouredly, striving to maintain her self-possession for her head was spinning madly at the very prospect of it all and the devastating effect the news would have upon her erstwhile suitor, Lord Tristram Fortescue. Indeed, it almost seemed as if Mr Penrose's fairy had waved her wand and granted her next most ardent wish because this Viscount Kleine sounded most excellent compensation for the loss of Tristram.

Suddenly her shoulders drooped disconsolately and the light vanished from her eyes. No, it was too utterly fantastic; too preposterous; too unreal. She smiled to herself, even laughed a little, then sobered as she opened the door to cruel reality.

"It is indeed very good of you to humour me in this way, Mr Penrose, when I have been plunged into the valley of darkness and despair," she thanked him wistfully. "I must own I am sorely tempted by your offer but I cannot believe you are in earnest—"

"Miss Northwood, I assure you I do not waste my time nor that of my clients in making worthless propositions. I am in *deadly* earnest."

"In all honesty, sir, you can't think me ideally suited to the role of viscountess—me! It seems so incredible when the man might have the pick of society."

"I know of none better suited, ma'am," returned he with due sincerity, fidgeting with his spectacles for it was quite out of character for an attorney-at-law to pander to the ego of any female. "Can you name one female in modern society who would agree not only to languish in

24

the outlandish north for the rest of her days, but who would not be besotted with fanciful romantic notions? For I stress, mistress, that this union will be a strict business arrangement in every sense—in other words, a *marriage de convenance*. And how many can boast any degree of intelligence?"

"You flatter me, sir."

"No, ma'am. I merely speak the truth as I find it. Moreover, if you will forgive the allusion, your recent trouble of the heart—of which I discreetly made no mention to his lordship—makes you an admirable candidate for you will not be vulnerable in this respect."

On the contrary, she felt extremely vulnerable where this tender organ was concerned, but she appreciated the point he was trying to make, that she would not readily fall in love with another.

"In evidence of my good faith, ma'am, I have already taken it upon myself to recommend you to Lord Kleine in the highest terms."

"And he has given his approval? Wouldn't he prefer to see my likeness first of all? I could send him a minature—:"

"No!" cut in the lawyer hastily. "That would not be wise—er—you see I suspect Lord Kleine desires a plain wife—even unattractive—though he has not said so in actual words, therefore I did not refine too much upon the topic of looks."

"How strange," remarked she.

"Strange indeed. However, I am convinced when my lord anon sees you he will certainly not cavil at your exceptional beauty—er—trusting you duly accept, of course," he appended sheepishly. "All that matters fundamentally is that you are endowed with all the essentials of a normal healthy female."

"And he himself, sir, is a normal healthy male?" countered she, suddenly cherishing qualms on this score. "He is completely sound of mind and body?"

"Indeed yes, ma'am. I have upon occasion met the gentleman—though some years ago. I assure you he appeared quite, quite normal and even tolerably handsome."

Francesca wrinkled her brow, puzzled. "Then perhaps it is his age—he is old? Senile?"

"No, ma'am. He is thirty-one."

"But there must be some drawback, Mr Penrose," she deprecated vigorously, for she was seized all at once by the irresistible feeling that the gentleman before her was not being as explicit as he might and was withholding something of vital import. "You must confess that it is somewhat unusual for a man in such an illustrious position to choose a bride in this off-hand manner, through his lawyer, as if he were buying a piece of property."

"Ahem—I-I'm inclined to agree, ma'am," accorded he, unable to meet her challenging eye.

"You are quite certain you have told me *everything*, sir?"

"Er—no, Miss Northwood," he stammered, squeezing two fingers within his linen stock to ease the sudden constriction round his throat.

"Ah! There *is* a slight drawback," she leapt to the immediate conclusion.

"No, ma'am,"—cough—"a substantial one named Villennay," groaned the attorney like a soul in purgatory.

"Villennay?"

"Sylvestre de Villennay."

"A Frenchman?"

"Of French descent. I believe the man himself has resided in England with the Viscount these twenty years or more and is, ostensibly, as English as you and I." Mr Penrose leaned forward confidentially, managing with difficulty to meet the lady's intent green eyes as she hung upon his every word, the proposition waxing more intriguing with each stammered syllable. "I shall be completely frank with you, Miss Northwood,"—and not too soon, thought she without the flicker of an eyelash—"and confess that I do not care for the man. I have found my encounters with him, though brief, unnerving to say the least."

"In what respect, Mr Penrose?" probed Francesca, feverish with curiosity, her eyes expanding to twice their size. "How much do you know about this Monsieur de Villennay?"

"Very little, I'm afraid," sighed the other. "Apart from the fact that he is aged about thirty-five summers, is a black-hearted unscrupulous rake, and exerts an unhealthy influence over my client!" he rounded off, quite passionately roused.

Francesca's eyes grew even bigger. "And you think this is also why the Viscount desires a wife of robust health? As some kind of protector, or saviour?"

"I am convinced of it, ma'am. I am equally convinced that she must needs be a female of outstanding determination, ingenuity, and resourcefulness, which is also why I recommended you, Miss Northwood."

"But why doesn't the Viscount simply evict this Monsieur de Villennay from his castle?"

Mr Penrose smiled at her naïveté. "Simply, ma'am? Because it could not simply be done, even if his lordship wished."

"You mean, he actually enjoys being dominated by this man?"

"You must understand that Lord Kleine has known the man a good many years. As a child he looked up to him as a boy might an elder brother, a hero, and then like a god. He is now wholly dependent upon him."

"Are you telling me, sir, that whoever marries Lord Kleine must also accept Monsieur?"

"Precisely, ma'am, unless the wife in question is strong enough to exorcise Villennay's influence—a truly formidable task for any female."

Francesca regarded Mr Penrose steadily, searchingly, a look the little lawyer met with unwavering sincerity. "And you consider I am that female?" she questioned with due solemnity.

"Indeed, I hope so, Miss Northwood, for his lordship's sake as well as your own. I admit quite openly that it will not be easy, for Villennay is nobody's fool. But win him to your side and you win the Viscount."

It was a very pensive Miss Northwood who, at length, returned to Clarges Street for she was utterly enthralled by all that had passed between herself and the attorney. So much so, that it was not until she was mounting the steps to her employer's front door she realised, to her dumbfounded astonishment, that not once during the past hour had Lord Tristram Fortescue entered her thoughts.

Three

To wed, or not to wed, is the most important decision in anyone's life, but particularly in that of Miss Northwood who was only too well aware that she would never receive an offer to equal this one, let alone excel it; and whereas she had long cherished the dream of marrying for love, she realised she must now put aside that dream and consider marriage in practical terms as one would an investment—in short, a marriage *à la mode*.

Such a decision was not to be made impetuously, therefore Mr Penrose granted her two full weeks in which to make up her mind; but the determined Miss Northwood required only two hours to decide where her best interest lay and the following morning was confronting the astounded attorney across his littered desk once again to inform him that she was quite adamantly set upon accepting Lord Kleine's generous offer. Following this, Francesca returned to Clarges Street and astounded her employer even more than Mr Penrose by breaking the news of her forthcoming marriage, though, in the most sympathetic words at her disposal. Two glasses of brandy and several inhalations of the aromatic bottle later, the Baroness was becoming accustomed to the idea, and upon realising that her companion was firmly resolved to wed this strange Viscount Kleine whom she herself knew not of and who therefore could not be all he was puffed up to be, she admirably swallowed her qualms and did all she could to assist Francesca in her objective, and even gave her her third favourite gown, of cherry lustring, in which to make her *début* at Kleine Castle.

Consequently, within the week Francesca found herself bag and baggage upon the public stage bound for Alnwick where she was to be met by his lordship's coach and four, and conveyed the rest of the journey to Kleine. The Viscount had most considerately imbursed her with sufficient to hire a private chaise and put up at the most reputable hostelries *en route* but she had sought to economise by taking the public conveyance and contenting herself with inns of modest means in order that she might spend the residue of the imbursement upon a new cloak of green camlet with silver frogs to complement her colouring and enchance her appearance.

Although the journey was compassed in the minimum four days it was nevertheless tedious, allowing Miss Northwood ample time to reflect upon the situation, upon her past and future, recalling her tearful parting from Lady Brindley one moment, and wondering with what manner of gentleman her life was to become so intimately involved the next. She declined to fall into conversation with her fellow passengers, but instead remained shrouded in her thoughts, breathless with excitement at the prospect of wedding her romantic prince and living in a real castle with servants to obey her every command—to suddenly panic in dire fear and question whether she had not acted a little too precipitately and would perhaps live to regret it. But then she would think of the pitiful Viscount, wilting under the ruthless tyranny of this Monsieur de Villennay when her sense of injustice would flare wildly and she would rigorously determine to take up the gauntlet in the Viscount's cause and beat down the French despot.

This was all very commendable in theory but upon ultimately arriving at The Morris Dancers, a noteworthy establishment in Pottergate, Alnwick, Francesca's crusading flame flickered a trifle at the curious reaction of the staff and local patrons to any mention of Kleine Castle, but in particular, the name Villennay. Precisely what kind of place she was bound for she was loth to contemplate any further upon the alarming discovery that she could not utter the name of her prospective spouse nor his plenipotential companion without despatching every lawabiding citizen hot-foot for their rosaries, rabbits'-feet, and sprigs of white heather in order to neutralise any evil the mere mention of these names might invoke. The only person brave enough to venture any opinion was an old rustic of some eighty-three summers who swore on his mother's grave that no one thereabouts had ever clapped eyes upon the elusive Viscount Kleine, so much so, that many believed that no such person existed. Concerning the Frenchman, however, the rustic was not nearly so forthcoming and hurriedly crossed himself before hobbling off to his humble abode as fast as his ancient limbs would allow.

As she partook of a cold collation in the inn's respectable parlour Francesca found it difficult to credit the strange attitude of the local townsfolk. Indeed, warlocks, demons, Rawheads and Bloody-bones—which had fallen from their lips with disconcerting regularity—seemed far removed from reality in such an attractive setting, of the quaint market place basking in the late afternoon sun with flower girls and fruit sellers shouting their wares, and yokels lazing about imbibing tankards of foaming ale or drawing a puff or two from long clay pipes. Miss Northwood smiled to herself as she gazed with affection upon the scene, thinking such simple folk might be prone to exaggerate somewhat and she banished their horrifying tales from her mind, refusing to be intimidated.

Fortunately, though many might have thought otherwise, she was not obliged to wait more than an hour when a chariot drawn by a team of four night-black stallions tore into the inn-yard and shuddered to a halt, and which was by no means the only thing to shudder in and around The Morris Dancers. Francesca did not need to be informed that the black rampant gryphons emblazoned upon the bright red coach panels was the coat-of-arms of Lord Kleine for the abrupt evacuation of the surrounding populace made it very plain indeed that they would not cease to marvel how the young lady was able to smile when *en route* to her obvious doom.

Not a moment was wasted in idle dalliance as coachman and postilion acquired fresh horses and two footmen in the Kleine livery of red and black leapt to attend Miss Northwood and her baggage, the whole manoeuvre being completed in less than fifteen minutes, as if the servants sensed their presence unwelcome.

However, it may be said that upon quitting the friendly town of Alnwick misgiving assailed Miss Northwood when the coach diverted from the regular turnpike road in favour of a somewhat precarious route across the moorland and mountains, a route favoured apparently by no other conveyance but theirs. This did not surprise her for she was flung about, twisted and jolted nigh out of her wits but was eventually forced to own that it had seemed to diminish the overall journey by a good forty-five minutes, enabling them to reach the castle ahead of the darkness which threatened.

It was as they approached Kleine and she leaned out of the coach window to obtain her first glimpse of it that she suffered the greatest misgiving of all to see the old fortress now little more than a ruin though it had been impressive at one time before the marauding Scots had reduced it to its present state. Little had evidently been done to restore it to its former grandeur let alone improve it, as if the owner were utterly indifferent to its fate. And as she thus gazed upon her future home in what could only be termed dismay, at the peculiar jutting towers silhouetted starkly against the twilight sky like skeleton arms waiting to embrace her, Francesca shivered and withdrew inside the coach. Suddenly the friendly faces of the Baroness and Mr Josiah Penrose seemed a terribly long way away, and the ominous tales and doings at The Morris Dancers began to assume an uncomfortable credibility. It was not until this moment that she devoted serious thought to precisely what her dire straits had inveigled her into, and why Mr Penrose had registered such a degree of surprise at her acceptance, almost as if he deemed Viscount Kleine, and not she, were getting the better bargain.

It was growing dark rapidly and she was obliged to strain her eyes through the window on her right to discern the mighty Cheviots rolling away along the Scottish Border, while on her left the wild hills and moorland swept down to Otterburn and Elsdon. A truly desolate spot and no mistake. The coach and four rumbled on through the massive barbican, the main entrance to the castle grounds, though she wondered why they bothered to manoeuvre the vehicle through the narrow aperture when the walls were virtually non-existent.

Shortly before nine, however, she entered the castle to gasp with admiration at the splendour within which contrasted markedly with the decay without, and although her knowledge of architecture was somewhat limited she was well able to identify the genius of Gibbons in the great oak staircase and wainscotting; the artistry of Verrio and Ricci portrayed upon the high ceilings; and dominating over all the baroque mastery of Hawksmoor. Nevertheless, she was not permitted to stand gaping for long before she was invited to ascend to her chamber by a dark whey-faced man of tall gaunt stature and garbed entirely in black.

Anxious not to be caught unawares by the Frenchman, Francesca lost no time in making her first *faux pas*.

"Sir, are you Monsieur de Villennay?" she fired at random, once established in her room where two chambermaids, and a personal maid called Martha waited to tend her.

The man stiffened frigidly to attention. "No, ma'am," he returned with dignity—or was it contempt? "I am Carter, the head footman."

"I-I'm sorry—I didn't realise . . ." Did one apologise

to servants? Evidently not if the expression of horror established on his features was anything to go by.

"I have been instructed to bid you welcome to Kleine on his lordship's behalf, ma'am," bowed he, ceremoniously. "Mr Villennay considered you would be wearied from your long journey and he has therefore postponed the formalities until the morrow. He trusts you will approve the arrangement," he appended in a tone which seemed to presume she would. "If everything is to your satisfaction, Miss Northwood, I shall retire and have supper sent up to you without delay."

Before she could give a yea or nay he was gone on the obvious assumption that she would be hard pressed to find a single flaw in his meticulous preparation. Needless to say, this presumption on the part of Monsieur did nothing but fan the flames of her already blazing prejudice against him; and it certainly did not help matters when she found herself obliged to own him victorious in round one of the contest and confess that she was rather tired. Moreover, had she been called upon to meet her future husband at such a time she would have given but a lamentable performance, and for her first encounter with Monsieur de Villennay she would need every ounce of courage and ingenuity she possessed.

As ordained, supper was served to her presently, a sumptuous meal borne in upon silver trays, and while she ate, a footman stood by to replenish her crystal wine-goblet whenever she so wished, which would seem to be his sole function. Throughout, she strove valiantly not to yawn despite the fact that her tiredness became most acute which was scarcely surprising following the longest journey she had ever undertaken in her life, not to mention the diligence which must surely have been the oldest in service and never missed a pot-hole, ditch, or the opportunity to abandon a wheel; and due to her economy measures she had not sustained a single good night's sleep.

However, that could not be said of her first night beneath the turrets of Kleine Castle for she slept amazingly well in defiance of her apprehension, and woke at almost eleven the following morning to find Martha awaiting her with the conventional cup of hot chocolate while her companions stood by with an impressive collection of gowns for their new mistress's inspection. As she was extremely anxious to appear before her lord looking her superlative best and Lady Brindley's cherry lustring, fetching as it was, clashed rather violently with her red hair, Francesca gave the gowns her fullest attention, especially as they were found to be of superb quality and style. And so she sipped the chocolate while the gowns were presented to her each in turn, and eventually chose one of turquoise damask together with a hoop of grandiose proportions to endow her with the dignity and confidence she felt she might lack.

As she undertook her toilette the gown was whisked away to be altered to fit her shapeliness more snugly and was returned within the hour, when it was found to fit to perfection. In fact the only fault to be discovered was that the décolletage was a trifle too low for decorum, particularly for a first meeting with gentlemen and during the cold light of day; therefore, a silk handkerchief was tucked within to spare her blushes.

By noon her toilette was complete and there seemed little else to do but sit by the window and wonder at what hour his lordship broke his fast for she half suspected she might be invited to eat with him. But no, as the previous night the meal was brought to her in her chamber at the conclusion of which she rallied courage to ask the wheyfaced Carter precisely when she could expect to meet his master, to be informed tersely that it would be 'before very long'.

Actually, it was almost three in the afternoon when Francesca was finally summoned to meet Lord Kleine in the round drawing-room. Upon entrance she was hardly surprised to find it completely circular being situated in the south tower but she was certainly surprised at the magnificence of the room which was by far the most splendid she had been privileged yet to see.

An exclamation of astonishment escaped her, swiftly followed by a sigh of relief to find the room unoccupied, which granted her an opportunity too wonderful to ignore to gaze her fill of all it had to offer. Glass-fronted lacquered cabinets bursting with porcelain treasures from Vincennes, Sèvres and Dresden lining the walls, complemented by gold and silver plate, elaborate girandoles, crystal chandeliers, ponderous gilt-framed mirrors and marble-topped boulle side-tables which matched the scrolled marble fireplace. In front of this the luxurious white fur pelt of a polar bear lay spread invitingly, while chairs and daybeds were scattered at random upholstered in purple velvet to enhance the rich embroidered hangings.

One need hardly state that Miss Northwood put the opportunity to excellent use and pried and peered in every cupboard, cabinet and casket, over the top of the tapestry screen and down upon her knees underneath the furniture. Precisely what she hoped to find—with the possible exception of Lord Kleine himself—remained to be seen. Having explored the rest of the room to her satisfaction she hastened across to the fireplace when she tripped and fell headlong —fortunately upon the fur rug where she sustained no injury to her person though much to her pride.

With a muttered incoherency she turned to view the object responsible and leapt up from the floor as if the bearskin had come to life, for what should the object be but a foot! A man's foot!—very elegant and encased in a silver buckled shoe. She gazed at it in abhorrence for several seconds, frantically willing it to disappear, before her eyes began their daunting journey from foot up shapely bestockinged leg, gartered at the knee, to the liberally cut skirts of a gentleman's coat in mulberry superfine, modestly trimmed with silver braid as befitting daywear—on to a cascade of purest white Flanders lace above which, as she was expecting, a face of the masculine gender met her vision; a face which held her entranced, spellbound. Why, she could not say, as it was not a particularly handsome face, though it had undoubtedly been so ten or fifteen years ago before licentiousness had begun to take its toll. Nevertheless, it was this very wickedness which had moulded its character and made it so arresting—the face of a man who had lived; who had not merely tasted but openly devoured the forbidden fruits of life; a pale face carved with contempt of mankind, and framed by an abundance of long black hair which hung unconfined about his shoulders.

But suddenly she was oblivious to all except the eyes, the most penetrating black eyes she had ever encountered and which she could feel shamelessly, remorselessly, seducing her mind; drawing forth her inmost thoughts and cherished secrets—or was it simply her own excruciating guilt?

"I trust you have sustained no serious injury, ma'am," he drawled in blasé fashion, seemingly unconcerned whether she had or no.

She sprang back further at the unexpected sound for he sat so still she had begun to wonder if he were alive or merely a wax effigy stuck up to keep the servants alert. The voice was lazy in character with its owner, yet she sensed, given the provocation, the man would leap to action with all the agility of a panther.

"May I boldly enquire, m'lady, precisely which feature of my dissipated visage so rivets your interest?" he furthered in similar vein.

"I-I beg your pardon, my lord," stammered she in a pother, hurriedly averting her eyes, for she had never been remiss of her manners before and could conceive no possible reason why she should be so now. Granted, the face was tolerably handsome as Mr Penrose had stated, but surely not handsome enough to blind her to common civility. "I did not mean to stare . . . I'm afraid you took me unawares. I thought I was alone."

"Evidently," he acknowledged, casting a significant glance around the room. "I presume everything is to your satisfaction? Pray feel at liberty to continue your inspection if you so wish," he invited cordially with cynical undertones, as if not really sincere in his offer but were seeking some diversion at her expense. "I vow I should

37

not hesitate to escort you but you appear to have incapacitated my right foot."

"Oh, I am so dreadfully sorry! I beg you will forgive me, Lord Kleine," she cried, frantic with concern. "Oh dear, and I *did* so wish to create a good impression. Perhaps if I were to chafe it a little?" she proffered by force of habit, her years of servitude difficult to break. "Lady Brindley often said I was gifted with the most comforting touch."

A salacious gleam flared in his eye. "That being so, ma'am, I grant you leave to incapacitate my entire leg whenever you feel disposed."

She drew herself up, striving to pocket her indignation.

"My lord, you mock me I think."

"I think I do, mistress."

"Do you know who I am, sir?"

"Miss Francesca Northwood from London," he replied suavely, rising lethargically to his feet to dwarf her five foot three inches with his six foot four. "And do you know who I am, ma'am?"

Doubt suddenly assailed her. True, she had been summoned to meet Lord Kleine had had naturally assumed . . . Once again was she compelled to look into those sinister eyes in obedience to his unspoken command, a command ordained by a will much stronger than her own and which she was powerless to gainsay no matter how she fought—and then she recalled the words of Mr Penrose: 'he is aged about thirty-five, is a black-hearted unscrupulous rake, and exerts an unhealthy influence over my client'

"L-Lord Kleine?" she faltered, stubbornly clinging to this forlorn hope.

"It harrows me to shatter your fondest dreams, ma'am, but our illustrious host is yet abovestairs striving to disentangle his curl-papers. He will be here presently."

"Then you . . . must be . . ."

"Alas, Sylvestre Villennay, the warlock, humbly at your service," he completed, sketching her a graceful leg. "Er—a glass of wine, perhaps? You look prey to the vapours."

Francesca managed against these overwhelming odds to execute a curtsy, and even ventured a weak smile while inwardly castigating herself at making such a deplorable start with the very man she had been so determined to outwit, though equally incensed with the man himself for not correcting her mistaken assumption at the outset.

"No, thank you all the same, sir, wine will not be necessary. I do assure you I am exceeding well. You merely caught me off guard."

"Off guard, mistress?" he queried shrewdly. "Do I detect a challenge?"

"Er—n-no, of course not . . . I simply meant unawares," she stammered in even greater confusion, cursing her slip of tongue.

She fell silent, which she deemed by far the wisest course, still seething and grudging him round two of the game while he brazenly surveyed her, his dark immaculate head to one side and eyes narrowed curiously as if he were reappraising this extraordinary female who had quite literally descended at his feet and who had chosen to take up the gauntlet, musing to himself whether she were to be enemy or ally.

"And I presume you are here, Miss Northwood, to wed my Lord Kleine—with my approval."

The man was being deliberately provoking!

"Your approval, sir?" she parried, taking umbrage at his presumption, tone, and the fact that he was now meandering round inspecting her as if she were on offer at a cattle mart. "Cannot his lordship decide such an important issue for himself?"

He did not readily reply but instead whipped off her modesty piece with a languid nonchalance to acquire a better view of her dangerously exposed bosom, about which she was able to do little apart from gasp, blush and fume with the greatest indignation.

"You will discover before long, mistress," he observed sardonically at length, "that my lord is incapable of doing *anything* for himself."

"Incapable?" exclaimed she aghast, her attention effectively diverted from his impertinence. "But Mr Penrose said quite emphatically that Lord Kleine was not physically disabled in any way."

"Neither he is, ma'am, to all appearances," he responded evasively, whipping off her cap.

"I do not perceive your meaning, sir," she rejoined with asperity, gaining the impression that it was not his intention that she should, while wondering which item of her apparel would next claim his attention, and how far she ought to let him venture before crying quarter.

He gave a wry smile, more a contortion of the lips. "You will, Miss Northwood . . . verily you will. Now would you oblige me by releasing your hair?"

"Monsieur de Villennay!" she protested.

"A simple Mr Villennay will suffice," he corrected abruptly, as if he were loth to be reminded of his origin, which was hardly surprising when the Seven Years' War had but recently ended.

"As you wish, *Mr* Villennay," she stressed acrimoniously, longing to gainsay him yet swallowing her resentment and mutely obeying for to object would be an open invitation for him to execute the task himself; and so removing the pins she allowed her devastating red curls to tumble down nearly to her waist.

If Mr Villennay were as devastated as she hoped he might be he kept it exceedingly well concealed. He certainly did not gasp and languish in admiration as the Lord Tristrams of society might have done for he had not earned his reputation by idle flirtation, and the most beautiful women in London, Rome and Paris had passed through his long sensitive fingers at one time or another. No, it required a great deal to surprise Monsieur, and he was never devastated by *anything*. However, he did fall strangely silent as with one elegant lace-draped hand he raised up her face to scrutinise her complexion for sign of a flaw. At length a pained expression crossed his face and his hand fell away in a gesture of defeat.

"Clarence won't like it above half," he sighed somewhat ambiguously, bestowing the appropriated garments into her hands and turning away.

"Won't like what, sir?"

"If I might volunteer a word of advice, Miss Northwood," he chose to ignore the question. "You could do worse than humour me, and remember at all times that I, and I alone, am your gateway between success and failure."

It sounded perilously like a threat, and the fact that she must own the truth of his words offered little consolation, for had not Mr Penrose proffered the same advice by indicating if she would win the Viscount she must first court the interest of Mr Villennay?—court his interest and then destroy him!

She was just summoning courage to query his advice when the doors flew wide and in paraded Kleine's lord and master with swaggering air. He was taller than she had expected, though not as tall as Mr Villennay, of slender build, and dressed most fastidiously from frizzed toupee to beslippered feet. His lilac coat was of the most costly brocade and the laced cravat at his indeterminate silk-smooth chin was every whit as white and fine as his companion's but unlike Monsieur he was very fair and his face was round, rather boyish.

Lord Kleine continued strutting arrogantly across the room, greatly impressing Miss Northwood who was seized with misgiving at how she was to fulfil the expectations of one so superior and self-assured when, to her amazement and Mr Villennay's despair, he suddenly flung aside the affectation as if it stifled him and dashed up to the Frenchman like a spirited young puppy, ruining the effect completely.

"Well, Sylvestre?" he breathed excitedly. "Did I do it right? Do I look like a beau of St James's, eh? Look! Look at my seals, my snuff-box, my mottoed garters! Aren't they grand?"

Mr Villennay elevated a disdainful eyebrow. "Aye, Clarence but I doubt prodigiously if a beau of St James's would gallop across a room like a filly in full tilt, wholly ignoring the presence of the sex."

Francesca was horrified to see the Viscount wilt before

41

her eyes and look crestfallen like a child in disgrace, his bubbling enthusiasm dying an abrupt death beneath the censure of Mr Villennay which, she was forced to own, had not been uttered harshly. But at this close range what stunned her even more was his looks, for Mr Penrose had pronounced him to be tolerably handsome which was wholly untrue. Indeed, he was not tolerably handsome— he was pre-eminently so! In fact, the term beautiful was the only description she could apply, a term she had never applied to a man before, probably because she had never seen one quite as beautiful. His complexion was peerless, excelling even the porcelain in his collection, and his eyes were beyond doubt the bluest she had ever encountered, fringed with golden lashes; and his rippling golden curls bid fair to rivalling her own.

But this was my lord at his superlative best for it was abundantly plain that he had taken immense pains to appear so. Indeed, but for whom?

It was then that she realised with pungent force that the long hours expended by his lordship prinking and preening himself had not been on her behalf at all, but on Mr Villennay's for he had not yet even noticed her. Once again were Mr Josiah Penrose's prognostications proved right; she had not come to Kleine too soon.

"Shall I go out and do it again, Sylvestre?" he muttered disconsolately, with drooping head.

"No, Clarence. You will make your bow to Miss Northwood who has been waiting a veritable age to greet you." He heaved a sigh of strained forbearance, availing himself of a pinch of snuff from Clarence's box and inhaling it with a practised hand and due deliberation. "There is no need to look so deucedly hang-dog, my dear fellow. Faith, I'll warrant the lady anticipates the laborious procedure with like disrelish." He paused, flicking particles of errant snuff from his impeccable person with languid waves of his perfumed handkerchief. "Pray give me leave, my lord, to present Miss Francesca Northwood." He then turned his indolent gaze upon Francesca who stood upon his right, devoured with apprehension. "Ma'am, be pleased to honour Clarence Edward James

Montague Fennistone, the ninth Viscount Kleine," he rattled off in a voice as bored as his demeanour.

Francesca sank into a billowing curtsy striving her level best to shield her liberally exposed bosom from the gentlemen's view, while Clarence fobbed his box, pocketed it then bowed his most elaborate bow hoping that this would suffice, but Mr Villennay frowned, clearly indicating that it would not, and so he forced himself with immense fortitude to kiss the lady's hand—though as quickly as possible then dropping it as if it were contaminated with plague. This did not bode well for his future bride for it would seem to indicate that my lord was not accustomed to entertaining females, moreover, found them distinctly unpalatable.

However, at least one good purpose was served for Francesca quite forgot her own anxiety in concern for that of the Viscount, and she even ventured a comment as the formal introduction had left a most disconcerting silence upon the air which neither gentleman felt disposed to break.

"You look very elegant, my lord, if I may . . . say . . . so . . ."

Her voice petered away as Clarence flung her a withering glance. No, apparently she was not at liberty to say so. Neither was her opinion to count for anything in competition with Sylvestre de Villennay's, the sun-god whom Clarence clearly worshipped if the blind adoration shining in his eyes was to be relied upon.

"Is this the woman you would have me wed, Sylvestre?" he questioned, trying not to grimace.

"Don't you like her?"

His lordship honoured Francesca with a longer look, and scowled petulantly.

"You promised she would not be beautiful. Look at her! She's almost as beautiful as I!"

Modesty would not seem to number among my lord's better qualities.

"If I must wed at all, why can't I wed Jenny Hobson?" he grumbled, peeved.

Mr Villennay raised his eyes ceilingwards. "Aristocrats worthy of the distinction, Clarence, do not wed dairymaids. It is essential that your offspring be of pure extraction."

Clarence shuffled awkwardly, casting baleful eyes at his prospective wife.

"Very well, I suppose she'll have to serve," came his deflating verdict at length, appending on afterthought: "Do *you* like this one, Sylvestre?"

This evidently implied that many had gone before whom the Frenchman had not, thought Francesca, bracing herself for his answer as Monseiur was the type of gentleman to openly deliver the contents of his mind regardless of cost in humiliation to his subject. Fortunately she had grown accustomed to insult since her reduction in circumstance, and was therefore able to weather it with a discreet silence when occasion demanded, though she was definitely not accustomed to gentlemen discussing her merits at such inordinate length as if she were not present when she quite obviously was.

Mr Villennay's unprecedented silence goaded the Viscount.

"Well, *do* you?" he persisted irritably.

"It doesn't signify, Clarence," he replied finally, again deftly evading the issue. "You forget, my friend, that *you* are to do the wedding, not I."

This, the Viscount did not enjoy being reminded of.

"Must I get wed, Sylvestre?" he whined. "Can't I simply—"

"You want a child, do you not?"

"Yes! Yes, more than anything!"

"Then you have no choice."

"But he will have red hair, and throw tantrums!"

"Not necessarily, Clarence. Do you throw tantrums, Miss Northwood?" he turned to query with commendable patience.

"If I did, Mr Villennay," she responded pleasantly, "don't you think I should have thrown one before now?"

The Frenchman indulged in a cryptic smile. "I think Miss Northwood will suit admirably, Clarence," he opined with languid amusement, his eyes not deviating from hers.

44

"Very well, Sylvestre, I'll wed her," my lord capitulated dismally, prepared to make the best of it. "S'pose I ought to have taken a wife years ago. Huh, kept putting it off like a tooth extraction."

Francesca was not very flattered with the analogy.

"Evidently it has not occurred to you, Clarence, that Miss Northwood may not wish to wed you, after all." Mr Villennay enlightened his lordship significantly. "You may not be quite what she expected, therefore it is only fitting that we grant her time to reconsider."

Monsieur was not mistaken. This had not occurred to Clarence and the stupefied expression upon his countenance would seem to confirm it. Indeed, he did not know quite what to say.

"Am I not what you expected, ma'am?" he asked Francesca with the ingenuousness of a child.

Frankly, no. Granted, she had expected a man somewhat quiet of manner and a little withdrawn—certainly not one who had been cloistered all his life and was so immature that she was convinced if she had suggested a game of hide and seek he would have preferred it infinitely to getting wed.

"No, Lord Kleine, I'm afraid you are not quite what I expected," she answered as tactfully as she could. "Indeed, you are a deal more handsome."

Sylvestre was pleased with this diplomatic reply, therefore Clarence was too.

"And would you like to marry me, ma'am?" my lord made bold enough to pursue.

Before she had time to phrase a reply Francesca found herself being escorted—though propelled would seem more apt — to the door by Mr Villennay at which unexpected manoeuvre she was too bewildered to feel annoyed.

"Forgive me, ma'am, but I suggest you reserve your judgment for the present," he cautioned in her ear when they were out of Clarence's range. "When you come to know his lordship a little better you may feel persuaded to decline his offer."

"Why, sir? Pray give me one good reason why I

ought," she challenged, suspecting the autocratic Frenchman of already attempting to manipulate her.

"I can give you several excellent reasons, mistress, but my lips are sealed in loyalty to Clarence."

"Can it be, monsieur, that you consider my prospective union with his lordship detrimental to your personal interests?"

"No, ma'am, detrimental to yours."

Four

Francesca duly settled in at Kleine and found life much easier than she had supposed it would be, upon the night of her arrival. However, it could not be denied that the atmosphere was tense, particularly between the two men, which she assumed was due to her advent, as if she had intruded upon some intimate scene, perhaps more intimate than the situation warranted. For example, neither gentleman was ever to be found alone which, she reluctantly conceded was not the fault of Mr Villennay but of my lord who seemed to dog Sylvestre's fashionable heels everywhere, so much so, that Francesca felt persuaded to doubt the supposition of Mr Penrose, and wonder if perhaps it were not Mr Villennay who was the oppressed, and the Viscount the oppressor instead of the other way about?

Throughout that first week she got the irrepressible feeling that Mr Villennay was every whit as anxious as she to further their discourse which the inevitable presence of Clarence rendered impossible. Consequently, she was not quite as taken aback as she might have been upon returning to her chamber one afternoon to find the Frenchman established therein, awaiting her.

He apologised most profusely for encroaching upon her privacy but explained that her chamber was the only room in the castle where Clarence dare not venture and there was a deal he wished to ascertain concerning herself, going on to assure her that her maid was in the dressing closet well within call should she feel at any time her honour was imperilled. Despite the adverse rumours in circulation about him, lack of self-control would seem to be the last thing Francesca had to worry about where Sylvestre de Villennay was concerned; and so she calmly seated herself upon a brocade stool and waited with an air of expectant civility for him to commence.

This appeared to be a sight more difficult than she would have supposed for one of his indomitable self-assurance, and a considerable transformation in disposition since their first encounter, for he did not remain seated upon the daybed opposite for very long but rose up to wander at will about the well-appointed room, as if her air of serenity somehow unnerved him, and he were unable to endure the unwavering gaze of her wide innocent eyes lest she stare him out of countenance.

"You have now met the Viscount, ma'am," he resumed finally. "May I ask what you think of him?"

"As a human being, sir? A man? Or a prospective husband?"

"As an individual," he added a fourth dimension. "Fear not to speak quite freely, Miss Northwood. Rest assured, I shall respect your confidence. I appreciate you have resided at Kleine only a sennight, nevertheless, I feel you cannot have failed to formulate some opinion of its master."

Yes, she had formulated an opinion, a very definite opinion, but doubted vastly if Mr Villennay were to be trusted as implicitly as he would have her believe.

"I find his lordship a little—er—youthful, perhaps ... somewhat immature," she submitted tentatively.

"Does it trouble you?"

"No. In fact, I find it rather refreshing."

"Would that indicate, ma'am, that you could eventually . . . care for him?"

"I'm sure I could—er—in a maternal way. It would be very easy to mother Clarence."

"Aye," he acknowledged with a degree of relief which puzzled her because a love which was purely maternal would scarcely beget his lordship the heir he craved. "I could ask no more, mistress, except that you judge not Clarence too harshly. He was bereft of the mother he adored at a very tender age and took it extremely ill."

"Then perhaps maternal care might be what he needs most of all, Mr Villennay. And with gentle nurturing it is feasible, is it not, that I may be able to help him develop into the man he ought to be?"

He threw her a calculating glance. "You would be prepared to shoulder such a burden? No, I beg you—wait." He restrained her with upraised hand. "I shall not press you for an answer until I am assured you are in full command of the situation. I presume the lawyer indicated that Clarence desires a child, an heir—not a wife. Alas, he cannot have the one without the other."

"Yes, Mr Penrose did say something to that effect."

"And that once the child is born it will not be a marriage in any sense of the word except that you and he will continue to reside beneath the same roof."

"I understand, sir," she concurred with complaisance, prompting him to hesitate in his perambulation to regard her curiously, for it was indeed extraordinary for a female to accept such an arrangement so calmly.

"It pleases me to note, ma'am, that you are not an emotional female with a proclivity to the vapours and hysterics. I make no secret of the fact that it was upon this assurance that you were chosen."

"Chosen by yourself, Mr Villennay?" she countered respectfully, but with a wealth of innuendo in her tone.

He smiled deviously. "Purely in concern for Clarence and his future well-being, mistress, for you'll appreciate I have my own life to pursue and I grow no younger." A graver note here entered his voice. "I have shouldered the responsibility of his welfare since childhood and am now a trifle wearied. Pray don't misunderstand me, ma'am," he made haste to clarify. "I love Clarence closer than a brother. However, there are times when . . ." He broke off with a helpless gesture and turned away. "It is not a natural relationship. Clarence has become too reliant upon me, a reliance he ought to be placing upon a wife."

Francesca mused pensively that this last statement was the only point on which the Frenchman and Mr Josiah Penrose would seem to be agreed.

"Surely it is not so imperative, sir, that he must needs wed immediately? He is still a young man. Perhaps in another year or two he might mature and—"

"No!" he cut in rigorously. "Clarence is becoming too set in his ways. Moreover, the situation has not improved over the years as I deemed it might. In fact, it has grown decidedly worse of late." He seemed as if he wanted to enlarge on this but refrained from so doing, no doubt aware that she might yet see fit to reject the offer, and his pace quickened about the room in evidence of the emotional disturbance within him. "If he is to be saved from himself it must be done now! Delay would serve only to aggravate the problem and I could not be answerable for the consequences!"

Francesca was awe-stricken by this voluble outburst and suspected that a deal more lay behind it than he was prepared to divulge; a point she did not hesitate to intimate.

"Your severe words and tone appear to indicate that the situation is much more serious than you have implied hitherto, Mr Villennay. Is there anything further I perhaps ought to know?"

"I have told you all that is necessary for the present," he rejoined curtly, almost rudely, advancing to the door as if suddenly anxious to be gone, but then he turned to submit a final word.

"Despite my impetuosity to have done with the sordid business I appreciate that the holy estate of matrimony is not to be regarded lightly, especially in this instance. I shall therefore grant you another seven days to weigh your decision. However, mistress, I do not deny that time is of the essence in your own interest as well as mine for every hour expended under this roof adds another smear to your reputation. Aye, Miss Northwood, that is another facet of life at Kleine you must accept if you elect to remain," he appended, taking his leave with a brief bow, "—gossip."

Following his departure Francesca sat a long while submerged in meditation trying to define the cryptic meaning behind his innuendoes, a meaning he adamantly refused to put into words and had elucidated as far as he dared and which she really ought to perceive yet for some peculair reason simply could not. What *was* it? What was the strange deception, the sinister aura which hung about Kleine and its inhabitants like a shroud? Was the Viscount an impostor? Or was it possible he was already wed to another? Francesca gasped at the horrifying thought, but gasped louder as she enlarged upon it. Perhaps Clarence had married and discovered afterwards that his wife was barren, incapable of bearing him the child he craved, and in a fit of rage had done her to death! No, not Clarence—Villennay perhaps, but definitely not Clarence. Indeed, Mr Penrose certainly had not exaggerated his opinion of the Frenchman whose uncanny power of perception enabled him to be always three jumps ahead of his adversary. And the man was so convincing. Even now, he had almost persuaded her into believing him as anxious as everyone else to see Clarence married with a son and heir—yet why should he be? Why should he be so eager to help Clarence attain that which would jeopardise his own position at Kleine and not only weaken his influence over my Lord Viscount but frustrate his efforts to seize Kleine's abundant wealth, which must surely be his prime ambition in life. Perhaps she did Monsieur an injustice, nevertheless she could not help thinking, had he longed genuinely for his freedom he would have gone long before now. She was inclined to believe Mr Villennay less than honest, and extremely cunning, especially when she refined upon their conversation and his intrinsic genius for saying a great deal yet revealing absolutely nothing.

In such circumstances a lesser female might have fled the scene and been upon her way back to London on the next available conveyance be it public stage or hay wagon, but Miss Northwood was not a female ruled by convention and was not easily deterred. On the contrary, apart from her feverish desire to be a viscountess and a rich one to boot, an impassioned interest in Kleine and its inmates was already fomenting within her which was, ultimately, to enmesh her inextricably in its web of intrigue.

But to do Francesca justice her motives for wedding my lord were not wholly mercenary or selfish but because she, even now, experienced a feeling of responsibility to Clarence, that same maternal feeling which filled her with a longing to cherish and protect him from what, exactly, she could not determine, for a peculiar instinct told her that it was not solely from Sylvestre de Villennay. Furthermore, it was infinitely better for Clarence himself to be wed to her rather than some avaricious self-seeking female interested only in his wealth and position, and who would deny him the tender nurturing and sympathy she felt certain she could give, also tolerance and understanding and, hopefully, the heir for which he so desperately yearned.

And so at the end of the week a very positive 'yes' was given in response to the unconventional proposal which pleased Mr Villennay—or appeared to—and because Sylvestre was pleased Clarence was too, anyway, for the moment. No sooner was her answer given than the contract was signed, sealed and witnessed, the Fennistone diamond was upon her finger, and preparations were set in motion for the quietest ceremony in marital history as no one was to be invited, and none was to bear witness from outside the castle walls.

During this period of preparation Francesca—when she was not being importuned by mantua-makers, milliners, jewellers or florists—made no attempt to obtrude herself upon her future husband, deeming it wiser to bide her time in the faint hope that *he* perhaps might condescend to come to *her*. And although, as expected, the hope proved forlorn indeed she did not repine for they sat down together at every meal (though invariably in the company of Mr Villennay) so that little by little she became familiar with her lord and was pleased to note that he was gradually coming to accept her, even if he never addressed her directly but included her in his conversation with Sylvestre. This, along with his indifference and rebuffs, Francesca realiscd she must endure if she was to make any progress in winning his regard and so bore up bravely, thankful to be accepted though it was in the mortifying capacity of a distant cousin.

However, she was given some indication of how stormy the future might be upon one morning when the three of them assembled for breakfast. It was obvious at a glance that Lord Kleine was out of countenance though it was a tolerable while before he gave voice to it and instead glowered across the flowers and silver plate at Mr Villennay, who was clearly the cause of my lord's ill-humour yet who went through the civilised motion of breaking his fast with the unruffled nonchalance borne of much experience.

"So, you're gallanting off again, your man tells me!" It was a statement, uttered with a vehemence his lordship did not seem the equal of, yet he apparently awaited an answer from Mr Villennay, the recipient of his verbal attack, at whom he continued to scowl while drumming the fingers of one effeminate hand upon the polished oak refectory table.

Mr Villennay gave no visible reaction but continued sipping his coffee with due deliberation.

Lord Kleine's scowl blackened to a thunderous degree. "Where is it this time? Dammit, not London!"

"No, Clarence," calmly returned his friend, rinsing the remains of ham and fruit from his long elegant fingers in a chased-silver finger-bowl. "All being well, I shall travel no farther than Durham and be gone no longer than a fortnight, so there is no need whatsoever to fly into a taking."

"A fortnight! Sylvestre, you can't! Hang it, you can't leave me here alone with—with—" His eyes swivelled anxiously in Francesca's direction making his meaning abundantly plain.

53

The Frenchman wiped his hands with meticulous care and flung his lordship a look of ill-concealed contempt.

"Clarence, I'm afraid being alone with Miss Northwood is something to which you will have to get accustomed."

"Yes! Yes! But not yet—now—today!"

"I have no choice," he replied laconically. "There are urgent matters to be attended to, for example, a licence to be procured if you wish the ceremony to take place in the privacy of your home. However, I urge you to reconsider and devote due thought to having your marriage solemnized formally in the Abbey at Hexham as your forebears have—"

"No! I won't hear of it! Don't even suggest it—I refuse absolutely!"

"You are breaking a great family tradition, Clarence."

"I care not what I break. I can't do it and that is final! Go, get your confounded licence! I'll survive, I suppose, as I've survived every . . . thing . . . else . . ."

"I shall be gone only two weeks, Clarence, not two years."

This seemed to be little consolation to his lordship who sat with chin submerged woefully in his starched linen stock as if his friend had predicted the end of the world.

Mr Villennay inhaled deeply and exchanged a glance with Miss Northwood, a glance pregnant with meaning.

"Please do not concern yourself, sir," she murmured discreetly out of Clarence's hearing. "I shall try my utmost to compensate to my lord for your absence."

He inclined his dark immaculate head in acknowledgment and smiled, but the smile lacked conviction.

"Thank you, ma'am," was all he vouchsafed, rising from the table and relinquishing his napkin.

As he rose Clarence's head jerked up anxiously. "Y-You *are* coming back, Sylvestre?" he queried on frightening afterthought, his eyes consumed with dread.

"Of course I'm coming back, Clarence. Where else should I go in the circumstances?"

He bowed briefly to Miss Northwood and progressed to the door where he turned to find Clarence on his heels.

"You won't go to any gaming halls? Or brothels?—or-or fight duels?"

Mr Villennay winced, flushed slightly, and overtured an apology to the lady on his lordship's behalf.

"No, Clarence, you have my word."

"Go then, while I am able to bear it," whimpered his lordship. "I think I'll repair to my rooms where I cannot witness your departure."

Francesca was abandoned, stricken and dumbfounded by the scene which bordered on the unnatural, and not a little shaken by it all, unaware that it merely scratched the surface of the formidable task before her if she elected to assume the role of Kleine's mistress.

Nevertheless it gave her much food for thought during Mr Villennay's absence when she sat in the chambers of the great draughty castle, alone and comfortless with her betrothed still languishing abovestairs in his rooms where he seemed destined to remain until Sylvestre returned. She allowed three days to expire in this manner before deciding to proffer the hand of fellowship to her lord for she was acutely aware that any effort to bridge the gap between them must come from herself.

She deemed it a good beginning to draw aside his valet de chambre and ask the man in confidence if he could advise her of any particular interest or liking his master cherished, something in which she might share and thus help him overcome his reticence. The valet clearly approved of the idea and replied without hesitation that his master was passionately fond of music and as a child had loved nothing better than to sit at his mother's feet while she played and sang. Indeed, if he (the valet) remembered correctly there was one piece in particular of which his lordship was especially fond, a somewhat remote song of Northumbrian origin, and with Miss Northwood's permission he would endeavour to find the copy.

Her permission was readily given and within the hour she found herself in the Music Room of the castle, poring over the frayed remnants of a much fingered manuscript. The song was a lament, of a peasant lass for her collier lover, with a plaintive beauty of its own and which would not prove beyond her musical ability once she had mastered the somewhat intricate rhythm.

The harpsichord at Kleine was, naturally, the most superlative instrument money could buy and by far the best Miss Northwood's dainty fingers had ever been privileged to grace. And so she practised the song throughout that day and the next in the hope of surprising Clarence with it should the opportunity arise.

The opportunity arose quicker than expected, namely, at the end of the first week of Sylvestre's absence when she found to her delight that she could play the song reasonably well. Nevertheless, it still required more practise to fulfil her ambition of overwhelming Clarence and she attacked the song anew, soon to become oblivious to all else, confident in the knowledge that her lord could not possibly overhear way above in his rooms which were situated in a distant part of the castle.

But Clarence was no longer in his rooms as Francesca presently discovered when his awe-struck face suddenly appeared over the instrument. She trembled with excitement but managed to maintain her outward calm and give an impression of being engrossed in the music and unaware of his presence lest she frighten him away. What would happen when she eventually ended the piece, as she needs must, she was loth to contemplate, but end it she did to sit gazing simply down at the black and white keys as if she believed herself still alone. On afterthought, she feared he might tip-toe out and so she struck up the song again to hold his interest when to her astonishment and joy Clarence actually spoke!

"That was . . . beautiful, ma'am," he breathed, rapt in wonder, his blue eyes shining just as they often did at Sylvestre.

"Do you like music, my lord?" she dared to ask.

"Yes! Oh, yes!" he responded eagerly. "My mother sometimes played that tune . . . w-would you play it again, please."

Francesca immediately obliged, yet throughout the song was unable to banish from her mind the soul-stirring reverence with which he had caressed his mother's name and which emboldened her to discreetly plumb the depth of feeling behind it when she finished playing.

"Did you love your mother very much, my lord?"

He looked crestfallen and nodded, hesitantly.

"I loved mine very much too," she quickly followed up to establish another bond between them.

"And did your mother love you in return, ma'am?"

"Oh yes, she quite ador-" Too late, she realised her disastrous blunder for it was plain by his pained expression that such had not been *his* case. Francesca bit her lip in annoyance and continued on, resorting to a little subterfuge to rectify the fault. "But I do not remember very clearly. You see, my mother died when I was still rather young, and my father soon afterwards."

"How sad," he sympathised ruefully. "And do you miss them? Does it hurt terribly to be without them?"

"Yes, my lord."

Clarence moved two steps nearer, solicitude written upon his angelic face.

"I understand how you feel, ma'am, because I suffer too . . . when Sylvestre goes away. Why should he punish me so? I have done nothing to displease him."

"And when you have, does he go away to punish you?"

"Yes," he whispered forlornly. "I-It hurts so dreadfully I'd rather he took a rod to my back."

"Do not repine." Francesca sought to discard the matter lightly. "It is only another week to Mr Villennay's return."

He brightened noticeably at this. "Yes! One more week and Sylvestre will be here."

"Is Sylvestre your friend?" she probed circumspectly.

Clarence nodded vigorously. "He is the dearest friend anyone ever had."

"Do you think he would be my friend?"

"No!" he objected in no uncertain terms with a scowl of blackest disapproval. "Sylvestre is *my* friend!"

"I'm sorry," she apologised hurriedly. "But I don't have a friend."

Apparently this had not occurred to his lordship. "No

friend? Oh, you *must* have a friend! Shall *I* be your friend, Miss Northwood?"

"Oh would you indeed, my lord?" gasped she, taken quite aback by this overture of intimacy. "I should love it above all things. And would you call me Fran as my dear father was used to do? It is much more friendly, and I'll call you Clarence, if I may?"

Lord Kleine giggled boyishly, obviously delighted with this new-found relationship.

"Very well—Fran," he agreed.

However, his lordship was no more delighted than Francesca herself at this miraculous break through his reserve, and could not cease rhapsodising how pleased Mr Villennay would be upon his return to discover how much progress had been made during his absence.

Neither was she disappointed for upon his return Mr Villennay *was* pleased, exceedingly so, though he gave as little evidence of it as he did any other emotion and his degree of pleasure was to be measured by the fact that he lost not a moment in drawing Miss Northwood aside to commend her efforts but, to her disconcertment, in a voice as cold as charity.

"I must applaud you, Miss Northwood. You appear to have wrought something of a miracle in Clarence. That is good."

"Is it, Mr Villennay?" she challenged pointedly, mistrusting his tone.

"Yes, why not?" he parried with candour. "Is it not what we mutually seek. Are we not steered upon the same course, ma'am, towards Clarence's ultimate benefit?"

"Clarence's, or yours, sir?"

"Mine?" he exclaimed in surprise. "I do not fathom your meaning. Pray how am I to benefit by your union with my Lord Viscount?"

As this was the question the answer to which Francesca herself would have willingly given her eyesight she was, alas, lost for an apt response and could do little but redden profusely and bite her tongue in vexation.

"Might I presume to ask, ma'am, what you *now* think of his lordship?"

"As an individual?"

"No, as a prospective husband. Do you find him attractive in the physical sense? In short, is he the type of man you would have chosen——er——granted the privilege of so doing?"

"No——neither are you, Mr Villennay!" she retorted tartly, instantly regretting it for she sounded quite childish.

His lip curled disdainfully. "Your opinion of me as a prospective spouse does not and never will arise, Miss Northwood. However, I shall presume to proffer a further word of caution, for your own benefit, and advise you, ma'am, not to become too emotionally involved with Clarence. Continue to care for him, by all means, but do not lose your heart to him."

Francesca stared at him incredulously. "Do you tell me, sir, that I must not grow to love him——as a husband?"

"Precisely. It would be fatal."

"Fatal? To whom?" she demanded with asperity, greatly resenting his interference to such an intimate level.

"To yourself, mistress. Clarence could never reciprocate such feeling. He is utterly incapable of love."

"He loves *you*, Mr Villennay."

He flinched and averted his gaze as her arrow struck its target.

"I would not have you make the same mistake, ma'am, and suffer like consequences. Be warned, do not offer Clarence more than he is willing to accept and which he is able to give in return."

Thus yet again did Mr Villennay leave Francesca in a dilemma with much to reflect upon, but with the same uncomfortable feeling that he was concealing a deal more than he chose to reveal.

Five

With the return of his beloved Sylvestre Francesca nurtured qualms that Clarence might revert to his former self and ignore her completely, but he did not. Granted, he was still a long way from trusting her and continued to seek only Sylvestre's opinion on everything right down to the most minor consideration, yet to his future bride's satisfaction he maintained a certain friendliness towards her and derived enormous pleasure from listening to her sing and play, and even assisted in the selecting of various materials for her trousseau which surprised her most of all. And when she threw up her hands and cried out appalled at his extravagance he chuckled like a babe and bought her even more, evidently enjoying this new experience of bestowing gifts upon a lady, so much so, that Francesca was given the distinct impression that my Lord Viscount was actually humouring her instead of the other way about.

During the final two weeks prior to the wedding little allusion was made to the event and life proceeded as normally as possible at Kleine lest its owner cry craven and countermand the whole thing.

Without further incident the wedding morn eventually dawned beneath the excellent auspices of brilliant June sunshine and the bridegroom's presentation to his bride (though traditionally *not* in person) of the family heirlooms, consisting of tiara, necklace, pin and ear-rings set with priceless emeralds, and which detracted somewhat from her wedding regalia yet which Francesca wore without demur in order to please her future husband.

The ceremony was to take place at noon and throughout the morning she carried out her preparations, attended by a host of maids who fussed and fawned upon her until she stood poised before her looking-glass at a quarter past eleven, her shapeliness enchantingly adorned in a billowing gown and petticoat of oyster satin embossed with silver, the sleeves of elbow length, from which showered treble lace flounces embellished with ribboned knots, while diamonds and pearls enhanced the stomacher and the fourreau back fell in an exceptionally long train. The gown was draped over a dome-hoop for the bride suspected the narrow aisles of the chapel would not accommodate anything larger. She herself was immensely pleased with her appearance for she looked quite as radiant as a bride ought; and contrary to first impressions she was now persuaded that the emeralds did much to enrich the colour of her eyes.

It was as she turned to compliment the maids upon their efforts that the door opened to admit Mr Villennay at sight of whom Francesca began to tremble. Why, she could not say except for the fact that he had never looked so magnificent dressed as he was in a full skirted coat of silver stiffened brocade, silver embroidered waistcoat, white silk hose, and ruffles of the purest white Mechlin lace at chin and wrists, the whole contrasting strikingly with his night-black hair which was styled in an unpowdered, though no less fashionable, queue at the nape of his neck. A solitary patch graced his left cheekbone, while a diamond ring winked upon the third finger of his right hand and a matching pin sparkled upon his breast.

He swept her an impeccable leg, which she endeavoured to repay with an equally impeccable curtsy despite the weight and magnitude of her apparel while inwardly querying the reason for his premature advent for it was quite lacking another thirty minutes to the appointed hour. She was not to wonder very long.

"I crave forgiveness for the intrusion, ma'am," he announced with the infuriating nonchalance he customarily affected which seemed to give the lie to whatever he professed no matter how convincingly he professed it. "I am come that I might grant my approval—er—or disapproval as the case may be."

Outrage flared within the bride! Was there no end to the man's presumption?

"Monsieur de Villennay," she fumed angrily, transposing his name into the French which never failed to exacerbate him, "I assure you that I am exceedingly capable of conducting my own wedding toilette with or without your approval!"

"I've no doubt you are, Miss Northwood," he returned with equanimity. "However, I am confident you will agree that I understand his lordship more intimately than your good self, and can therefore be better relied upon to estimate precisely what will and will not please him. I am equally confident, mistress, that you do not need to emphasize how disastrous 'twould be for all concerned were we to offend Clarence—the perfume, he won't like it, I suggest *eau de violette*—at this crucial stage, for I guarantee the most infinitesimal flaw could well despatch him to his rooms to seek solace in a bout of spleen."

Fume as she might Francesca was forced to own his reasoning valid and held her peace—though with difficulty—while he undertook his inspection in a disconcerting silence, flicking a curl aside here, patting a love-knot into place there, and provoking her self-control to extreme by removing a silk patch from the curvature of her shoulder to reposition it alluringly upon the voluptuous crest of her right breast where it emerged from its bed of silver lace. She drew in her breath sharply and he paused, anticipating some objection, before he turned with a cryptic smile to address her tire-woman.

"The train is a ludicrous length. Curtail it by two yards."

Before the bride could voice her strongest indignation Monsieur forestalled her.

"Clarence might take exception to it and bethink you were endeavouring to outshine him," he clarified affably.

"Do you mean Clarence or yourself, Mr Villennay?" she snorted resentfully as the maids set to work with deft fingers and scissors upon the long train in order to have the task completed in time.

The question elevated his right eyebrow. "Myself? Nay, mistress, I mean Clarence in all truth. What you deign to wear is not of the slightest personal interest. Faith, you may swagger to the chapel yonder in nought but a blush—you certainly would not be the first—but alas, Clarence—"

"—wouldn't like it!" she flung back acidly, colouring profusely. "Is there anything else you feel my Lord Viscount might not like, sir?"

The question was scarcely airborne when she regretted it for his dark passionate gaze began to meander over her face and form once again, omitting not an inch, an indeterminate look in his eye yet which increased her embarrassment an hundredfold.

"No, ma'am," he murmured at length, as if the words were loth to leave his tongue. "My lord will be hard pressed indeed to find anything else amiss."

Who but Mr Villennay should lead her down to the Fennistone family chapel in the courtyard below, where Francesca found the servants fully assembled from head footman to ostler, and housekeeper to kitchenmaid, while my lord's personal musicians played an *allemande* in the flower-bedecked gallery above but at so slow a tempo that it bore more resemblance to a dirge.

Clarence was conspicuously absent which engendered some misgiving in her maidenly breast that he had perhaps cried off after all. However, her escort certainly did not appear to share her misgiving and upon reaching the

63

centre of the aisle sure enough her husband-to-be appeared, leading his own short procession from the direction of the chancel.

Bride and 'groom converged at the altar where Francesca bravely ventured a glance at her lord and emitted a gasp, for if she had thought him beautiful before he now looked unbelievably so, clad in a suit of virgin white satin encrusted with silver, diamonds, and pearls of varying size while his long silken hair hung like liquid gold about his shoulders, with rebellious curls framing his exquisitely handsome face.

Francesca dragged her eyes away from him and sank into a profound curtsy at his diamond buckled shoes which, following an imperceptible nod from Mr Villennay, Clarence honoured with a graceful bow, about to kiss her fingertips when he hesitated. Sylvestre frowned, and Francesca held her breath bethinking her lord was about to be perverse and create a scene before the congregation of gaping servants. But nothing was further from his intention for if Francesca was stricken by his exceptional beauty he was equally so by hers and stood staring, bemused, while his bride's heart leapt into her mouth as she wondered frantically what he would do, when to her speechless amazement he bent forwards and, instead of kissing her hand—kissed her cheek, and whispered something about her looking like a fairy princess.

Yes, Mr Villennay was also pleased, or was he merely relieved? This boded well indeed for the night ahead which Francesca had been dreading a deal more than was customary for a bride, for the ordeal of consummation would prove quite intolerable if the bridegroom were reluctant to take what the bride was naturally reluctant to give.

Although the wedding ceremony was appreciably quiet it did not lack dignity and splendour as befitting a peer of the realm and was conducted by the Fennistone family vicar who felt it incumbent upon him to bestow due reverence and honour on the bridal pair by elongating the ritual with an amplitude of prayers, blessings and a sermon extolling the 'groom's finer qualities and generosity to his servants in allowing them to abandon their tasks for a whole hour in order that they might bear witness to the occasion.'

Throughout, Francesca's attention was given ample opportunity to wander round the interior of the twelfth century chapel in admiration of the wrought gold and silver-work, the stained glass windows, colourful frescoes, carved choir stalls and altarpiece, and the impressive fan-vaulted roof, all gaily adorned with flowers. But strange though it may seem, she found her eye wandering involuntarily in the direction of Mr Villennay, positioned upon her left, who remained oblivious to her interest until their eyes suddenly met and he smiled a furtive smile, as if he were enjoying some private jest at her expense, concerning the docking of her train, perhaps—or was it another surprise he had secreted up his elegant sleeve?

Here she was brought up with a start as Clarence took her hand to make his vows, his hand as cold as ice. On impulse she squeezed it to generate some warmth but he immediately snatched it away and, to her horror and everyone else's dropped the nuptial ring.

There fell a deathly silence followed by a hubbub which rippled round the superstitious congregation presaging everything from eternal damnation to offspring with cloven hooves.

"I-I'm sorry, Sylvestre," Clarence panicked, nonplussed, as the servants scrabbled about to assist the vicar in retrieving the errant article and caused a degree of commotion upon the blue velvet dais. "I didn't mean to drop it, I swear! I don't know how it—"

"There is nothing to be sorry for, my lord," cut in the frigid tone of Mr Villennay, while Francesca quietly seethed.

Why? Why did Clarence so demean himself to this Frenchman? What was the mysterious power he held mercilessly over her lord's noble head, a power strong enough to reduce him from a proud peer of the realm to a quivering mass of cringing servility? Needless to say this did nothing to elevate Mr Villennay in the bride's esteem and she determined that her first concern as Viscountess

Kleine would be to sever this bond and break down the Viscount's slavish subservience to this sinister man who dominated all as if he were master of Kleine, and who would be given more than enough encouragement to quit the castle to live his own life at the earliest possible opportunity in accordance with his alleged desire. Kleine was now to have a mistress, which Monsieur de Villennay was to learn to his cost!

Despite the tumult within her breast Francesca made her vows in a calm clear voice loud enough for all to hear, including Mr Villennay, and mark well her determination, following which the ring was blessed by the vicar and placed upon her finger by Clarence. A feeling of exultation swept through her at the presence of the little solid gold band round her finger, pronouncing her to be Francesca Elinor Catherine Northwood no longer, but instead, Francesca Elinor Catherine Fennistone, Viscountess Kleine.

The Viscountess closed her eyes to pray but also to luxuriate in the wonderful exhilarating feeling and upon opening them was pleased to find Clarence smiling down at her, a warm smile of almost—dare she think it?—affection? She was delighted for he smiled all too rarely but no doubt he had little cause to, or perhaps Mr Villennay did not allow it? Well, before long there were going to be some changes at Kleine whether Mr Villennay approved or not. This overbearing dictatorial Frenchman was going to find his nose pushed back into place and Clarence was going to enjoy himself! For the first time in his life he was going to do exactly what he wished in his own castle—even step a lively *contre-danse* on the dining table if he so desired.

Following the ceremony the three sat down to an elaborate feast in which the vicar, steward, housekeeper and head footman were permitted to participate in order to help compensate for the pathetic lack of guests. Nevertheless, the banquet was rendered even more pathetic by the seating arrangement which decreed that bride and bridegroom sit at opposing ends of the extensive table while the remaining five redressed the balance in between.

As it was shockingly out of place for any of the 'guests' to address the Viscount without his lordship first addressing them conversation was reduced to a stony silence with nothing but the tinkle of china, clatter of cutlery and exchange of apprehensive smiles to be remarked, for Lord Kleine was clearly not disposed to converse though there were times when he looked as if he might. In fact the only person present to appear utterly impervious to the embarrassing atmosphere, though which was hardly surprising, was the very person who ought to have sensed it most acutely, namely, Mr Villennay, who remained his inimitable nonchalant infuriating self throughout.

But to be honest, Francesca did not feel greatly tempted to converse; neither did she feel tempted to eat despite the delectable array of dishes, the *pièce de resistance* of which was swan stuffed with olives and anchovies, for her thoughts were understandably centred upon the night ahead and how she and Clarence were to face each other across the nuptial bed without suffering the most excruciating embarrassment on both sides if Mr Villennay were not to allow them the rest of the day to better their acquaintance. Though she never would have dreamed it possible some months ago she was more concerned on her husband's behalf than her own due to his painful shyness in her company, as if he had never entertained a lady to tea let alone to the hallowed confines of a bed, which would seem somewhat difficult to credit for a man of his unusual beauty and thirty-one years.

As soon as was considered seemly the Viscountess excused herself and rejected the lamentable gathering in favour of the Gallery and the blissful solitude it afforded. Here, she expended the subsequent hours pacing up and down the polished wooden floor beneath the supercilious gaze of generations of Fennistones, while she duly meditated her problem, wishing Sylvestre de Villennay would take himself off and leave her and Clarence alone as they ought to be. But it would seem Mr Villennay was firmly resolved this day of days that bride and 'groom were to remain apart, the one from the other.

The three met again at five o'clock in the Tudor Chamber to take tea in the English manner but little passed between them other than small-talk, certainly no allusion to weddings, marriage beds, and the like.

In fact, the remainder of the day following the wedding-breakfast was spent in much the same way as any other, that is until shortly before supper for which Francesca was in the middle of her preparations. She was selecting a necklace to flatter her gown of apricot sarsenet when the door burst wide and someone rushed into her room. She closed her trinket box then turned, stunned to find her visitor was Clarence! Clarence had dared to enter her bedchamber! Moreover, his face was flushed and excited like a child who had just been given the moon.

Hastily overcoming her confusion she rose to curtsy dutifully as he approached but to her further astonishment he grabbed her arm and pulled her up onto her feet.

"Never mind about that, Fran—come! Come! You must come and see!" he chuckled infectiously. "I've something wonderful to show you."

Francesca was too dumbfounded to protest, had she wished, and suffered him to almost drag her from the room, along the passage, through several chambers, up two long flights of stairs and after traversing the length of another passage they halted suddenly outside a stout panelled oak door.

"This is it! Close your eyes, Fran. Are you ready?" he cried eagerly.

She closed her eyes wondering what on earth was toward but intending to humour him at all cost, and permitted him to guide her by the hand into the room, adjuring her the while not to look until the door had closed upon them.

"There! *Now* you may look."

Francesca looked, to fall back with an exclamation at the breathtaking scene which met her vision though at first it all seemed a blur of dazzling silver and shimmering silks and gauzes of white, pink and lavender. But what astounded her even more was the fact that it was obviously the bridal chamber yet Clarence was quite as enthralled and overjoyed about it as she herself; about the celestial bed in the centre shaped in the likeness of a huge pink shell and adorned with white muslin, ribboned love-knots and silver bells; at the festoons of flowers scattered all about the room in myriad colours and perfumes; the marriage tokens, and the white sumptuous sheepskin rugs upon the floor.

"Isn't it beau . . . ti . . . ful," he breathed, deeply moved.

Francesca was moved too, not merely by the room but by her husband's tone and the bemused, rapturous look in his blue eyes.

"It is truly, truly wonderful, Clarence," she supported fervently, uncertain if he appreciated the implication behind the elaborate trappings and nuptial splendour which she was about to query in her most prudent manner when he unwittingly answered her.

"It's for you, Fran . . . this is where you will sleep tonight."

The envy in his voice was unmistakable.

"What about you, my lord? Where will you sleep?"

He heaved a disconsolate sigh and pointed briefly to a door on their right.

"In there," he informed her. "That door leads to my apartments."

"Aren't you going to sleep in the beautiful bed too?" she probed as tactfully as she knew how.

"With you, Fran?" he exclaimed in surprise as if such an arrangement had never entered his head. "No, of course not." Appending on afterthought: "I-I'd like to, mayhap, but . . ."

"But?"

He gave a helpless shrug. "Sylvestre would never allow it."

Francesca could not credit her ears. "H-He *what*?" was all she could stammer.

Clarence met her horrified gaze unflinchingly, a look which warned her to beware what she said about Sylvestre, the man he worshipped and whose word was law at Kleine. Francesca realised she was balanced upon a precipice, to plunge headlong to her doom if she failed to school her temper which had flared at this newest and most infamous presumption on the part of the Frenchman. Curbing her wrath she tried to reason with her lord as she might a raw youth, which indeed he was however absurd the notion might seem when he had resided beneath the same roof as the degenerate Mr Villennay for a quarter of a century.

"Clarence, you do know that ladies and gentlemen are at liberty to share one bed when they are married one to the other?" she intimated as sympathetically as she could.

"Yes, I know that, Fran. I'm not an idiot."

"Well, now that we are wed don't you think we ought to do so too?"

A tortured expression crossed his face. "I-I'm not sure, Fran. You see, I've never done . . . anything like . . . that before."

"Neither have I, my lord."

This did little to console Clarence who was clearly racked with anguish, and Francesca turned away, feigning further admiration of the decoration lest she add to his discomfort, a discomfort she also experienced in no small measure for was it not the *bride's* prerogative to be blushing, modest, and apprehensive of the night ahead? Inspiration prompted her to fire a shot at his most vulnerable spot—his yearning for a child, alas, the begetting of which was going to be a deal more arduous than she had hitherto foreseen.

"Clarence," she whispered, anxious to preserve the aura as she approached him with a soft rustle of silks and gently laid a hand on his arm, a familiarity he did not appear to resent. "Is not it your dearest wish to have a son of your very own? Is not that the reason our marriage was arranged?"

"Yes! Oh yes!" he enthused, his soulful eyes misty with longing as he gazed entranced at the bed.

"Then you will come to me tonight . . . t-to sleep . . . in the beautiful . . . b-bed?" she managed to articulate, seared with shame for she had never made such a proposal to a man before, even if he was her legal husband, and anticipated the fulfilling of it with even greater dread but she was, nevertheless, determined to keep her avowal.

To her relief— or was it fear?—his arm hesitantly encircled her shoulders and he drew her nearer to him, his eyes still feverishly fixed upon the bed.

"Yes, Fran . . . I'll come . . . I promise," he murmured like one under a spell—then abruptly asserted himself and all but pushed her away. "What about Sylvestre?" he cried out aghast, devoured with guilt.

"You must not tell Sylvestre, Clarence!" she urged him. "Give me your word on sworn oath that you will not divulge your promise. It is to remain a secret—*our* secret, Clarence. Do you understand?"

Yes, he understood well enough; the question was, would he consent to deceiving Sylvestre?

Clarence stared back at his wife, his sweet face deathly serious in full appreciation of precisely what she was asking of him, and suddenly a gleam sprang into his eyes as the idea of having a secret from Sylvestre began to appeal to his boyish nature; then he smiled, giggled, and planting a kiss upon her cheek he dashed off to disappear through the door into the sanctity of his chambers, from where Francesca heard the distant click of a lock.

Six

Such excellent progress with Clarence helped considerably to quell Francesca's blazing anger at Mr Villennay's unwarranted interference in this exceedingly personal issue and instead of departing in hot pursuit of him, as was her first intent, she paused to reflect upon the possibility that Mr Villennay with his gifted perception might well inveigle her, before she was aware of it, into revealing her cherished secret. She certainly had no wish to make him as wise as she, especially when, according to her husband, he was so adamantly opposed to the plan.

But why, when he had been eager for Clarence to wed her did he now seek to drive them apart? Was it jealousy? If so, of whom—of her, or Clarence? Did he now resent her becoming the dominant person in Clarence's life, taking the initiative and depriving him of his influence over his lordship, just as Mr Penrose had foretold? But surely this conflicted violently with all he had professed to her face about growing wearied of the responsibility and wanting to live his own life. Or was it that he had suffered a change of heart and did not relish, any longer, the prospect of Kleine having an heir? An heir who would undoubtedly prove an obstacle between himself and Clarence's wealth.

Whatever Mr Villennay's motive for such incongruous behaviour Francesca appreciated she must tread very warily for it would seem by his most recent prohibition that he was determined no heir should be begot, though why he should persuade the Viscount to take a wife in the first instance if their union was not to be consummated was something she could not wait to discover. Meanwhile, that night should bear witness to some interesting developments . . .

The Viscountess returned to her boudoir to put the finishing touches to her interrupted toilette then, infinitely calm and self-possessed, she descended to supper clothed in her apricot sarsenet and a feeling of jubilant expectancy.

Once again the three sat down to dine, this time informally upon a cold collation of beef, larks' tongues, chopped vegetables and oysters, followed by fruit, syllabub and wine. As the table on this occasion was round, about some six feet in diameter, it gave each the advantage of perusing the other but the disadvantage of being perused in turn, though for the most part Lady Kleine could sense Mr Villennay's dark eyes upon *her* probably because hers were, for the most part, upon *him*.

Clarence, his wife was pleased to note, was quite chirpy and rattled merrily on throughout the meal impervious to whether the two listened or no, and covered every topic from the haymaking revels, to how many days it was lacking to Michaelmas. This it would appear, gave some indication of his inward elation to which Mr Villennay gave an impression of total disinterest, responding in monosyllables when absolutely necessary, between which he frowned down at his plate and across at the Viscountess alternately as if something burdened his mind, something he was loth to divulge, or perhaps was unable to if the expression of confusion and suspicion suffusing his countenance was anything to go by. It was almost as if he

73

sensed there were something toward and were trying to establish precisely what.

The Viscountess's pleasure waxed to delight for this would imply that Clarence had not divulged the secret as she supposed he might. Nevertheless, if Mr Villennay was suspicious he was equally cautious as if he too had elected to play a waiting game, no doubt in the hope that her ladyship might betray herself without his generous assistance.

Following supper they took hands at cards, Francesca more to divert Mr Villennay's suspicions and assure him that everything was quite normal rather than any inclination to play. Even so, Clarence enjoyed it all prodigiously for there was nothing he loved more than playing games, especially when he continually won which seemed guaranteed upon this particular evening due to his opponents' abstraction of thought.

However, her ladyship did not play for very long. Being anxious to maintain the deception that nothing was changed she retired at her usual hour of ten and to her own room, where Martha and her two assistants were waiting to prepare her for the marriage bed. Her curvacious form was arrayed in a white gossamer-silk bedgown, flounced with the finest cobweb lace and trimmed with pink rosebuds, while her long flaming hair was brushed until it rippled down to her waist in all its shimmering glory. Upon her own insistence every trace of paint and powder was removed from her face and thus, her beauty unadorned as nature intended, she finally donned a swansdown robe and suffered the maids to escort her in true marital custom to the bridal chamber to await her lord.

It was not until she was duly established in the marriage bed that she fell to pondering why Mr Villennay should go to such elaborate pains to arrange this nuptial splendour when he evidently nurtured no intention of allowing the nuptials to be consummated? It was passing strange . . . but doubtless she was not destined to find the answer to this until she unravelled the rest of the enigma shrouding Kleine Castle and its inhabitants.

And so there seemed little else to be done but settle down and await patiently—as patiently as she could contrive—Clarence's advent, that was, if he condescended to come. Indeed, she could not have despised him for failing so to do for her own courage was rapidly evaporating at the prospect of what lay ahead.

However, even her inventive imagination could certainly not have envisaged the wedding night which lay in store and which, had she but known it, was surely to go down in conjugal history as one of the strangest ever recorded.

Much as he may have wished Clarence did not cry craven though the hour was well advanced by the time he chose to emerge from his rooms, and the solitary candle had long since spluttered into extinction, throwing the room into abysmal darkness for the flowered velvet curtains draping the windows were of an extraordinary thickness and allowed not a glimmer of moonlight to filter through.

The muffled rattle of a key in the lock of the communicating door was the first intimation she had of her husband's approach, as if he were anxious to creep in unobtrusively lest she be sleeping, though how she be expected to sleep upon such a night was beyond her comprehension. A louder click sounded followed by a tense silence as he paused, wondering if he had woken her, then the door creaked faintly as he entered, bumping himself on the furniture and tripping over a rug before finally gaining the bed where he paused even longer. Despite the turmoil of her own emotions Francesca strove to maintain the deception of sleeping lest he take fright at the sudden sound of her voice.

He was breathing quickly, with excitement or trepidation would be impossible to say, as he discarded what seemed to be a dressing robe for she felt it fall across her feet as he flung it on the bed. Once decided upon getting into the bed he did so with some alacrity yet with barely moving the bedclothes, so much so that she would not have known he was in at all but for the much closer proximity of the breathing. Having progressed thus far he apparently deemed himself a prince among men for he then lay as still as a rock, keeping well apart from his bride.

Clarence maintained this rigid position for well over an hour and seemed like to do for the rest of the night which Francesca could not allow yet knew not how to offer encouragement to a spouse who was obviously more nervous than she, and who at her first advance might abandon the bed in panic to seek refuge beneath it. But clearly an advance of some kind was called for and so she pretended to become restless in her supposed sleep and flung out a hand accidentally, though carefully aimed, in his direction. This proved disastrous. At sudden contact of her arm with his body he began to tremble violently, indeed so violently that the whole bed shook and before long he was bathed in perspiration. Francesca grew alarmed bethinking he was taken ill.

"Clarence?" she breathed urgently. "Are you unwell? Shall I summon your physician?"

A groan escaped him. "N-No, Fran. No physician can cure . . . m-my sick . . . ness."

"What is it? What's wrong?"

He unleashed a strangled cry and leapt from the bed to flee in refuge to his rooms. Frantic with concern she hastened after him but upon reaching the door was brought up short by a nauseating sound, the sound of him retching and vomiting most distressingly.

Francesca was stricken, and in the circumstances saw no point in pursuing him further; and so, leaving him to the tender ministrations of his valet she closed the door and groped her way back to the bed, not a little piqued that the prospect of making love to her should evoke such a feeling of abhorrence in his breast.

She lay quietly in the darkness, brooding over the complex character of the man she had married and how she was to beget him the child he desired when he found her so physically repulsive. At length she heaved a sigh, certain of one thing, namely, if the marriage were to be consummated at all it was not going to be *that* particular night; and having thus reconciled herself to the fact, she snuggled down in the comfort of the bed and sought repose. This was not difficult for it was almost three in the morning and the strain of the last twenty-four hours had long since begun to take its toll of her nerves. Therefore, within seconds she was drifting into a sound slumber, content in the knowledge that her sleep would remain undisturbed.

For fully half an hour Francesca was correct in this belief—until she was roused by a sudden movement close by. Her eyes flew wide in panic, banishing her erstwhile tiredness, and she lay shivering, tensed, at being taken unawares, clutching the coverlets up to her chin and waiting with bated breath for further developments. Yes, he was there again beside her in the bed for although she could neither see nor hear him she could sense his presence.

Surprisingly, he seemed to be recovered and his composure restored for there was not even the sound of breathing as he lay still as at first—perhaps a little too still, inspiring his bride to wonder if the terrible ordeal of compelling himself back to the marriage bed had proved too much for his constitution.

"Clarence?" she whispered doubtfully. "Are you all right?"

"Yes," was all he returned, almost inaudibly.

She inhaled a deep breath and lay back, undecided whether to rejoice or repine the fact that she was, after all, going to be called upon to fulfil her wifely duty. By now she was fully awake with every sense on the alert, every muscle taut, waiting for him to make the initial overture for she had no intention of assuming the initiative as before only to suffer the same calamitous result of despatching him to his closet—or possibly his grave.

She had not long to wait this time. With scarcely a conscious movement he manoeuvred beside her, but not too close; close enough to place a hand on hers and take it in a light clasp. When she did not withdraw it he became a little bolder and his hand progressed to her arm, then her naked shoulder, his touch comforting, caressing, as if he were seeking solace from her nearness . . . a soothing touch, infinitely tender and which gradually coaxed all the

77

tension and anxiety from her being until she too relaxed, luxuriating in the warmth of his proximity and the wonderful feel of his fingers as they continued their course from her shoulder to her neck . . . on and up into her long hair. Indeed, so relaxed did she become and abandoned to his caress that when he eventually slid an arm round her body and drew her gently into his embrace she almost welcomed the overture—though the sudden contact with his naked flesh made her start. His grip tightened rendering escape impossible and soon she overcame her modesty sufficiently to snuggle into his shoulder and even venture an arm about his waist.

Why Clarence had dreaded the experience was something she could not cease marvelling at for he seemed extremely able to assume command of the operation. Exactly what had wrought this transformation in him she was unable to determine until her nostrils were assailed by a strong aroma of brandy.

His lips brushed her left ear and a vibrant shiver ran through her, a shiver not of fear, nor revulsion; neither could it be desire for she did not actually love Clarence . . . did she? Her breathing quickened as his lips now traced the course set by his fingers, from her ear on down her neck where he loosed the ribbons of her night-shift to expose the full rounded contours of shoulder and bosom. Her cheeks flamed at this intimacy for although he was her husband and therefore legally and morally permitted to take such liberties he was, nevertheless, a man, and no man—not even Tristram—had ever been allowed to do more than kiss her upon the face and hands.

Never had she been more thankful for the sympathetic darkness which obscured her blushes from view as his lips slowly but inexorably made their way down towards that voluptuous region where none of his sex had been privileged to venture, and she stiffened accordingly. This he must have sensed for he stopped, waited, then diverted his strategy by drawing her deeper into his arms to comfort her awhile before recommencing the ritual, tenderly kissing her hair . . . her closed eyes . . . her soft cheek . . . along her jaw . . . to her delectable mouth.

His first kiss was quite brief; likewise the second. Even the third was nothing spectacular. Nevertheless, each time he felt her a little more breathless and eager than the last, as if he were working to a formula which had been previously tried and tested; a book of rules which he seemed to have mastered to perfection, enabling him to gauge each overture with expert precision—spontaneous, yet not impetuous; and upon kissing her a fourth time he left her gasping, her heart pounding vigorously and bosom heaving in unison.

Francesca averted her face to regain her breath but he forced it back and sprang to life, kissing her as she had never been kissed before; devouring her lips in an explosion of wildest passion guaranteed to brand her memory, her heart, her soul into eternity, and create devastation in her breast. She dissolved beneath his blazing ardour, unable to deny him even had she wished. But to her own astonishment she did not so wish! On the contrary, she was more astounded than ever and not a little frightened to find a peculiar feeling awakening deep within her, a feeling which prompted her arms to embrace her lord as fervently as his were embracing her, and her desire to rage in fierce competition with his own which was scaling to unprecedented heights—his arms now crushing her to him, brutally, savagely, as if the desire *she* was awakening in *him* were racing out of control.

Francesca clung to her lord desperately, her eyes tightly closed, offering up gratitude to heaven that they were indeed wed for, were they not, there was extremely little she could do to preserve her honour at this stage which was perilously near the point of no return.

Now she floundered in delirium; a wonderful erotic delirium as his hands—such beautiful hands—played upon her most vulnerable weaknesses; weaknesses she was not certain she cared to have played upon yet knew not how to prevent him, to then realise unashamedly that she did not *want* to prevent him. His touch was no longer gentle but demanding, almost cruelly demanding; demanding everything she had to give and willing to settle for nothing less, oblivious to her finger-nails clawing his naked back

79

and shoulders in an agony of longing as her entire being cried out for she knew not what though he seemed to know well enough and assumed still more powerful command of her will . . . her desires . . . her body.

"Oh Clare . . . ence," she groaned in ecstasy. "How little . . . I have known . . . you."

He did not respond or even grunt in acknowledgment, so absorbed was he in his conjugal duty. But was this the sole reason?

All at once the doubt which had lain dormant in her mind beneath the passion and euphoria surged to the fore, doubt which grew and grew, persuading her to think it uncommonly strange how not a single word had been spoken; how the entire proceedings had been blanketed in silence from the very outset, a disconcerting silence broken only by her gasping, groaning, and the deafening thud of her heart with, curiously, not a sound from her noble lord.

Suddenly in this moment of reckoning and rebirth of her conscious mind an alien sound penetrated the uncanny silence—the sound of anguished weeping, wailing and moaning far, far away. At first she thought it due to the wind sighing in the great empty chimney until it struck her with a pang that it was the sound of a human being in direst distress.

"Clarence, listen!" she exclaimed of a sudden, bolting upright to prick her ears in the direction of the sound. "I can hear someone weeping."

But seemingly Clarence was too passionately roused to pay the slightest heed to the abnormality and dragged her down onto the pillows to complete the act of consummation, smothering her protests with his lips.

"Clarence! Stop!" she managed to cry out at length, struggling beneath his weight. "Please . . . if you love me—"

This he was about to prove categorically, though not in words, when a strong premonition that something was wrong, terribly, terribly wrong, seized Francesca and she bounded out of the bed in one nimble movement before he could stay her. Rushing across to the long narrow casement she wrenched aside the heavy velvet curtains, allowing the bright moonlight to streak across the room, piercing the inky darkness and revealing in the beautiful nupital bed, not Clarence her bridegroom as she might have expected, but instead his overlord—Monsieur Sylvestre de Villennay.

Seven

Outrage! Blazing unmitigated outrage consumed Viscountess Kleine like a holocaust as she stood trembling uncontrollably by the window, her ague due more to the aftermath of her profound emotional experience than her rage though nothing in the world would have urged her to confess it. Nevertheless it was a rage so intense that it excelled the excruciating humiliation battling for second place and temporarily blinded her to the fact that her state of dishabille, together with the brillance of the moon, was leaving remarkably little to the Frenchman's imagination.

"How dare you!" she eventually articulated after three abysmal attempts, choked with venom as she suddenly donned her swansdown robe with some alacrity. "How dare you take so much upon yourself and usurp my husband's rightful place! In the name of heaven, sir, this is the ultimate!"

No, Mr Villennay did not leap from the bed and fall upon his knees in abject contrition to petition her forgiveness as she deemed any decent mortal might. Instead he merely rendered his person more comfortable amongst the feather pillows, hands clasped behind dark head while he surveyed her through languid eyes in obvious anticipation of a stormy scene.

He could hardly own the lady's affronted outburst unexpected. Although he had taken pains to darken the room with extra thick curtains and a deficiency of candles he was under no delusion that an astute young woman like the new Lady Kleine would remain hoodwinked for long though he had hoped she would remain hoodwinked long enough for him to accomplish all that was necessary. Apparently he had not mimicked the bungling swain as well as he ought.

Consequently, he endured her tirade with stoical forbearance volunteering not a single word of self-vindication while she rampaged up and down the room lashing him with her tongue and designating him every vile name she could call to mind.

"How could you use me in such heinous manner, sirrah—even *you*?" she flared, her green eyes flashing a virulent accompaniment. "Despite your licentious past I thought you had been reared a gentleman, not a villainous vulgar barbarian! Surely there are wenches aplenty in the local taverns for you to seduce at your pleasure, or have you exhausted the supply? Well, monsieur?" she demanded, struggling to steady her voice which shook at the affront she had been accorded but perhaps more in the knowledge that the man was capable of rousing her emotions to such unprecedented heights. "Why do you choose me, sir, to wreak your lecherous designs upon? Why? Why me?" she screamed at his supine form for her words seemed to be falling by the wayside.

Indeed, she suspected he had gone completely deaf for not the slightest indication did he give that he was hearkening to her words though her volume of voice granted him little choice. Neither did he move but remained unnaturally still while his black sinister eyes, glinting like a cat's in the semi-darkness, followed her irate figure up and down the room with unwavering steadiness until she stormed to a halt and drew herself up, her bosom still heaving tumultuously in defiance of her wishes.

"Sir! As you refuse to answer me, though I appreciate even your power of ingenuity would be hard pressed to concoct a plausible excuse for this appalling act, I order you to leave immediately!"

As she half expected him to ignore her order, she was hardly disappointed.

"Do you hear me, sir? I command you to leave this instant? If you refuse you will give me no alternative but to summon the servants and have you removed by force! Very well," she snorted, marching round the bed towards the communicating door, "perhaps Clarence himself might be interested to discover precisely how his peerless idol conducts himself when his lordly back is turned."

Before she could suit action to words his hand shot out, seized her by the swansdown robe and dragged her roughly to the bed where she found herself pinioned in his brutal hold and gazing up into his face, the expression of which defied all description.

"You will not bother Clarence with this trivality, mistress," he adjured her on a note of unmistakable menace.

Not until this moment did Francesca appreciate fully the true character of this man called Villennay, just how ruthless he could be and how imprudent it would be to seriously provoke him, as his dark ferocious eyes seared her being, the eyes of a vicious black panther, and she suffered not the slightest doubt that he would prove equally savage if roused. Again she trembled, but this time in trepidation, wondering for the first time if her coming to Kleine had been a wise decision after all for she sensed a peculiar feeling that the degradation she had undergone at the hands of Monsieur was, somehow, not to be the limit of her tribulations.

"Will you suffer me to vacate the bed as I am?" he appended in the same tone. "Or shall I robe myself?"

With a cry of protest she hurriedly averted her eyes as he flung back the bedclothes to rise. How he managed to don his scarlet brocade dressing robe without relinquishing hold of her was a feat of dexterity she cherished no predilection to witness, but when she did dare venture a look she found him respectably attired. She flinched as he transferred his hand to her arm, bethinking he was about to strike her for all the insults she had hurled at his head, but instead he drew her across to the communicating door to Clarence's rooms where, to her bewilderment, he gently yet firmly placed her cheek against the door panel.

"Listen, Madame la Vicomtesse," he invited calmly enough, though granting her no alternative. "Tell me what you hear."

Francesca duly listened and once again detected the sound of distraught sobbing and weeping but this time much more distinctly, before she sprang back wide-eyed from the door.

"I-It isn't Clarence? It can't be Clarence!" she gasped.

"Who else, ma'am?" he parried laconically.

She struggled in his hold. "But I must go to him! I can't bear to hear him so stricken—I must try to comfort him."

"No, mistress," he discouraged her in no uncertain manner, his tall, invincible, brocade-clad figure barring the way. "It would serve no purpose."

"Why?" she cried as he propelled her across the polished floor and fur rugs back into the room away from the door, where he released her. "Is it because you forbad him the marriage-bed on his wedding night, sir?"

"No, ma'am. He is distraught because he disobeyed me."

"And you seek to punish him most heinously by locking him in his chamber while you ravish his bride!"

The Frenchman reined in his temper with super-human control.

"I admit it rather seems that way but, I assure you, nothing is further from the truth. Even I should cavil at descending to such despicable depths."

"Be honest, sir! Why else would my lord lie weeping on this night of nights?"

"Why not? Surely it isn't the singular prerogative of the bride?" he flung back with blistering scorn.

Francesca ignored the gibe and boldly confronted him, striving to meet his gaze which was as hard as flint.

"On oath, sir, did you coerce my lord into this marriage?"

"Correct me should I be at fault, ma'am, but I laboured 'neath the delusion you deemed me the proverbial spoke in the nuptial wheel?"

Monsieur was right, of course, as Monsieur was *always* right. To be completely frank, Francesca was not at all certain in which direction the Frenchman's pendulum of loyalty swung, for or against; but having tried the one and been found wanting she had a mind to try the other. However, of one thing she was absolutely certain, that in either event the pendulum would swing to no one's advantage but his own.

"Er—that was so, monsieur," she admitted at length, commensurately shamefaced, "but you must confess this present crisis alters the situation somewhat. Perhaps there is something personal about me he doesn't like?"

He shrugged non-committally. "Not to my knowledge. At least, no more than any other."

"So much so that his stomach rebels and he must flee in retreat to his closet?" she challenged him forcefully. "Do you tell me, sir, that other females affect him so?"

"Yes."

"They make him sick?"

"Violently."

She gaped at him in open-mouthed incredulity. "Why? D-Doesn't he like women?"

"No. They sadly disillusion him, as you yourself did scarce ten hours ago."

"*I*—disillusioned him? In what way?"

His black brows drew together marring his forehead, as if he were reluctant to pursue the topic any further, but this her ladyship refused to allow.

"Please, Mr Villennay, you must tell me what I've done to upset Clarence," she pleaded, swallowing her bitterness at his reluctance to speak out. "Don't you see, I might inadvertently upset him again, apart from which I'm his wife! I've every reason to know!"

He paused, then capitulated with a sigh. "Very well, ma'am, I shall be candid. I have reason to suspect you did encourage him in the fatuous belief that he might consummate his own marriage."

A deathly hush greeted the disclosure which took some tolerable while to penetrate her ladyship's dazed brain, while Mr Villennay stood viewing her questioningly as if awaiting confirmation of his words although they had been uttered in a statement of fact.

"I-Is there any reason why he should not?" she stammered faintly.

He flung away from her as if the issue rearing its ungainly head were repellant to him, and were desperately seeking a way to evade it, a way which did not, alas, materialise.

"I know not how to phrase it . . . I had hoped it would not be necessary," he began, to break off with a futile gesture. "To be blunt, ma'am, your husband the Viscount is—is—"

"Yes?"

"Impotent."

"Im . . . po . . . tent?" she mouthed aghast, her numbed senses battling to refute the diabolical interpretation her brain was putting upon his admission.

"Do you comprehend my meaning and exactly what it implies?" he turned to question tersely. "Or would you have me clarify it in all its sordid detail?"

"There can . . . be no mis . . . under . . . standing?" she probed, struggling to quell the nausea mounting inside her.

"None whatsoever. It has been established beyond doubt."

"And you were both aware of it when you invited me to Kleine?" she queried significantly, indignation assuming command of her emotions. "You knew when I married Clarence that he was unable to beget a child yet you did not confess it? You deliberately deceived me?"

He winced, then nodded.

With a strangulating sob she turned from him in shame, the most crucifying shame it had ever been her

87

unhappy lot to endure and she knew not how she would ever be able to look either of these men in the face again, Mr Penrose, Lady Brindley, Tristram—or indeed anyone! The past weeks flashed before her eyes and ambiguous, perplexing events now assumed a crystal clear meaning. Experiences which had not only confounded but actually frightened her suddenly had a reason, a purpose, not least of all the weird atmosphere of the old castle, as if the very walls were party to the conspiracy and exuded the same strange character of its inmates. And the never-ending stream of innuendoes which seemed to infer that their relationship ran much deeper than they would have her believe.

Oh, how naive could any girl be? How consummately foolish of her to believe that a viscount of such enormous affluence would condescend to wed her and lavish upon her everything his wealth could buy, endowing her with title, power and privilege without seeking something in return! She had been so flattered and overwhelmed by the offer, bethinking he wanted her solely for herself, that her conceit had blinded her to any ulterior motive he might harbour. It was now that Sylvestre de Villennay's words struck her most poignantly—that Clarence was incapable of doing *anything* for himself.

The whole room gave a sudden jolt and began to spin madly, and Francesca clung to her head with both hands, her eyes tightly closed, trying to still the maelstrom howling round her, threatening her sanity—when she felt a hand on her arm and she looked up through thick swirling mists to discern the vague image of de Villennay by her side, an expression suffusing his countenance which, had not she known him better, she might have termed compassion.

"This has obviously dealt you a substantial blow, ma'am," he overtured in concern. "Be pleased to be seated—"

"Don't touch me, sir!" the Viscountess shrank from him with all the revulsion in her being infecting her voice. "I am well able to sit myself wherever I choose."

And to corroborate this she stumbled across to the

nearest chair into which she sank—or more aptly, collapsed—serving only to confirm his doubts. Following this curt rebuff Mr Villennay retired to the farther side of the room where he proceeded to light the candles in the candelabrum while her ladyship sat rallying herself, fanning the flames of her indignation until it flared into the most raging fury at the abominable way these two purported gentlemen of the upper class had plotted her downfall; had, flagrantly connived to snare her in their nuptial net with not a single thought to her own fate, how she was to survive such gross abuse of her honour and innocence, nor even considered her opinion on the matter!

But vying in close contention with her anger was stupefaction for try as she might she simply could not believe Clarence capable of such intrigue, such devilish cunning, behind which she detected the subtle brain of the Frenchman, upon whom she now turned.

"Am I to assume from this burlesque, monsieur," she questioned, seething at the recollection of her recent humiliation as she gestured with disgust towards the bed, "that it was your foul intent to beget the desired offspring in my husband's stead?"

Mr Villennay had the grace to colour as her brutal candour struck his impervious conscience with punishing force, and he nodded briefly.

"What kind of woman do you think I am, sir?" she challenged him, incensed.

"One of admirable high principle, ma'am," he returned without hesitation.

This merely heaped fuel upon her fire of insult. "Why insist upon a woman of high principle when any vulgar woman of the town would have served your vile purpose and guaranteed my lord his heir?"

"But not guaranteed her silence," he pointed out, a wealth of meaning in his voice. "Conversely when a woman of your moral standards loses her virtue thus 'tis not the sort of thing she cares to boast about."

Francesca blushed furiously. "You appear to have considered every aspect, monsieur!"

He bowed his acquiescence as if he were being complimented.

"It was not my intent that you should remark the substitution. I confess I stand guilty also of underestimating your degree of perception."

Francesca was momentarily bereft of words, undecided whether to applaud his barefaced audacity or condemn his total lack of moral rectitude.

"Mr Villennay, do you have the effrontery to tell me that, had you succeeded in your wicked ploy, you would have suffered no qualms of conscience in so deceiving me?"

"No, ma'am. Why should I? A servant obeys his master without question and does not presume to doubt his judgment. I merely execute the commands of my Lord Viscount."

Her ladyship fell back a pace, aghast. "Sir! Is there no limit to your impertinence? Surely you do not expect me to believe that Clarence ordered you to commit this unpardonable sin? Or that you, Mr Villennay, would demean yourself to the level of his servant and deign to do his bidding?"

The Frenchman met her derisive green eyes with his steady guileless black.

"Alas, I have little choice, my lady. He holds all four aces in his hand and the devil knows how many up his sleeve."

"I don't quite understand you," she faltered, doubts beginning to circulate in her brain that she had not yet heard the worst.

Cynicism curled Mr Villennay's callous mouth. "You will learn before you are very much older, Madame la Vicomtesse, that your noble spouse is not the wide-eyed ingenuous babe you deem him."

"Do you now choose to slander him, sirrah, and transfer the blame for your heinous deed to his sweet innocent head?" she rounded on him hotly.

"Heaven forbid, ma'am. Doubtless you will not appreciate the wisdom of my words until you see him in his true colours."

"What do you mean? You speak in riddles, monsieur!"

"I mean, your ladyship, that my lord will scarce be overjoyed to learn that my first attempt to beget his heir has proven abortive."

"First attempt!" she blazed anew. "Do you presume to think there will be others?"

"Unquestionably, ma'am," he replied with unflinching candour. "If my Lord Viscount commands."

"That remains to be seen, Mr Villennay, and what *I* command!" she hurled at him scathingly. "It is well to know precisely where we stand."

"You seem to forget, madam, that you vowed in all honour to beget the Viscount a child otherwise he would never have wed you."

"Exactly, sir! And it is in all honour that the child will be begot or not at all! I shall not be party to this scandalous arrangement. You must engage another sacrificial virgin to participate in your pagan rites."

"A substitute is inconceivable, mistress. You must realise that as well as I," he rebuked her as he might a refractory infant. "Permit me also to point out, had not you infected his lordship's mind with fanciful notions of begetting his own heir this awkward situation might never have arisen."

"How, sir? Do you foolishly believe I should not then have detected the subterfuge?" she ejaculated, contempt in her eyes and voice. "Do you think Clarence, remotely capable of kissing me as you did? Not to mention the wealth of . . . of experience in . . . your . . . your . . ."

"You are an exceedingly beautiful woman," he cut in swiftly, in a tone she might have termed sincere had it belonged to anyone else. "Is it so difficult to accept that I momentarily forgot myself? I shall endeavour to exercise greater control the next time."

The Viscountess leapt to her bare feet. "You do not seem to understand, Monsieur de Villennay, there is to be no next time! This farce is at an end!"

"With all respect, ma'am," he rectified with a magnanimous bow, "the farce, as you so aptly term it, is just beginning. I'm sorry if the very concept offends your sensibilities but, alas, there is no help for it. All must cede to my lord's will, even his lady wife—and her sensibilities." He sauntered nonchalantly to the outer door which he unlocked, then turned. "I trust you will forgive the deception. I sought simply to make the nights which lie ahead less painful for us both."

"Do you imply, sir, that you would insult me further by committing me to your dastardly will by force?"

"If needs be, and my lord commands."

"Whether my lord commands or not, monsieur, you will not lay a hand upon my person!" she charged him, taking full advantage of her superior position. "You overlook the fact that I am now a viscountess while you remain a scurvy misbegotten French refugee." She glowed with satisfaction to see her dart pierce his imperturbable guard and his black eyes flare, though evanescently. "You will deign to treat me with the respect my elevated status demands or suffer the consequences of your reprehensible actions. I think you will discover anon to your cost, monsieur, that I also have an ace or two up my sleeve."

Without further comment he retired, but leaving my Lady Kleine somewhat less confident than she sounded. Granted, she readily acknowledged that Sylvestre de Villennay was not the most trustworthy of mortals, and indeed, every whit as unscrupulous, devious and cunning as Mr Penrose had declared him to be. Howbeit, there was something in his manner, his tone—she could not say what—which generated a feeling of discomfort, prompting her to doubt, pause and reconsider, and ultimately ponder the question if it were at all possible for there to be an element of truth in his claim?

Eight

Although it was almost dawn by the time Francesca climbed back into the marriage bed, sleep eluded her. This may have been due to a gnawing anxiety that Mr Villennay might condescend to pay another visit and surprise her while she slept, though how even the astute Frenchman was to accomplish this with a chest of drawers placed across one door and a daybed across the other would be difficult to say. Alternatively it may have been the sense of burning outrage which continued to smoulder within her as she lay in the darkness reliving every harrowing moment of the degradation she had been accorded, and cursing Sylvestre de Villennay from his raven-black hair down to his elegant feet, while imprecating heaven to punish him most severely for his inexpiable sin; granted a sin he had not actually committed but nonetheless had intended to, and assuredly would have done but for a fortuitous prompting of her conscience.

Ice-cold perspiration bedappled her forehead as she recalled how close she had been to relinquishing her all to this French reprobate, and she trembled in wrathful remembrance, refusing to acknowledge the possibility that her trembling could be due to anything other than the appalling concept of being so dishonoured and by such an one, for what else could it be? What indeed! After all it certainly could not be due to any ominous feelings deep within that the man had evoked such passionate emotions in her that for one brief moment she had actually wanted him to commit his dastardly act, French reprobate or no.

Moreover, it may have been this same feeling and the realisation that Mr Villennay had it in his power to dominate her as he did Clarence which incited her hatred and hostility towards him. Perhaps it was his dark seductive eyes and the way they swept her up and down as if able to perceive a deal more than she intended they should, or the way he swiftly veiled them with his thick black lashes whenever she sensed he was observing her. Or was it that sinister yet attractive aura which shrouded him? The aura Mr Penrose had warned her about and which she must be strong enough to gainsay.

No! Monsieur de Villennay was not going to hold his evil sway over her. She was forewarned! True, she had come perilously near to defeat but all was not lost for she now saw through his fiendish cunning and how he had deliberately tried to poison her mind against her husband with a farrago of lies. Poor, sweet innocent Clarence. How could one believe such vile insinuations about him? Yes, she was prepared to concede it feasible that he was unable to beget his own child, but wholly repudiated the suggestion that he was party to the iniquitous scheming.

It was in this firmly biased attitude of mind that the Viscountess betook herself down to break her fast the following morning, though it was almost noon, her guns run out and ready to fire at the first indication of war by dint of provocation from Mr Villennay. But nothing would appear to be further from the Frenchman's intention who, throughout the meal, was the quintessence of urbanity as if there were nothing more untoward between them than the Viscount's hang-dog expression. And although the repast proceeded quietly with little conversation, it did so without incident. Moreover, Clarence's inability to command even himself let alone anyone as outspoken as his friend, together with his obvious longing for the floor to open and swallow him up chair and all, would seem to give the lie to Mr Villennay's claims and prove them irrefutably false.

On the contrary, it was Mr Villennay himself who, as always, held full sway over the breakfast table and who did not fail to admonish the hapless Viscount whenever the occasion so warranted, and once or twice when it did not. Clarence refused to be drawn out and remained silent the while, toying indifferently with his food, his eyes downcast and cheeks a dull red as if he were overwhelmingly conscious of Francesca's presence and the terrible indignity he had suffered the previous night. In fact, his mortification became so acute that before the meal was over he was craving Sylvestre's permission to adjourn to his rooms, permission which was granted and at which her ladyship was hard pressed not to laugh out loud. Why should Clarence feel obliged to crave permission of anyone to quit his own table? And so Clarence slunk from the room leaving his Viscountess to endure the same discomfort alone in Mr Villennay's company as he himself had in hers.

Her ladyship did not linger long after her husband and presently rose, excusing herself upon the pretext of writing some letters, but before she had taken three steps towards the doors—guarded by the inevitable sober-faced lackeys in the Kleine livery—she found her path barred by Mr Villennay.

"If I may make so bold as to proffer a word of advice, ma'am," he murmured softly in order that none should overhear.

"More advice, sir?" she rallied him facetiously.

He ignored her ill-conceived humour. "His lordship labours cheerfully under the delusion that his marriage was—er—was—"

"Consummated? Is that the word you seek?"

His eyes progressed ceilingwards, a sign that her provocation was having its desired effect.

"Consummated," he repeated as if the word choked

95

him. "You would do well to foster this delusion if you wish to avoid any unpleasantness."

"Unpleasantness for whom, sir? For you, me, or my lord?"

"For all of us. Your servant, mistress," he dismissed himself with a curt bow, thus foiling any further requital hovering upon her lips, and sauntered off leaving Madame la Vicomtesse battling with the irresistible urge to drum her dainty fists in his velvet-clad back.

That night, understandably, Francesca took every possible precaution to safeguard her chastity from further violation by placing her scissors and silver back-scraper readily to hand at the bedside and, should these prove ineffectual and the worst happen, a small primed pistol appropriated from the armoury under her pillows. With her stronghold thus fortified against surprise attack she settled down between the comforting silk sheets, content in the knowledge that her honour would remain intact and that the doors were firmly locked—though this alone could scarcely be relied upon to keep her enemy at bay.

My lady reflected upon this awhile and eventually decided to adopt more stringent measures by rolling herself up tightly in one of the sheets and so render it an utter impossibility for Mr Villennay to fulfil his dastardly ambition without waking her—that was if she unwittingly fell asleep which she certainly had no intention of doing. Granted, her movement and breathing were somewhat restricted but this she was more than willing to suffer in order to confound the Frenchman's amorous advances. Indeed, she was so pleased with her stratagem she even indulged in a chuckle or two as she lay prone in the flickering light of one candle, her gaze riveted to the outer door—until her eyelids began to droop and she fell into a sound sleep.

But Mr Villennay did not attend the nuptial chamber that night. At least he certainly did not appear to have done when her ladyship extricated herself from the sheet the following morning to sit up and gaze round the room. Everything was exactly as it ought to be. Even the doors were still locked, upon inspection, and these she hastily opened lest her maid be suspicious when she arrived with her customary cup of hot chocolate.

Perhaps it was a little premature to applaud her efforts as yet, nevertheless she was relieved, if not daring to be elated, at this initial success in deterring Mr Villennay. Of course, it was quite feasible that he had fallen asleep, taken ill, or merely decided to grant her a night's respite and would in all probability spring his second attack that very next evening.

But neither did he appear the next night, nor the one after. And night rapidly succeeded night until they lapsed into weeks, then months, when Francesca felt justified in pronouncing herself truly victorious. In retrospect, however, she could not own herself surprised for it was now screamingly obvious that Mr Villennay had taken fright at her threat to confront Clarence with his trumped-up excuses for heinously daring to seduce his lady. This she could have felt perfectly happy about but for one tiny misgiving, namely, why he should request her most earnestly to encourage her husband in the deception; to engender the belief that he had actually committed the foul deed? But this was too trivial to entertain when the evidence weighed so heavily against the man. Therefore the matter was despatched from her mind though she continued assiduously each night with her precautions, nonetheless.

In fact, she now saw virtually nothing of the Frenchman whom she assumed to be hiding his face in shame and for the most part found herself left very much to her own devices as Clarence, since his disastrous experience upon the wedding night, was also unable to look her in the eye, and even the simple task of bidding her a good day seemed to place a formidable strain on his self-control to such a degree that he eventually declined to dine with her altogether and remained enshrined once more in his rooms.

The situation came to a boisterous climax one day when, to relieve her boredom, Lady Kleine decided to go riding and explore the beautiful rugged countryside of which she had seen extremely little outside the castle walls since her

97

arrival which seemed to beckon her more forcibly than usual on this cold but sunny September morn.

At length, garbed in a fetching riding habit of strawberry pink superfine trimmed with silver, lace steinkirk, and matching cocked hat sporting a sweeping peacock feather, she cantered out of the castle upon a sleek chestnut, unable to see what harm she could cause in so doing for she had her maid, Martha, and a groom to bear her company lest she fall foul of the mountainous area and lose her direction.

Once through the barbican she was suddenly overwhelmed by an exhilarating sense of freedom as she gazed upon the range of sweeping hills and wild desolate countryside outspread before her which seemed to invite her more strongly than ever to come and join them in their abandonment, to liberate herself and sample the fruits of the wilderness.

Francesca did not wait for a second bidding and digging her heels vigorously into the mare's flanks shot off at a break-neck gallop across the heath and moorland. Thus she rode like the wind, leaving the servants far behind and having much ado to keep within calling distance, laughing as she galloped at the wonderful indescribable feeling of shaking off the past and beginning life anew at Kleine; blowing the memories of Mr Villennay's sordid little interlude from her mind with the knowledge that Clarence would, alas, be obliged to relinquish his desire for an heir and accept his defeat gracefully.

Breathless and excited with the stimulating ride she eventually drew rein at the foot of one of the surrounding hills and waited for the servants to come alongside. She then dismounted, declaring it her intention to climb a short way up the hill and admire the view therefrom, and invited them to accompany her if they so wished. As the maid had not recovered from the exerting ride it was the groom who accompanied her ladyship up the hill to the desired spot where she could command an awe-inspiring view of the landscape with the Cheviots in all their grandeur on one side and the moors on the other, stretching down to the rural village of Otterburn and rolling away into the distance as far as the eye could see, to Hexham and the Tyne valley, while to the left ran the turnpike from Elsdon to Rothbury beyond which lay the flourishing market town of Morpeth.

She strained her eyes along the horizon, trying to discern the pit-heaps along the Tyne but this was demanding too much of even her excellent vision, and so she turned her attention to the other side of the hill. As she did so she spied a house not far away, a house of comparatively modern design which certainly could not have been more than fifty years old, and which the groom informed her was the dower House. It had been constructed for the sixth Viscountess Kleine upon her relegation to Dowager—a veritable dragon of a woman by all accounts—yet who had occupied the house for a mere six months before the invading Scots had forced her, brave as she was, to flee for sanctuary within the castle walls, and the house had stood empty ever since.

Francesca continued on round the hill to the farther side which looked out upon its elder brothers and sisters, hills of greater stature, and upon the most breath-taking sight of all, namely, her home—Kleine Castle. She had never viewed it from such an angle before and found it strangely impressive, almost bewitching, set thus amongst the splendour of the purple hills and raised upon a broad knoll which had helped render it invincible against the marauders during its turbulent lifetime, though it bore the scars of many a border skirmish, scars which its indifferent master had not chosen to heal. Nevertheless it stood out in defiance, bold and noble, with three of its four jutting towers quite unscarred and sketched majestically against the blue skies. But as she lingered thus admiring the ancient fortress the less admirable it suddenly became, and it transformed before her eyes into something hideous; into a gruesome demon's head, not with towers but with horns; and the castellated battlements were now huge blackened teeth grinning at her grotesquely, mocking her, until with an articulate cry she sped off down the hill to her horse upon which she leapt and galloped away, leaving maid and manservant to follow in her wake as before, striving as she went to convince herself against insurmountable odds that it was not an ill omen, nor an evil prognostication of what was to come.

Until this catastrophic moment so alluring had been the scenery that Francesca did not realise she had tarried longer than intended. Even so, all she anticipated upon her return was some mild disapproval and, perhaps, concern on her behalf—certainly not anything like the welcome she was accorded, and before she had as much as overstepped the threshold she found a flunkey hastening towards her to inform her in anxious tone that she was awaited most urgently in the Plantagenet Chamber. Her appearance was a little unkempt to say the least and she was about to hasten abovestairs to tidy herself and change into more becoming attire before presenting herself, but barely had she mounted two stairs of the ponderous Jacobean oak staircase when martial footsteps resounded upon the floor of hewn flint and a masculine voice called out peremptorily.

"Madam! I would have speech with you—now!"

As the servants scurried away like mice to their holes Francesca turned in some astonishment to see Clarence framed in the doorway of the Plantagenet Chamber, an expression upon his face which could only be termed thunderous, and utterly alien to his nature. Indeed, it was quite some time before Lady Kleine could collect herself for she had never witnessed such an expression upon anyone's face let alone that of Clarence her husband, and most timid of mortals. Upon ultimately regaining her composure, or as much of it as she could muster, she thought it wiser to obey without remonstrance and so followed her lord into the room in question. Not surprisingly she was a trifle shaken for she had not yet recovered from the effects of the ghastly vision and now felt persuaded to accept its ominous portent with some degree of credibility.

Why the Plantagenet Chamber was so named would be difficult to say for apart from a suit of armour displayed in a tall glass-fronted cabinet and a huge daunting stag's head looming over the fireplace there was little else reminiscent of the fourteen monarchs from the houses of Anjou, Lancaster and York. On the contrary, the furnishings were quite modern and the very best that money could buy, boasting brocade upholstery and carved walnut, and a luxurious carpet of an oriental flavour before the fireplace wherein logs blazed merrily upon this fine but chill autumn day.

It was across to this gaping orifice of sculptured stone that Lord Kleine strode, dismissing the footmen with an irritable jerk of his head to then march up and down, refusing to utter a syllable until the doors had closed upon the last liveried back, when without more ado he launched his attack.

"Who, may I ask, madam, gave you leave to go galloping off to heaven knows where, giving licence to your own selfish pleasure and hazarding the precious life of my unborn son?"

Her ladyship's mouth fell appropriately ajar in amazement.

"I-I'm afraid I don't understand you, my lord."

"Don't you?" he snapped acidly. "You cannot deny that you could at this very moment be bearing my future heir within you!"

"I both can and do, sir!" retorted she, her anger flaring on a par with his own. "Most emphatically!"

A cutting silence descended upon the scene, his lordship's eyes narrowing suspiciously.

"How can you be so certain, madam, when you have ceased to be a virgin these three months past?"

Francecsa flushed to the roots of her dishevelled red hair as she swept it back from her face with an outraged gesture, realising that it was time for blunt speech. So infuriated was she, in fact, that she blurted out before she could foresee the consequences—or indeed, that there were any to be seen—of her hasty words.

"I beg your pardon! I assure you I am still in full possession of my virtue and shall remain so until the day I die rather than abandon myself to the wanton lust of your Monsieur de Villennay!"

My lord's countenance was a picture to behold, a classic study in bewilderment and disbelief. Disbelief eventually won the day.

"You lie!" he snarled.

"I do not lie, sir!" she snorted, taking most indignant exception to his tone, manner and choice of phrase. "If you doubt my word, my Lord Viscount, you may summon your physician to verify my claim any time you wish."

This time my lord was wholly bereft of words for his lady seemed to be telling the truth, a truth he could have simply verified; but to admit so was to lay open to question every human instinct he possessed concerning the character of the man with whom he had lived for twenty-five years.

However, it need hardly be said that her ladyship was also dumbfounded for her own judgment of character had been dealt a shattering blow and she could not credit that the snarling monster before her was Clarence—her timid, pitiful, sweet Clarence. But worse was the daunting knowledge that she must own Mr Villennay the victor, the man she had reviled, scorned and condemned as liar, and that she must now accept the painful facts. Every word he had testified and which she had contemptuously flouted was proven and made manifest. Clarence *had* commanded him to commit this cardinal sin; had confirmed it from his own lips. She was trapped with no way of escape! She was wed to Clarence and would therefore be obliged to do his bidding. She was his wife, his chattel, to do with as he pleased; even sell her in the market-place if he so desired, or have her subjected to all manner of cruel punishments to discipline her to his will and correct her forward ways. And if she fled from Kleine, whither would she run? Certainly not to London where news of her marriage would already be spread abroad by Lady Brindley and Mr Penrose. She would be an outcast, rejected by all and sundry for even the lower classes thought very poorly of a wife who deserted her husband. Alas, she could not hope to evade Clarence's wrath for very long.

But how could she possibly contemplate the shocking alternative of allowing Sylvestre de Villennay to have his lecherous way? How could she relinquish to this rake, this profligate who respected neither God's law nor man's, her most valuable gift, the gift she had vowed before heaven to relinquish unto no man but her legitimate husband? But had not she vowed with equal fervour and reverence to obey her noble lord? And if he saw fit to command her to bear the child of Mr Villennay ought not she so to do as a dutiful wife? No! No! Not Sylvestre de Villennay, her heart cried out in protest. Some other man, perhaps, but not he. If Clarence were obdurately set upon this plan then she must prevail upon him to at least humour her whim to select another man; a man of gentle amenable disposition, who would respect her status, and who had not tumbled every wench in the entire county.

"Do you tell me, madam, that Sylvestre has deliberately deceived me?" the Viscount's irascible voice obtruded upon her deliberations at this point.

His wife knew not what to reply. She had no desire to incriminate Mr Villennay any more than was necessary, and furthermore was acutely aware of the danger in provoking Clarence in his present unpredictable mood when she sensed a mere word or misplaced gesture could well result in physical violence. Therefore, instead of turning on him in a torrent of outraged modesty as conscience dictated she decided to try to reason with him, philosophically.

"Clarence, surely you do not expect Sylvestre to blacken his soul by committing this terrible deed?" she digressed diplomatically round his question.

He returned a disparaging look. "I do not understand you, ma'am. How can anything become blacker than black?"

The gibe was not intended as such, she sensed, and the disparagement was seemingly directed at her rather than Mr Villennay.

"That's as may be, my lord, but what of *my* soul?" she spoke up anxiously. "Would you have me tarnish it by breaking God's commandment?"

This was a mistake, for nothing was guaranteed to exacerbate Clarence more than allusion to his Creator.

"Do you dare to defy me, mistress?" he erupted anew,

his eyes alight with a kind of madness. "Would you break *my* commandment rather than that of your God?"

Francesca fell back in horror. "Sir! You blaspheme me!"

"Why should I honour a god who has cursed me with this vile incapacity? Why?" his tongue lashed her in biting disdain. "I did not seek to be thus afflicted!"

Despite her revulsion Francesca was seized with sudden compassion for her husband, for she began to suspect that the violence of his emotions concealed great suffering beneath.

"Clarence," she ventured cautiously. "Have you ever thought to invoke His clemency?"

"Clemency for what? You speak as if I had committed some misdemeanour. I have done nought to merit such punishment, madam. I did not even ask to be born."

"But if you were to pray for help and guidance perhaps—"

"Help!" The Viscount drew himself up with a regal air, his head aloft and manner aloof. "Are you perchance suggesting, ma'am, that I, Clarence Edward James Montague Fennistone, should humble myself on my very knees to a being whose existence I know not of? That I should grovel and supplicate for aid in amending a wrong which is no fault of mine? A wrong which has not been inflicted upon others more deserving of such!"

Francesca shrank before her husband as he stood tall and haughty confronting her with the blood of generations of arrogant Kleine overlords coursing vigorously through his veins. No, this was not the Clarence she knew. This was not her Clarence, the man she had played with, sung and laughed with. But just how well did she know him? Was not it conceivable that the proud unfeeling aristocrat now poised in front of her was the *real* Clarence, the Clarence who would beget his heir by fair means or foul?

"I granted your God until Eastertide to redress the injustice," he went on with unmistakable malice in his voice, "but He has chosen to spurn my ultimatum."

"One does not threaten the Supreme Being with ultimatums, my Lord Viscount," she could not resist enlightening him, self-righteously.

"Nonetheless, you must see that I now have no alternative but to redress the injustice in my own way, as I think fitting."

"It's wicked! Sinful! Iniquitous!"

"But effective."

"No! I won't! I can't debase myself in this shameful way."

In two strides he was at her side with her right arm paralysed in a grip of iron, a grip she would never have dreamed him capable of but for the fact that her arm seemed about to break.

"You can and will, madam, because I your lord and master command it!" he hissed between clenched teeth. "You are my lawful wife and will obey me implicitly in all things. Is that understood?"

"Yes! Yes! M-My arm . . . it's breaking," she gasped, almost fainting with the excruciating pain.

He released her roughly and stalked back to the fireplace as she sank weakly onto a Derbyshire chair, tenderly caressing her bruised arm, surprised to find herself actually longing for Mr Villennay to come for he, if anyone, could surely bring Clarence to his senses.

"Am I to be granted no voice in the matter?" she faltered at length.

"No!"

"Not even concerning the father of my child?"

Up jerked his fair head, his eyes two glinting icicles. "Take care what you say, madam!"

"Clarence," she besought him placatingly, "must the father be Sylvestre? Can't you choose someone else?"

Too late, she had courted disaster. Clarence stormed across the room towards her as if he would rend her limb from limb then pulled up short, trembling, livid with rage by her chair into which she recoiled in fear.

"You-You harlot! You Jezebel!" he screamed at her, incensed. "No man but Sylvestre will ever be granted the privilege of bedding my wife! What do you take me for, woman? I give you warning, madam, I will not tolerate being made a cuckold and mocked by every clodpole in the county!"

"I-I'm sorry, Clarence, I did not quite think what I was saying . . . p-please forgive me," she pleaded, trying desperately to humour him as he towered above her, his hands clenched rigidly until the knuckles shone white.

"I'll suffer you to bear the child of none other but Sylvestre—"

"Yes! Yes! Whatever you suggest," she endorsed hurriedly—when a new interpretation of his words was suddenly borne to her and she raised her head, a strange misty look in her eyes. "Clarence . . . is it possible?" she breathed in wonder. "Would you be . . . jealous?"

"Jealous? Of course I'd be jealous! D'you think I'm inhuman?"

"Oh Clarence!" she enthused, starry-eyed. "Is it because you truly love me, and feel that Sylvestre is the only man you could bear to touch me in such a way?"

An odd expression suffused his countenance. "Love you?" he exclaimed with a chuckle, then a laugh—an unnatural laugh with the spine-chilling ring of insanity. "Love you? Of course I don't love you! I could never love you! If you want the truth of it, I *hate* you. I have hated you since I first set eyes on you. I hate you for being beautiful; for hurting him; for what you've done to him. Oh my lady, how I indeed despise you for the insult he has borne at your behest! How could you spurn a man like Sylvestre? How?" Tears sprang to his eyes as his voice broke suddenly and he flung away from her lest she observe his distress. "I love Sylvestre! I love him more than my very self, and only *his* child could I cherish as my own. Don't you understand—I *love* him!" he cried out in torment, tears now coursing freely, unashamedly, down his cheeks. "You're a fool! A blind ignorant fool!" he sobbed. "How I loathe you for rejecting his love, his passion, the feel of his arms encircling your body—arms for which I have yearned desperately throughout the past agonising years yet which he has constantly denied me. La! Do I shock you, ma'am?"

Yes, she was certainly shocked! Too shocked to utter a

syllable. Clarence was right; she had been blind and ignorant not to have realised it from the outset. This was it! This was the strange feeling she sensed and which Sylvestre de Villennay had sought to convey without words during that first meeting in her boudoir, a meaning she had not been able to comprehend—or perhaps had not wanted to? Surely it had been there hovering inexorably the while in the back of her mind, battling for the recognition she stubbornly refused to grant lest it open the floodgates to the most crucifying pain, heartache and humiliation it had ever been woman's accursed lot to endure. Clarence! Only Clarence, driven by the force of his perverted emotions had been able to summon sufficient courage to phrase the crux of Kleine's sinister aura into words—Clarence, the effeminate weakling had finally proved the strongest of all; but it was a strength motivated by a soul-destroying virulent pernicious jealousy.

"Can you appreciate the agony of soul which has been mine during the past months, envisaging you languishing in those same arms every night? Can you?" he spat contemptuously, prowling round her chair like a leopard scenting its prey. "The intolerable agony of imagining him caressing you, kissing you, while I lay in my chamber alone and dejected, unloved and unwanted. An agony which in one fell blow you have set at nought, and which I must endure all over again! By Satan, I could kill you with my naked hands—"

"Clarence!" The voice of Sylvestre de Villennay cut through the air like an axe.

Nine

Lord Kleine leapt back as if stung by a hornet to stand blinking stupidly at Sylvestre as if waking from a profound sleep, then the madness fell from him and he transformed before his wife's eyes into the lovable innocent she knew.

"Sylvestre!" he cried excitedly, dashing across to greet his friend like a devoted spaniel, seizing his right hand and kissing it with great fervour which Mr Villennay resented yet tolerated though his austere expression deepened as his eye alighted upon Francesca who was so overwrought she could not bring herself to curtsy nor acknowledge his advent in any way.

It would have been howlingly apparent to someone far less perceptive than Mr Villennay that something was sorely amiss. Precisely what remained to be seen though he could well imagine if Clarence's closing speech was to be relied upon. Without averting his gaze he elevated one long slender forefinger to summon a flunkey of whom he requested brandy and glasses before turning his attention to Clarence who still fawned at his side.

"Tell me, my lord, what has occurred during my absence to overset her ladyship to such a degree?" he invited with equanimity, gently disengaging his dove-grey superfine sleeve from Clarence's clutching fingers to stroll across to the log fire and extend his hands to the welcoming blaze.

"Overset? Fran isn't overset, are you, Fran?" replied he with beguiling innocence, following breathlessly on Sylvestre's heels. "Please, Sylvestre, don't 'my lord' me," he begged plaintively. "Don't be angry with me, I beseech you! I-If you only knew how I . . . suffer when you are gone . . . the anguish and torment . . . you would not punish me so. Where've you been?" he now demanded, his deeply disturbed but equally disturbingly beautiful face staring up at his obdurate friend. "You have been gone so long I vow I was about to send forth servants to search."

"That is not the impression I was given upon arrival," drawled the Frenchman with caustic undertones. "You were quite hysterical and threatening her ladyship in a most hostile fashion."

"I wasn't hysterical, Sylvestre." He forced a laugh which was interrupted by the entrance of the footman regally bearing the requisitioned brandy and glasses, and the discourse did not resume until the double oak panelled doors had closed upon him, allowing his lordship a moment's respite in which to rattle his fevered brain for a plausible reply. "I was merely shouting, or rather talking loudly—w-we were playing a game."

"May I enquire which game necessitates a man encircling a lady's throat with his bare hands?" pursued his friend, casually measuring a few drams of the spirit into a glass and proferring it to Francesca.

Clarence gave a nervous cough. "I'm afraid I lost my temper, Sylvestre. You know what a shocking loser I invariably am—"

Mr Villennay slammed the solid gateleg table with his lace-draped hand, silencing Clarence on the instant to the jangle and tinkle of bottle and glasses.

"Do not seek to cozen me, Clarence! It ill becomes

you," he thundered furiously. "I discovered you in the act of assaulting your wife just now and I would know why?"

His answer came from an unexpected quarter. "My lord was anxious to know why I was not yet with child," submitted her ladyship, surprisingly calm though vastly subdued.

Monsieur choked on his brandy but made a miraculous recovery.

"And you enlightened him, I presume?" he countered, frowning in vexation.

"Yes, sir."

Clarence meanwhile was no less uneasy than Mr Villennay and hung about the doors ready to make his escape when he felt his absence would not be remarked.

"You lied to me, Sylvestre," he could not resist reproaching his friend, the pain in his voice clearly defined. "You led me to believe the sordid deed done."

Mr Villennay sipped the brandy—of which my lord had declined to partake—with grave deliberation and the respect it deserved, seeking a means whereby he might vindicate himself and at the same time protect the Viscountess at whose door the blame largely lay.

"It cannot be hurried, Clarence," he opined at length. "Your wife is not one of the local doxies to be seduced at pleasure but a young lady of breeding and refinement whose existence has been somewhat sheltered. Your patience must endure a while longer, my friend."

"Damnation, Sylvestre! How much longer? You've had three whole months!"

"I'm afraid it is not in my power to predict."

His lordship was not slow to perceive the implication.

"Confound it! Why do you stand on ceremony and permit her to thwart you? You, of such wide experience. Damme, you've never let a woman defy you before. Show her who's master, man! Show her the *real* Sylvestre de Villennay!"

The Frenchman smiled a contemptuous smile, though in contempt of what or whom would never be known. Suffice it that he would scarcely have been human had not he experienced a certain measure of satisfaction at my

110

lord betraying his colours so openly and obligingly before his lady.

"Are you suggesting I ravish your wife, my Lord Viscount?" he queried blandly.

"Yes!" approved Lord Kleine zealously, his eyes agleam at the prospect, which would at least ensure that his wife would not lose her heart to Sylvestre—the thing he personally dreaded most in all the world. "Ravish her! Compel her to your will just as you did the Squire's—"

"No!"

"Why not, blast you?" shouted Clarence, confused by this peculiar attitude of his friend who had never nurtured a grain of tender feeling throughout his entire life.

"I will not take her by force, Clarence!" he rasped irritably, no less confused by his change of heart. "I refuse to make amorous overtures to an embalmed mummy."

If Clarence did not appreciate the significance of this his lady certainly did, and her sharp intake of breath resounded in the poignant silence which greeted the declamation for it proved irrefutably that despite all appearances to the contrary Mr Villennay had indeed paid visits to her bedchamber while she slept. How he had gained admittance undetected, however, was something she could not fathom for she sprinkled starch powder upon the floor and balanced porcelain vases behind the doors yet neither trap had been disturbed and it was utterly impossible for anyone of mortal flesh to have entered without so doing.

She sat tensed, bewildered, her eyes glancing from one man to the other as her fate was batted back and forth between them like a tennis ball and of equal importance, both expressing liberal views and judgment upon how, when and where she was to be defiled yet concerning which vital matter she herself was not allowed to even form an opinion, still less express one.

In spite of rigorous efforts at self-control Clarence was beginning to flounder as his reigning passion slowly emerged; the mad glare was in his eyes and his breathing was laboured as he confronted Mr Villennay across the expanse of tessellated floor.

"You've never suffered qualms about doing so on your

own account," he snarled maliciously, his body perspiring and rigid. "Why suffer them on mine? Why do you now suddenly develop a conscience?"

"Calm yourself, Clarence!" flashed back the Frenchman, a razor-sharp edge to his voice. "Or I shall be forced to take stringent measures."

The Viscount's madness waned as rapidly as before, leaving him trembling, ashen, and only too ready to accede to anything his friend might suggest.

"No! Sylvestre—p-please, I implore you, have mercy! Forgive me! I-I didn't mean to shout at you. Please don't punish me . . . d-don't leave me . . ."

Mr Villennay was disturbed and frowned accordingly down at the empty glass he still held which portrayed the Kleine crest. Past events had engendered the belief that Viscount and Viscountess actually enjoyed each other's company for he himself had not infrequently chanced upon them happily indulging their mutual love of music together, and sometimes with their heads bowed low over a game, giggling like carefree children. And whereas he had acknowledged it inevitable that Clarence must needs discover the truth when his lady was loth to maintain the deception, it was somewhat unfortunate that he should have done so in such a way and at such a critical time.

"You cannot dislike her," Clarence felt urged to point out sullenly. "You vowed most adamantly before I wed her that she was to your taste otherwise I should not have done so."

"Aye, Clarence, she is very much to my taste," murmured the other, pensively regarding the wilting defeated figure of Lady Kleine, "but alas, that is not enough."

"Plague on't, what more do you want?" expostulated my lord.

"Her cooperation."

Clarence's jealousy welled anew. "Cooperation? Nothing more?"

"No, Clarence. You need not fear, my good friend, my heart is not in danger. I give you my word, I shall neither take nor bestow upon your lady wife more than is absolutely necessary to achieve your ends."

His lordship seemed pleased with this reassurance and he brightened—as his lady rallied her remnants of strength to rise in preparation to abandon the nauseating scene of which she had stomached more than enough. But instead of proceeding directly to the door she proceeded first to Mr Villennay.

"Mr Villennay," she faltered, her voice reflecting the despair burdening her heart, "I hope you will forgive me for mistrusting you . . . I-I was grievously wrong . . . I'm sorry . . ."

And before he could make any response she fled the room with a stifled sob, leaving her husband to gaze thunderstruck after her fleeting form and wonder what all the unpleasantness had been about, while Mr Villennay stroked his smooth chin in some perplexity, asking himself why this new submission on the part of her ladyship should disturb his peace of mind.

Ten

Viscountess Kleine had admitted defeat; she was prepared to accept the inevitable; and although her lively ingenuity might yet have devised ways and means whereby she could elude her fate she had neither strength nor will to fight any longer and failed to see that any benefit was to be derived from merely postponing what she must suffer eventually, and which she would infinitely prefer to bestow, however reluctantly, rather than have taken by force. Yes, she would prejudice her soul by yielding to the vicarious arrangement; would accept Mr Villennay in lieu of Clarence and succumb to his demands with the same tolerance and fortitude, while battling to overlook the fact that her lawful husband was lying in the adjacent room writhing in anguish and rending his pillow asunder in a frenzy of jealousy, not for love of his wife, but of the man seducing her, lest she seize his heart in recompense for her honour.

It was almost midnight when Francesca stood by the lattice gazing wretchedly out upon the moonlit gardens below as she awaited the coming of her executioner. This time no snares were laid, the doors were unlocked, and she had chosen a shimmering bedgown of ice-blue Indian silk to tempt his fastidious taste; a gown baring her shoulders and cut provocatively low lest he accuse her of being uncooperative.

Her flesh was warm, inviting, and assumed a translucent glow in the pale light, while her glorious red hair fell in rippling waves, free of its pins, combs, and anything else which might discourage his long sensitive fingers from revelling in its aesthetic beauty.

She stood proud and regal like the peeress she now was with the abundant riches she had craved and the guaranteed life of luxury but, though she would never have envisaged it six months ago, these worthy assets had not brought the happiness she anticipated they might. And suddenly amid her tribulations and woe there was Tristram! There appeared before her eyes a vision so realistic of the debonair young lord she had loved who, alas, seemed to belong to another world, a world of gaiety, laughter, music and dancing, now so contrary to her own and for which she yearned desperately. And as she recalled those long gone nostalgic days with the fashionable witty Lord Tristram Fortescue her spirits drooped more disconsolately than ever, for it was impossible to think of her lovable reckless Tristram without suffering the most searing pangs of remorse which would seem to indicate that a spark of affection still burned within her heart and that she yet loved him in defiance of her stringent efforts not to. Nevertheless, it was to be marvelled at precisely how little Tristram had occupied her thoughts since her arrival at Kleine where so much had happened to obliterate the pain of her heartbreaking loss.

Indeed, why he should occupy them now was something she could not reason for upon this night in particular her thoughts ought to have been consumed by a man diverse in every conceivable way from Tristram; a man who was the epitome of everything Tristram was not, and to whom she was to be sacrificed; the privilege which was rightfully Tristram's, the honour she had cherished through the years for him alone, was about to be conferred upon another who was not even her lawful wedded spouse!

A wave of the most racking self-pity overwhelmed her together with a bitter longing to see her Tristram once more, to hear his gay laughter and have him embrace her again gently, timidly, as if she were as brittle as an eggshell; to feel his light kiss upon her cheek, and the fond clasp of his fingers on hers as they strolled through the verdant glades of St James's Park.

To her surprise Francesca found herself weeping, for those magic moments would never be recaptured and appeared so much more endearing in this tragic hour. Tears rolled down her cheeks to splash upon the windowseat and she sobbed—then gasped as the candles suddenly went out. She waited tensed with bated breath in the semi-darkness for the next move to herald the arrival of her seducer, she lacking the moral courage to turn and look as she sensed his presence not many feet away.

Her heart gave a violent jolt as hands suddenly touched her arms from behind, but they were gentle hands, even gentler than Tristram's; hands which drew her back to rest against a satin-cushioned muscular chest whereupon she rested her head in comforting oblivion for these same hands might well have belonged to Tristram . . .

"Why do you weep, Francesca?"

The voice of Sylvestre de Villennay shattered any illusions and she made to spring away but his grip tightened upon her.

"Do you weep in anticipation of what I must do?" he whispered close to her ear. "Or that I, Sylvestre de Villennay, must do it?"

She could not speak; she could not move! In fact, it required every ounce of energy and will she possessed to simply prevent herself fainting outright at his feet.

"And why do you tremble? Is it with fear, or revulsion at my touch?" he continued in the same velvet tone, as his hands graduated slowly from her arms to her naked shoulders and she stiffened in alarm at this man's uncanny ability to evoke the most shocking emotions in her breast; how, with a mere caress, gesture, or even tone of voice, he was able to reduce her resistance to shreds, play havoc with her inhibitions, and leave her prey to excruciating desires; desires she had never experienced with Tristram who, incidentally, had always requested her express permission before kissing her, and *never* with such passion, nor for longer than six seconds let alone until her body was quite drained of breath. But her seducer must have misinterpreted her reaction, to add: "Do you hate me so intensely, Madame la Vicomtesse?"

"I-I don't hate you . . . Mr Vill . . . ennay," she gasped weakly.

"Would you prefer another in my stead?"

"No. There is no man on earth able to banish my shame. Why do you do this, sir? Why seek to corrupt us both?"

"I am already corrupt, ma'am."

"And I?"

He unexpectedly released her and turned away. "I'm sorry, Francesca," he confessed hoarsely. "I cannot deny that it troubles me despite my infamous repute, though I'm hanged if I know why. However, it consoles me to know that if it were not I then it would be someone else, someone who perchance would not be quite so mindful of your maidenly scruples, nor appreciative of your delicate rearing and beauty."

She rounded on him to challenge forcefully: "If it pains you so sorely, monsieur, why did you propose such an abominable plan in the first place? And I pray you will not insult my intelligence by pronouncing it to have been Clarence's idea!"

Monsieur had the grace to look discomfited. "Clarence wanted his offspring and I wanted my freedom," he stated simply, as if this were ample vindication.

Confusion marred her ladyship's brow. "I cannot see any connection. Why should Clarence's inability to produce an heir compel you to remain at Kleine?"

He hesitated, then shrugged helplessly. "Alas, I have little choice. I too am at his mercy."

117

"*You*, Mr Villennay?"

"Aye, ma'am. He has it in his power to discredit me most effectively and I've no doubt would do so without the slightest compunction should I refuse to honour his demands—er—or rather, requests. As you see," he appended on an ironic note, "we are wholly dependent one upon the other. He needs me . . . but I also need him."

A cutting silence greeted his admission as Francesca fought to refute the only interpretation she was able to put upon his words, namely, that the relationship between the two was anything but honourable. Neither did she deem her qualms unfounded when she weighed the disturbing confession Clarence had made that very day, added to Mr Villennay's present inability to look her squarely in the eye. Obviously she could not ask outright and therefore sought to guise her curiosity beneath the auspices of provocation.

"I do not seek to encroach upon your personal life, monsieur," she flashed at him scornfully, leaping upon this hallowed province with both feet. "What you and my husband choose to do in the privacy of your rooms is entirely your own affair."

Mr Villennay pulled up short and turned on her, livid with a rage it was demanding all his strength of will to control.

"What exactly do you imply by that remark?" he rasped, choking back his anger. "Tell me, ma'am, what you suspect we do in the privacy of our chambers?"

"It is not my duty to estimate, sir, but a matter between you and your conscience."

"Govern your tongue, mistress! You tread a precarious path."

"It is no more than Clarence himself did imply only this afternoon when I—"

"I care not one whit what Clarence said! I have never laid an ignominious finger upon him in my entire life and may God strike me dead if I speak the breath of a lie!" he asseverated strongly, passionately roused. "Why do you think the atmosphere here at Kleine is so strained?"

"Perhaps *you* would tell *me*, monsieur?" she countered, a deal braver than she felt, her anxiety for the future compelling her to ignore the misgiving gnawing at her heart. "Moreover, why its owner, a peer of the realm, should bow down and worship you, an underling?"

He flinched as her arrow hit its target.

"And the love he bears you—"

"It is unnatural, I agree," he acknowledged reluctantly, his step graduating to a march in evidence of the perturbation running rampant within him.

"Mr Villennay," she overtured fervently as he paced up and down, his expression guaranteed to daunt the most courageous spirit. "I beg you will not misconstrue my motive. I am concerned only for Clarence, my husband, and the success of my marriage. Believe me, sir, I want in all earnest to make him a good wife but I know not where to begin when he will not even trust me. You indicated before the marriage that you were wearied of the responsibility and that it ought to be shouldered by a wife—well, I am now his wife! I ought to be the closest person in the world to him yet whenever I make the slightest overture he flees in panic to his rooms or throws a fit." His pace was slowing noticeably as her plea wrought some effect and she hurried on. "Please, monsieur, if you would be frank with me I should then be in a better position to understand Clarence and help him overcome his problems."

As her voice tailed away he came to a standstill by the fireplace to lean heavily upon the ornate chimney-breast which boasted a magnificent Titian complete with carved frame of gilded pinewood, and he gazed despondently down into the lifeless heap of log and ash which seemed so in harmony with his mood.

"You must think us an incongruous pair," he stated at length. "I charge you, ma'am, have you ever witnessed such exquisite beauty, such peerless complexion as my Lord Viscount possesses? Is it not quite as delicate as the very Dresden which graces his table? In truth, have you ever seen such attributes bestowed so liberally upon a mere male, and enhanced by such lustrous golden tresses which the most fastidious lady of St James's might justifiably envy?"

No, she certainly had not and had been about to say so on more than one occasion.

"I confess, Mr Villennay, his beauty quite takes one's breath away. Indeed, he is more beautiful than any female."

He turned from the fireplace to cast her a look laden with portent. "Is it small wonder, then, that I should also deem him so?"

Francesca stood rooted to the floor her anxiety and interest soaring to fever pitch as he wandered over to the pedestal table at the bedside where he relit the candles then sank onto the bed with a groan as if the troubles of the universe burdened his shoulders, running his long pallid fingers through his black hair in torment.

"You are right, of course, Francesca," he conceded apologetically. "It is high time I was honest with you and divulged the whole. I realise only too well that I ought to have done so sooner but—" He broke off, obviously at a loss. "I plead only Clarence's welfare my excuse . . . I trust you will forgive me."

He inhaled deeply, glancing about the room as if seeking some intoxicant which had become increasingly essential to him over the years but of which commodity the bridal chamber was, alas, conspicuously devoid.

"His looks were always deceptive," he eventually resumed. "Even as a boy he was frequently mistook for a girl, so much so, that he oft disguised himself as one and derived immense pleasure from playing pranks upon the local tenantry. As I was raised with him I—"

"May I ask why you left France?" Francesca blurted out on impulse.

The question caught him unawares and drew a disconcerting frown to his forehead as he deliberated awhile.

"My mother was forced to flee my father's cruelty," he replied briefly at length, as if the topic pained him. "My brother, Raoul, was heir to the title therefore I felt it incumbent upon me, as the younger son, to accompany her hither to England."

"Your father—was a French nobleman?"

"Yes," was all he vouchsafed.

"I—I'm sorry . . . I had not realised . . . I shouldn't have—"

He waved her apologies aside with a languid hand. "My mother was an intimate friend of the late Lady Kleine. Alas, neither of them lived to see thirty-two."

"How tragic," lamented she. "And you were raised here with Clarence?"

He inclined his head in agreement. "Consequently I developed an immunity to his extraordinary looks. Both parents died before he was fifteen which struck him a forcible blow—especially the loss of his mother. I comforted him to the best of my ability and became a kind of guardian though I myself was a mere nineteen. Following the death of his father I left him in the care of his old nurse and tutors and returned to Oxford. We did not meet again for several years as I went from thence to Italy upon the Tour and when I returned Clarence himself was at Oxford. It was here at Kleine we finally met to discover we had both changed, alas, not for the better. We were now men and obliged to live alone together in this vast stone fortress, furthermore, Clarence was a viscount, a peer of the realm, and looked every inch of it. The disparity in our status was acutely felt—by me, at least, though I must stress that he has never taken advantage of his rank."

He paused, inhaling deeply, his eyes roving round the exquisite ceiling painted by Sebastiano Ricci and which portrayed, most appropriately, the goddess Juno surrounded by a multitude of cherubs.

"I told myself that nothing had changed, that we were older but rational mature men and everything was exactly the same between us, stubbornly burying my head in the past and refusing to acknowledge all the obvious signs, choosing instead to place innocuous interpretations upon overtures and gestures which I now realise could only be termed dubious." A tortured expression crossed his face. "I endured with forbearance his need for me to kiss and fondle him bethinking it was due partly to the deprivation of his mother when young, and partly to his belated development to manhood."

Now that he approached the most crucial period in his narrative Mr Villennay found he could sit still no longer, and rose from the bed to resume his pacing about the room while his listener sat hanging upon his every word.

"Clarence was very subtle in his seduction. I vow 'twas all of two years before I realised his boyish adoration of me had taken an unsavoury turn, that his hero worship had gone sour. In a desperate effort to rectify the situation I forced him into female company which he positively abhorred, yet suffered for both our sakes, though deep down I must have known it was all too pathetically late. The gates of Kleine were flung wide and all manner of entertainment given—balls, parties, masquerades; the best musicians were brought from Italy and the most dazzling women invited. They stormed the battlements night after night and the castle resounded with laughter, music and gaiety. Alas, it was then that his affliction was discovered," he groaned, passing a well-manicured hand over his eyes as if the recollection were too much for human endurance. "Excuses were hastily made to the women involved lest the truth be suspected but as far as Clarence was concerned the damage was done. He was devastated by the blow that he could never father a child despite the fact that he must have nurtured suspicions for some time. He was inconsolable and eventually made himself quite ill."

"At length he recovered and I sent him post-haste to Paris to convalesce and, hopefully, forget the past—and me. I ordered him to remain abroad for twelve months, to enjoy himself and live recklessly, but he returned in three, worse than before! His demands upon me increased; they were beyond reason and left nought to the imagination; demands to which I could not, would not, submit!"

His shoulders heaved spasmodically as he stood with head bowed over a chair, gripping the back with rigid fingers.

"He implemented every art and subterfuge known to man in his efforts to inveigle me to his bedchamber, a manoeuvre which both angered and disturbed me. It resulted in the most shattering quarrels and one night I lost my temper and actually struck him." He cringed at the poignant reminder. "Following this harrowing climax I spent long periods away from Kleine, battling against futile odds to forget both it and its owner. I revelled in every form of vice and corruption to blot out my excruciating memories—I'm sorry, I would spare you this but—"

"No! No! Please continue, I beg!"

He heaved a sigh as if not very pleased with the picture he was having to paint of himself.

"I ashamedly confess I drank, gamed, and wenched from dusk unto dawn and consequently amassed mountainous debts which I could never hope to repay. Eventually I was obliged to flee the Capital. Alas, where could I flee but back here where I found Clarence prey to the most crippling depression. At sight of me he wept with happiness, killed the fatted calf, and all was revelry and joy! Indeed, he was so delighted at the prodigal's return he was ready to agree to anything I had a mind to suggest, therefore, we—er—I formulated the plan for him to wed, and me in secret to beget his offspring in exchange for which service he would pay my debts and render me a free man. The rest you know."

Francesca would have been the first to acknowledge the tale an unpleasant one yet elation bubbled inside her as she stood barely four feet away from Mr Villennay, not daring to move or even breathe lest her hopes be dashed, though hopes for what, exactly, remained to be seen.

"Is that . . . all?" she ventured anxiously.

"Isn't it enough?" he flung back sardonically.

"You are certain you have told me everything, Mr Villennay?"

"Everything, ma'am. What more do you want?"

"Oh, please *do* forgive me, sir," she enthused nonplussed. "I don't mean to cause offence but—but—"

"Well?"

"Am I to understand that you are bound to Kleine *only* by debts?"

Monsieur reined back his indignation with admirable control.

"What else?" he parried with blistering disdain. "By the death, ma'am, if 'tis not your deliberate intent to be offensive I should be loth to encounter you when it is! Profligate I may be but I assure you there are limits to the depths to which even I should sink in spite of the fact that I have been incarcerated in this God-forsaken wilderness with Clarence for the devil knows how many years. Had we been in London the while, I doubt prodigiously if I should ever have been tempted."

"You admit, sir, that you were tempted?" Francesca leapt upon the word.

"Quite unreservedly," he rejoined with admirable candour. "But I resisted!"

"What of Clarence?" she pursued doggedly. "Can you be sure he remains equally unblemished? That it is all, as yet, only in his mind?"

"Yes, ma'am. He would have none other but me, if that is what you imply," he confessed frigidly, unable to see much cause for celebration.

Her ladyship heaved a sigh of overwhelming relief. All was not lost. It was not too late for her husband, marriage and whole future to be saved, she pertinaciously told herself, repudiating the stirrings of conscience that this was not the sole reason for her elation and sense of relief.

"And until I yield you will continue to be a prisoner here, Mr Villennay. Is that correct?"

"Aye, mistress. Once I have made Clarence a father I shall be free to quit Kleine and go to perdition in my own way."

For several seconds challenging green eyes met calm calculating black at his natural assumption that she would eventually yield, concerning which Francesca chose not to comment.

"Does Clarence know of your plan to quit Kleine, sir?" she elected to enquire instead.

124

"I have made it abundantly plain though he chooses not to heed," he murmured, almost as if he did not wish her to hear, his eyes wavering suddenly and falling away. "I trust he may be brought to appreciate that I cannot obtrude myself between husband and wife."

"But Kleine is your home, sir. Surely you belong here?"

"Heaven forbid!" he rebelled vehemently. "I abhor this execrable place—this great stone devil-infested tomb. Gad! At times I think I'd have fared better in the Fleet! It corrodes and maligns my very soul like a damnable cancer."

"Do you think it will corrode mine, monsieur?" she probed in idle curiosity.

He turned his gaze full upon her, a wry smile banishing the severity from his face.

"It will prove an interesting experiment, will't not, ma'am?" he countered evasively, the smile playing mischievously about his lips as he awaited her verdict for as far as he himself was concerned everything had been said that needed to be. He had revealed his hand quite openly and all that now remained was for Madame la Vicomtesse to bestow her stamp of approval by relinquishing her virtue.

"So," observed her ladyship at length, as if divining his thoughts, "my honour is to be sacrificed for your freedom—"

"Nay, mistress. You will sacrifice nothing on my account. It is for Clarence you make the sacrifice, and yourself, for until he gets his way you cannot expect any happiness with him. Once the child is—er—guaranteed I shall retire gracefully from the domestic scene, bestowing the responsibility of my lord's welfare into your capable hands, and we will all live happily ever after going our divers ways . . . Clarence will have his child, you will have a husband, security, title and wealth in abundance—"

"And you, Mr Villennay, will have your debts paid, your freedom, and the added satisfaction of seeing your son duly become tenth Viscount Kleine, or your daughter a very wealthy heiress," she completed significantly.

"Surely 'tis a trivial price to pay to be relieved of my onerous presence?" he parried with a knowing glance, then despatched it with a shrug. "However, the choice is yours. Even at this eleventh hour you are under no obligation. If you come to me it must be of your own volition."

"What of my lord's command? Your freedom?"

"Despite my lord's command your honour will remain inviolate. I pledge my solemn word, ma'am. Clarence will never learn of it from me. After all, our endeavours would not otherwise be guaranteed to bear fruit, therefore why should he suspect aught amiss?"

The Viscountess could not contain her amazement. "You would seek to protect me though I should persistently deny you, sir, and thwart your bid for freedom?"

"Aye, m'lady," he responded shrewdly, as if he were able to determine her mind better than she. "But do not forget that I am your only gateway to Clarence and your future happiness."

Francesca knew not what to say and could only gape at him dumbfounded and puzzled for it was quite unlike Mr Villennay to be chivalrous to the point of denying himself on *anyone's* behalf. Was it possible she had misjudged him yet again?—or merely his degree of perspicacity?

And as she thus ruminated, the subject of her thoughts remained standing by the bed, quietly surveying her the while, his austere handsome face devoid of expression, giving no intimation of his feelings—if any—concerning the part he was called upon to play. The poignant silence continued unbroken for seemingly an eon of time during which the candles, one by one, petered and spluttered into wisps of thin grey curling smoke, leaving nothing but the moon's sympathetic beams to filter into the room through the leaded casement.

Finally Lady Kleine turned from the window, her decision made, and with pride and dignity befitting her station came to stand before Mr Villennay, to meet his black inscrutable eyes bravely, and attempt to discern the mind beyond just as he was discerning hers while the moonlight

126

glinted upon her glorious red hair as it rippled down over her full rounded breasts which were scarcely concealed by the thin diaphanous gown.

No vestal virgin had ever looked more breathtakingly alluring than she at this moment as she poised briefly, conveying the message in the lustrous depths of her green eyes before she pronounced it with her lips. Even Diana herself could not have looked more beautiful though whether Mr Villennay thought so was not to be determined for his expression never varied despite the fact that he had long anticipated her answer.

"I am ready, monsieur," she murmured, a tremor in her voice. "Take of me what you will—I shall no longer gainsay you."

Monsieur did not appear convinced and placed one aristocratic forefinger beneath her chin to turn her face from the shadows into the pale light, to search it for the most minute sign of doubt, anguish, aversion to this touch; but all he could see was a degree of trepidation which was to be expected. Still he remained sceptical, and in one swift movement whipped down the silken nightgown.

Francesca bit her lip but did not flinch as her sole means of attire fell crumpled to the floor, exposing her nakedness to his dark ruthless gaze which slowly, inexorably, traversed every contour of her sensuous flesh.

"I give you fair warning, ma'am," he enlightened her in the softest whisper, "it will mean total surrender . . . you understand?"

"If you in turn will understand, monsieur," responded she in the same gentle tone, "that I offer myself not in obedience to my husband's commands, but to gain your long-desired freedom."

It was a rather confounded Sylvestre de Villennay who swept the Viscountess up in his arms to bestow her yielding voluptuous form in the nuptial bed for he could not quite deduce whether her ladyship's sudden capitulation was simply a noble gesture in sympathy with his cause, or prompted by a feverish desire to have Kleine rid of him once and for all.

But in either event, before the first cock crowed at dawn that morn the Frenchman had won the third round of the contest, and consummated the union between the Right Honourable The Viscount Kleine and his Vicountess.

Eleven

A transformation now fell upon castle, and if the atmosphere was not actually jubilant it was undoubtedly a deal more genial. Granted, Mr Villennay did not undergo any noticeable change but was, as always, the quintessence of courtesy in the everyday running of the estate. Howbeit, if one felt disposed to mark any difference in his attitude it was, understandably, towards her ladyship in whose company he was to be found a trifle more than occasion warranted yet for which minor indiscretion, to appease my Lord Viscount's peace of mind, he could invariably volunteer an excellent reason.

No, it was Francesca who experienced the change most of all and whose spirits were almost buoyant. One can only assume this was due to the fact that her future happiness with her noble lord was now, hopefully, assured for one would not presume to suggest her elation was in any way connected with her emotional and physical ordeal at the hands of Mr Villennay which, though she dare not confess it even to herself, had not been quite the ordeal she had anticipated.

Just how seriously Mr Villennay intended to take his connubial duty her ladyship had no way of telling though if he was in such frantic haste to quit Kleine as he would have her believe she supposed he would avail himself of every conceivable opportunity to further his cause. This led her to expect his advent upon each and every night and twice an hour between, but her judgment could not have been more at fault for he did not indeed appear until the third night, and proceeded to do so upon every third night thereafter, evidently of the opinion that this was quite adequate to achieve his aim.

His visits continued thus for almost a month when, for no apparent reason, he became inconstant and after attending her upon two consecutive nights abstained for almost two weeks then came again. Furthermore, his affability began to erode beneath which emerged a taciturn nature. He grew moody, irascible, as if she no longer appealed to him, and at times almost truculent in his manner as if he hated her and could have killed her, shortly after which his visits dwindled to nothing but a memory.

One might have expected her ladyship to view this as a blessed release and to assume Mr Villennay had finally elected to spare her any further indignity and shame, but this her vanity—or so she chose to term it—would not allow. And whereas she thought it strange that she experienced not the relief expected, she thought it stranger still that she should actually suffer disappointment, pique, and ultimately despair at his puzzling neglect. Perhaps it was even more incongruous that she should call it neglect when only a few months previously she had called it quite the reverse, and what had revolted her beyond belief she now found herself craving with an intensity which shocked and alarmed her. In the circumstances she could scarcely voice complaints to her husband that his hired Lothario was not fulfilling his conjugal duty without him leaping to the absurd conclusion that she was falling in love with Sylvestre, and what could be more ludicrous?

But most alarming of all was her own change in temperament which was soon the very antithesis of the lightheartedness she had experienced a few weeks ago.

Indeed, she was become so volatile and splenetic that she feared she might betray herself completely unless she learn to control the malady and exercise circumspection. Scolding the maids without reason and fretting over merest trifles to the point of tears was certainly not the erstwhile Francesca Northwood who had weathered all manner of adversities in her young life with a calm philosophic attitude of mind bordering on the stoical.

Try how she might she simply could not see that her peevishness could be due to anything other than Mr Villennay's cruel neglect of her; and whereas she was partly correct, for her malady was undeniably due to Mr Villennay, it could not possibly be designated neglect in any interpretation of the word! However, in one impetuous moment she determined to confront the Frenchman when next the opportunity arose, and solicit his reason for avoiding her when she had done nothing to offend him— or had she? Perhaps she had let fall some careless word or gesture without realising it?

The next opportunity did not arise for almost a week and even then not without some contrivance on her part to the extreme of secreting herself behind an unwieldly japanned cabinet wherein nestled a display of pottery boasting its origin from the Tang dynasty, and was situated in the corridor leading to Monsieur's chambers in the North Tower. Fortuitously she did not have long to wait thus cramped in position before the confident tap of his heels set her heart in a flutter which waxed as the noise grew louder, heralding his approach.

Barely had he drawn level when Francesca swirled out from her hiding place with a rustle of silks.

"Monsieur!" she hailed him forthwith.

He stopped short, a mingled expression of astonishment and annoyance suffusing his face but recovered himself on the instant and bowed courteously.

"My lady?"

"Would you be pleased to grant me a moment's speech?"

He could hardly refuse when her voluminous petticoats distended by an enormous hoop monopolised the entire

131

passage. He frowned, and with a glance all around to ensure they were not observed drew her swiftly into the privacy of an adjacent unoccupied chamber and closed the door.

"Your servant, ma'am," he stated abruptly, evidently not relishing being accosted thus, nor what he already perceived the topic was to be.

Francesca's heart sank with mortification to find him standing stiffly upon ceremony behind his barrier of officialdom, impervious and aloof, when she had hoped he might be his amiable nonchalant self, ready to grant her a sympathetic hearing. Moreover, it did nothing to alleviate the problem when he roamed about the room like a caged lion, as if her very presence exasperated him.

While she strove to compose herself and her words my lady's resentful gaze followed his tall immaculate form, which was clad to perfection in an exquisite figured damask of deep rose pink, stressing the impeccable whiteness of his starched linen and the intense blackness of his hair, confined at the nape of his neck in a large petersham bow, and which hung down in wanton ringlets in defiance of his wishes.

"I shall not detain you long, sir," she began, her chagrin turning to asperity as she steeled herself against the emotion mounting ever higher within, for the last thing she wanted was to make a fool of herself before him—especially in his present humour—by giving licence to the tears and megrims which had plagued her of late. "I desire to ask only one question."

"Well, your ladyship?" he prompted, flavouring the formal address with more than his customary degree of contempt.

Francesca bit her lip in dismay. This was not the Sylvestre she knew, the man who had held her vibrant pulsating body next to his own and loved her with a torrid all-consuming passion until she had sobbed wildly, deliriously, with the turbulence of her emotions. Perhaps it would be wise to postpone the raising of her sensitive topic until he was in a more conducive mood.

132

"Your question, ma'am," he reminded her in growing impatience, granting her no reprieve.

"I—I would simply know, sir, why you have been avoiding me recently?"

"Avoiding you, mistress? How mean you?"

The art of putting her meaning into dignified English threw her ladyship into greater confusion.

"It is almost six weeks since . . . I mean, you have not been to—to er—y-you have not yet fulfilled your obliga-. . . tion."

"No, ma'am."

She had not expected him to be in such blunt agreement.

"Clarence will be angered at—"

"Damn Clarence!"

"I-I'm sorry," she apologised though unable to say why, then paused before querying apprehensively: "Do you intend . . . do-doing so . . . ere long?"

He swung round on his heel, presenting his back to her which aggravated her perturbation for although Mr Villennay had been guilty of many indiscretions he had never been found wanting in good manners since she became Viscountess.

"I am unable to say," he flung over his shoulder, a trifle incoherently. "Alas, I begin to think the task . . . quite beyond my . . . capabilities."

"Beyond your cap—" Her voice failed her in disbelief. "On the contrary, Monsieur, you would seem to be more capable than most!"

"You misunderstand."

"Then tell me, I pray, what you would have me understand?" she cried in a thin quivering voice, wrestling to restrain the tears already pricking her eyes as she inwardly castigated her weakness.

But it would seem Mr Villennay had his own problems to contend with and if he noticed her crumbling emotions he certainly gave no evidence of it as his beautiful white hands gripped the bedpost so rigidly that the knuckles threatened to pierce his flesh.

"Francesca . . . I cannot continue . . . I must abandon the task to another."

"Oh no! No! Sylvestre you can't do this to me!" she sobbed, rushing forward to seize his arm then suddenly curbing the impulse. "I couldn't bear it! I couldn't!"

"Forgive me, but for the sake of you and Clarence I must," he confessed hoarsely, face averted from the wretchedness distorting her face. "Circumstances beyond my control would indicate that—"

"No! No! I don't believe you! Why can't you be man enough to speak the truth?"

"This *is* the truth?"

"No! You lie to spare your conscience. Be honest, sir! Say how you have grown wearied of me," she wept unrestrainedly. "Say how you long for the fashionable ladies of St James's—how you despise me! Tell me what loathsome creature I am for allowing you to—"

"Francesca!" he remonstrated aghast. "What devil possesses you?"

"I-I don't know . . . I can't think what's wrong with me," she wailed at his feet. "I weep incessantly and sometimes . . . feel quite ill."

"Ill?" he prompted, stooping to gently raise her up.

"At times I feel truly, truly dreadful. I was violently sick last Tuesday and blamed eating too much marchpane. But I was just as sick today despite not—"

"You were *what*?"

He grasped her by the shoulders and drew her round to face him, his eyes sweeping her up and down. Not a word was spoken as she gazed up at him through her misery while he stared back at her, a mixture of strange indeterminate emotions overspreading his countenance. Thus they remained for some considerable time, silent and motionless, she wondering what she could have said to have wrought such a dramatic change in him while he seemed to want to savour the moment as something very special yet was not quite sure whether he dared . . .

"I-I was just—sick," she clarified hesitantly.

"Oh, Francesca!" he rejoiced aloud to heaven, kissing

134

her on both cheeks. "You greenhorn! Don't you realise what this could mean?"

No, apparently her ladyship did not and failed to see what cause he had for such elation when she felt about to collapse with the strain he was inflicting on her poor nerves and delicate constitution.

"Can't you see, it could well mean my obligation is fulfilled and that you are already—"

"W-With child?" gasped she, and swooned outright in his arms.

Twelve

Yes, that the Viscountess Kleine had conceived of a child was ably confirmed by no less than three physicians summoned within a radius of forty miles of Kleine by eight o'clock that same evening, news which gave cause for the wildest celebration the like of which the surrounding populace had never witnessed before. The castle gates were flung wide and all from squire to village idiot invited—or rather, commanded—by the Viscount himself (whom it was naturally assumed was the proud procreator) to come within and join in the festivities.

Bearing in mind the unsavoury rumours in circulation about Kleine and its inhabitants, and the fact that no invitation of any kind had ever been issued hitherto, the locals were somewhat slow to respond. But the temptation of free food and drink—as much as they could consume—proved too much and soon all and sundry were storming the castle in their hundreds as news travelled far and wide.

A banquet fit for the King himself was prepared during which the musicians played their liveliest jigs and wine ran like fountains in praise of Baccus and the father-to-be. Indeed, having imbibed two bottles of his best champagne my Lord Viscount was ready to cast dull care aside with vengeance and sang, danced and generally besported himself amongst servants and peasant folk, and bloated gout-ridden gentry until the early hours.

In fact, it would seem the only people not to partake in the Kleine revels were the two responsible, namely, Madame la Vicomtesse and Monsieur de Villennay. But Monsieur had other plans in mind which would necessitate a very clear head and so he merely lingered in the background sipping the odd glass and observing the jollification with more than his customary cynicism, smiling a smile of supreme satisfaction for his task was now complete and all that was left to do was lure his lordship aside and prevail upon him to fulfil *his* part of the bargain by recompensing him (Monsieur) accordingly for services expertly rendered.

It may be said that Clarence did not take very kindly to his friend imbibing a paltry two glasses instead of his customary two bottles and felt persuaded to interpret it as an insult to the unborn offspring, that is, until he himself became too whittled to recall the reason for the celebrations in the first place let alone how much liquor Mr Villennay was consuming.

Meanwhile, Lady Kleine lay abovestairs in her bedchamber, her head pounding with the din below as she strove to little avail to capture the repose she urgently craved for the three physicians had acquitted their examinations most diligently before finally affirming that she was, in fact, with child.

This, however, was the only fact upon which they had been unanimously agreed, for while one had stood poised by the bed, meditatively stroking his grizzled sidewhiskers and holding his pocket-watch suspended over her ladyship's abdomen, his companions had embarked upon a heated exchange concerning when the child was to make its entrance into the world, one advocating a period of six months and one week, while the other averred just as dogmatically that the conception could not have taken place more than two months ago. This, his associate adamantly refused to accept, declaring it a sheer impossibility to form a diagnosis in so short a time. And while the two had wrangled thus the first medic had added fuel to the fire of contention by pronouncing that the child would, without doubt, be of the masculine gender, evident in the fact that—if everyone would observe closely—his pocket-watch was revolving significantly in a clockwise direction which was a sound indication that the child was a boy for this method of discerning the information had proved infallible throughout his twenty-eight years of medical practice. Not surprisingly, when the three learned gentlemen had eventually adjourned they had done so leaving the Viscountess little wiser but considerably wearier than when they had arrived.

My lady shivered and a maid hastened away to procure more logs for the fire, returning anon with logs and the news that it was snowing heavily and his lordship had prevailed upon the three doctors to stay the night for it was not a pleasant experience to be lost in a blizzard after dark thereabouts. And while the girl's broad Northumbrian brogue droned on, relating various mishaps and tragedies which had befallen victims in the area, Francesca reclined in her bed and warmed to the cheerful fire and the knowledge that she was to be a mother, concerning which vital fact she had not been granted a moment's reflection.

It was December, soon to be the start of a new year and with a new life within her. She was creating a living being, a child . . . Sylvestre's child. Despite its ill-starred conception the knowledge pervaded her with a pleasurable feeling, of excitement, anticipation, but most of all, fulfilment. And with a smile of sheer contentment curling her lips Lady Kleine sank into a blissful sleep.

Some time afterwards the cacophanous revels gradually diminished, the locals returned to their homes, and by four that morn everyone was in their beds including the servants; everyone, in fact, except the Lord of Kleine and his henchman, Sylvestre de Villennay, for my lord did not elect to retire yet awhile despite having reached advanced stages of intoxication several hours ago. Nevertheless, he still managed to stand on his feet and as long as he was able to do so refused to adjourn to his bed lest the reason for the celebrations vanish like a dream in the cold light of day.

Mr Villennay applauded himself, deeming he had chosen his moment well though many might have advocated waiting until the morrow in fairness to his lordship when he should be refreshed from his slumbers and, probably, able to consider such a request with greater application of mind. This the Frenchman had no intention of doing. On the contrary, he believed his interests would be much better served if my lord were a trifle bereft of his senses and therefore unable to appreciate, in all its dire meaning, what he himself was demanding of him and the ulterior purpose behind it.

But for the first time in their long association Mr Villennay misjudged the mood of the Viscount and what he had presumed to be complete intoxication on the part of his friend chanced in reality to be proportionately excitement. In consequence, his efforts to hoodwink Clarence met with frustration, and upon overturing his claim for the service he had discharged he found my lord obdurately opposed, maintaining that he (Sylvestre) had not fulfilled the agreement *in toto* for he (Clarence) did not yet have his son and heir as guaranteed. No, Sylvestre must needs wait until her ladyship was delivered and should the fruit of her womb be female then, alas, it would entail Monsieur rendering his services once again, and yet again until the desired son was forthcoming, and not a penny piece would he get from the Kleine coffers in the meantime.

De Villennay was furious and accused his lordship of playing him false, of going back on his word of honour for he understood the arrangement had been to beget a child, nothing more, and declared it nothing but a despicable ploy on my lord's part to keep him prisoner at Kleine all the longer. Neither was Monsieur much mistaken in this supposition which Clarence made no attempt to deny, and the most bitter feud broke loose between the two, but no amount of shouting, cursing and threatening would persuade the Viscount to recant his decision. Indeed, the Frenchman was so enraged that it demanded all his strength of will not to settle the difference by the sword—for he himself was not quite as sober as he was wishful to think—and might well have done but for the nagging realisation that Clarence's perversity was generated by love and an innate dread of him quitting Kleine forever. Love, perhaps, but of an unhealthy strain; a love which was evil, noxious, and which one day would surely destroy them both unless one of them were strong enough to fight it now by taking the appropriate steps.

Whether Clarence deemed the hallowed environs of his apartment more conducive to persuading Sylvestre to his way would be difficult to say, but it was here that the major contention, begun in the Banqueting Hall below, came to a vociferous climax, and why Francesca found her sleep disturbed.

She did not waken immediately but lay in a semi-comatose state striving to regain command of her senses while hearkening to the bellicose exchange in the adjacent room. She presumed it to be the festivities still in progress but soon appreciated that this din was not in any wise festive. All at once her eyes flew wide at the volume of anger between the two men, and she lay anxiously in the darkness debating whether or not to interfere when the voice of Mr Villennay, incensed with rage, was heard to bellow even louder at Clarence whereupon the outer door slammed and all fell quiet.

Francesca fell asleep and when next she stirred it was to the muffled sound of Clarence's convulsive sobbing. She turned over with a groan bethinking he had, once again, been endeavouring to inveigle Sylvestre to his bedchamber when she sensed something unusual, as if she had not woken voluntarily but by a sound, or the strange feeling of another presence in the room. She bobbed up to strain her eyes in the darkness but could see nothing for the thick curtains did not permit even a chink of light, if light there chanced to be upon this bitterly cold winter's night; then she called out but which proved just as futile, and so she lay down again, shrugging the feeling aside, and fell off to sleep once more.

Her ladyship now slept continuously until late morning when Martha brought the customary chocolate drink and drew back the curtains to declare it the coldest day she had ever known and that there had been further heavy falls of snow. Her mistress made no comment but snuggled deeper within the bedclothes and sipped the hot beverage, her thoughts centred upon the night's boisterous and peculiar events, while the maids set to work to re-kindle the dead fire. Then she thought of the unborn child and her hand involuntarily travelled to her abdomen, to touch it dubiously, apprehensively, wondering if the physicians' opinions were to be relied upon after all because she certainly did not feel any different today. Most surprisingly, she did not even feel sick. No, it could not all be a dream as she had first suspected for Martha was chattering on excitedly, while setting out her mistress's apparel and cosmetics in preparation for the morning toilette, about how the celebrations had continued well into the early hours and how she had not known whether she had been on her head or her heels. Upon her ladyship soliciting news of her husband and Mr Villennay she was respectfully informed that it was assumed the gentlemen would sleep well into the afternoon for they had contin-ued revelling long after the domestics had retired to their beds. And when Francesca discreetly delved into whether or not anyone had heard any noise *after* the revels had ceased all three maids replied with giggles that they had been so merry with ale and tired that they would not have even heard the cannons on the battlements explode.

With the fire blazing cheerily and her misgiving thus al-layed Francesca rose and suffered Martha to assist her into a dressing robe of quilted cream satin trimmed with ermine, then took a glance at her reflection in the glass while her tub was prepared. At length she discarded the robe and was about to discard her bedgown also in order to commence her ablutions when the communicating door burst wide and crashed against the wall. Mistress and maid leapt back in alarm, but not to be compared with the alarm which seized them at sight of Lord Kleine established upon the threshold.

A look of frenzied desperation blended with the most consummate anger would, perhaps, best describe his expression as he stood motionless, breathing heavily in evidence of the volcano smouldering within him about to erupt at any moment. It was obvious at a glance that his lady had once again done something to warrant his displeasure; exactly what, remained to be seen, but there was nonetheless that same madness in his glazed blue eyes which Francesca had witnessed too often to be mistaken. Not until he stepped into the room did she see clutched ominously in his right hand a heavy full-length horsewhip, more suited to driving a cart-horse than a coachhorse and which left pitifully little to the imagination.

Martha recoiled with a cry of horror, her arm raised to ward off a blow as if anticipating her employer's wrath were to be unleashed upon her. But his rage was clearly directed at his wife who needed no official proclamation to realise it, and remained outwardly calm while inwardly battling against overwhelming odds to conquer the dread consuming her, her hands clasped across her bosom in an effort to still her palpitating heart.

"Get out!" he screeched at the girl as if she were to blame for his misfortune, his fingers curling and uncurling around the carved ivory handle of the brutal instrument he held, seemingly anxious to put it to use.

Despite her paralysing fear Martha assumed a protective stance, arms outflung, before her mistress, choosing to defy the terrible fury of her master. However, although this heroic act earned Francesca's profound admiration it was plain to see that the maid's presence was aggravating his lordship's humour and so she besought the girl to adjourn to the dressing closet, though she could have benefited from Martha's moral support, if she was capable of little else. Upon the reassurance that my lady would call out if need be Martha dropped a dutiful curtsy and reluctantly retired from the room.

Long after the door had closed upon her humble figure both lord and lady remained stationary, neither speaking, staring unwaveringly across the room at each other—my lord at my lady with the most daunting scowl, and my lady at my lord with mild disapproval as if she were about to rebuke a recalcitrant child which she considered by far the best attitude to assume in the precarious circumstances for there was no way of knowing to what extreme Clarence's dangerous mood would carry him.

Though it cost her dear she continued to meet his ferocious gaze calmly, steadily, nurturing the quaint belief that as long as she could manage to do so he would stay where he was, but the moment her eyes deviated from his he would leap to action which, were she to own the truth, was precisely how she had schooled a mad dog upon one similar occasion some years ago, and which had proved quite effective. On second thoughts she doubted whether the situation were so similar after all as his lordship's breathing quickened and his chest heaved spasmodically before the tempest fomenting within him finally broke loose.

"Do you realise, madam," he spat out mordaciously, his voice shaking to such a degree it seemed as if he might lose it altogether, "that my life is finished? That I have nothing to live for? I have lost everything, and it's all due to you!" His tone waxed in pitch to terminate upon a shriek of outrage as he took three huge strides further into the room, brandishing the whip to give emphasis to his claim.

"I-I don't know what you mean, my lord," faltered his lady, unable to understand the logic of his reasoning as she took three commensurate paces back to maintain the distance between them.

"I mean, ma'am, that you have ended my life as assuredly as if you had slain me with the sword! You have driven out my very soul; ravaged my heart of all feeling; cut off my last breath! You have eclipsed my sun—"

"Clarence! What is it? What's happened?" she cried in all innocence, still unable to comprehend the reason which was carved clearly upon his anguished face.

"You have robbed me of everything! Gone! Gone is the only thing I ever truly wanted—repelled by that accursed

143

clacking tongue of yours! I shall have it torn out by the roots and fed to the crows!"

"My lord! In what way have I betrayed you? Tell me, I pray?" she implored, revolted by the prospect of this barbarous unjustified penance.

He halted only a matter of feet away, his breath now coming in gasps and his eyes suffused with an insanity the like of which she had never before witnessed—even in Clarence.

"Sylvestre—he's gone!"

"Gone?" she mouthed like an imbecile though the meaning was lucid enough, as a flame suddenly perished within her and a pang of fear mingled with dismay wrung her heart, an emotion she could not accurately define yet which for some strange reason outweighed all the insult and humiliation she had borne—even the anomalous consummation of the marriage. Granted, freedom had been his avowed intent but somehow she had believed, as Clarence had, that he would never actually go; and all at once it was inconceivable that the great castle should be bereft of his tall dark confident figure because Kleine was where he belonged; he was part of it! "H-He can't have gone."

"Of course he's gone, you lunatic!" stormed Clarence. "Would I be rampaging about like this if he hadn't?"

"But why? Why so soon?"

"Why?" he rounded on her barely able to control his wrath. "Because you, dear wife, could not keep quiet! You had to proclaim your condition from the battlements!"

Francesca gasped with affront for Clarence had done more such proclaiming than anyone.

"I assure you, my lord, that I did not wittingly divulge the information to Sylvestre."

The scowl blackened. "And unwittingly?"

"He detected the fact for himself long before I—"

"Damn you, woman! Why didn't you conceal it?"

"I wasn't aware at the time that there was anything to conceal, my Lord Viscount," she rejoined, her own temper wearing thin as her indignation waxed with the force of her conviction, bethinking if he seriously intended putting the whip to use he would have done so before now. "I could not have concealed it indefinitely, apart from which you would have been compelled to forgo your festivities and bribe the physicians into silence."

Alas, the rationality of her reasoning together with the fact that he could summon no apt requital served only to exasperate his lordship the more, and from his position there was only one way to redress the imbalance. He had suffered a bitter loss which he knew not how to endure except by wreaking the full crucifying vengeance of it upon someone even weaker than himself. This role his wife filled to perfection and he now charged at her like a fiend out of hell, wielding aloft the whip to cut her down in one fell stroke and, hopefully, alleviate his soul-destroying grief.

Francesca stood petrified, not daring to credit what now seemed painfully evident until the crucial moment when she shrank back in the window embrasure, bracing herself to receive the paralysing blow of the cruel lash, while crying out in frantic alarm for the life of her precious babe.

"Clarence! Stop! The child—you'll harm it!"

Her piercing cry fell upon him like an enchantment and he hesitated, whip suspended, as if the anguish in her voice had magically restored his senses and the knowledge that he was not suffering alone. He glanced about him in bewilderment, then at the whip he still held aloft, wondering how it came to be there in his hand before he cast the vicious weapon from him with a violent shudder and, to his wife's stupefaction, collapsed at her feet devastated with remorse at the terrible thing he had almost done, while she sank trembling onto the window-seat.

How long she sat thus stricken, numb, listening to Clarence's heart-rending weeping Francesca could not hazard a guess but it seemed an eternity before he eventually raised his pitiful tear-streaked face from the haven of her petticoats to sob brokenly:

"I'm sorry . . . F-Fran. Can you forgive me . . . p-please? You don't understand . . . the pain, it's so intolerable, I simply must blame someone . . . I don't want the child at such a price . . . I'd sacrifice my entire inheritance to recover that which . . . I-I've lost."

"Clarence, you haven't lost Sylvestre," she tried to reassure him, though nurturing forlorn hope. "He'll come back, you'll see."

"No, no—not this time," he contradicted, shaking his head as if nothing in the world would persuade him otherwise. "I've lost him!" he bewailed anew. "He's gone for good—Sylvestre, gone! And all because of a mere brat!"

Francesca swallowed her resentment at the responsibility of Sylvestre's leaving now being ladled upon the innocent head of her child.

"Don't you want a child any longer, Clarence?"

"Not if I must forgo Sylvestre," came his sullen response.

"Sylvestre wants his freedom, my lord, whether you have a child or not. He simply tried to soften the blow of his leaving by giving you a wife and family. But make no mistake, he would have gone anyway—so please don't blame anyone, Clarence."

He did not rebel at her words as she anticipated he might but instead sat quietly pondering them at her feet with his head in her lap and his arms around her legs, hugging them to his body as if they in some way brought him comfort. Then he looked up into her face, revealing his beautiful distraught features; his blue eyes glistening with unspent tears and his golden hair falling in soft waves about his shoulders.

"Fran," he whispered, trying to control the trembling of his lower lip, "tell me what I must do. Please help me to win back Sylvestre . . . I can't live without him."

Francesca's heart sank in despair. "Don't you like me, Clarence?"

His eyes widened in surprise. "Yes, Fran! Of course I like you," he replied with genuine fervour though obviously wondering what her question had to do with his request. "We have had some very enjoyable times together, you and I, making music and playing our games. I'd miss you terribly if you were to go away."

146

She heaved a sigh of abandoned hope. "But not as much as you miss Sylvestre, apparently."

His head fell onto her knee again, face averted. "That is unfair in you, Fran. Sylvestre is different—quite, quite, different. I have known him almost all my life and he is not to be compared with anyone else."

"Couldn't you grow to like me as much as Sylvestre?"

"No! Never! I like you as a sister, nothing more."

"But I'm your wife, Clarence."

"What does that signify?" he parried petulantly. "I didn't want you to be, Sylvestre did. I married you to please him and this is how he repays me! Oh, why did he have to go now, this very day? Why couldn't he have stayed just a little while longer?"

Although she did not see much purpose in Mr Villennay remaining at Kleine merely to postpone the inevitable parting, Francesca was forced to own herself in full agreement with Clarence concerning the feverish impetuosity in which Monsieur had quit their portals. Yes, she had an answer, a very good answer, but one she did not care to divulge for it was scarcely complimentary to herself having, as it did, such painfully significant connotations with his embarrassing neglect of her. However, she could not prevent a dull red suffusing her cheeks which she trusted Clarence would not notice.

"Do you wish me to despatch a servant post-haste, Clarence, to find Sylvestre and prevail upon him to return?" Did she suggest this capitulation on her husband's behalf, or her own? "The snow lies deep—he cannot have travelled far—"

"No!"

Both his answer and the vehemence of it took her aback, prompting her to query if it had any connection with the heated contretemps during the night. Exactly what had caused this she had no preconceived idea and harboured the opinion that it had been an emotional difference rather than a business one.

"Don't you want Sylvestre to return?" she probed, caution ceding to curiosity.

"Yes, but he must return of his own free will. I will not—grovel!"

Neither did it seem he would, thought she, silently noting the proud jerk of his noble head as the blood of the arrogant Fennistones appeared to surge more quickly in his veins. She deemed this an auspicious sign, encouraging her in the hope that she might use this family pride as a wedge to drive between her lord and the Frenchman, and one day penetrate the impregnable barrier Clarence had erected around himself—but the unexpectedness of his next question left her wondering if the barrier were, in reality, as impregnable as she was wont to believe.

"Fran, do *you* like *me*?"

She paused, selecting her words with extreme care for he was regarding her curiously agog, as if her reply were of some importance to him—perhaps once again, more than she was wont to believe.

"Yes, Clarence, when you are gentle and kind to me."

The sweeping golden lashes swiftly veiled the intensely blue eyes, setting her heart aflutter at the extraordinary beauty of this man.

"I'm sorry, Fran," he apologised anew, with a slight nod in the direction of the discarded whip. "I wouldn't have hurt you, really. At least, not as much as Sylvestre has hurt me." His head descended to her knee as before and he seemed blissfully content to remain thus, as she thought he would have loved to have done as a child at his mother's knee. "Could you love me, Fran? Am I lovable, do you think?"

Francesca gazed wistfully upon the golden head. "Yes, my lord . . . it would be very easy to love you."

"My parents didn't think so," he yawned wearily, as if it no longer mattered. "No one has ever cared about me . . . except Sylvestre."

He made no demur when she caressed his head with a tender hand, brushing the tendrils of hair from his damp soft cheek as she envisaged Clarence the angelic infant and wondered how, in the name of mercy, the woman who mothered such a child could have spurned and rejected him so cruelly. Overwhelming pity stirred deep within her heart and she whisked away a tear as she studied her sleeping husband, marvelling that he was indeed the same man who had rampaged into the room brandishing a horse-whip barely thirty minutes ago; but most of all she marvelled at her own ability to becalm him from a ferocious beast into the sweet childlike boy slumbering on her knee yet who was a grown man of almost thirty-two.

Her ladyship closed her eyes and offered up a silent prayer, importuning God to aid her in her most rigorous determination to save her lord from the diabolical cancer within him, and to grant them the strength to fight and conquer the sovereign influence of Sylvestre de Villennay which hung over them like impending doom. Was it too much to ask? Dare she hope?—or were they already destined to languish under the curse of the Frenchman for the rest of their lives, to live in an eternal threesome with him in spirit if not in flesh? In short, was she expecting too much of her husband to be content with her alone . . . expecting a miracle which he, perchance, was powerless to effect?

Thirteen

In fairness to my Lord Viscount let it not be said he did not try to overcome his disability; indeed he did, as far as it was in his power, and no wife, be she dame or viscountess could surely ask more.

My lady was also tireless in her efforts, offering encouragement and friendship, and spending every conceivable moment in his company in order to help divert his mind from his loss, though he would sometimes brood alone in his rooms. And during the cruel hours of darkness when the visions of Sylvestre and yearning for him became unbearable, my lord would venture to his wife's bedchamber and creep trembling into the bed beside her for no other purpose than to be comforted, and eventually he would fall contentedly asleep, cradled gently in her arms.

Francesca was exceedingly proud of Clarence and the progress he made throughout these initial difficult weeks, and whereas she appreciated only too well that their marriage was destined to be an incongruous affair he was, nevertheless, growing to trust her more each day, gradually relying upon her as he had upon Sylvestre, and with careful nurturing she believed in time he might come to love her. Even so, if their relationship merely continued thus as brother and sister it was mutually pleasant and infinitely more successful than many marriages of the day.

However, her ladyship was proudest of all at the price he was willing to pay in toll taken of his looks, nerves and appetite, to achieve what many might have regarded a modest success. For example, when they played piquet together by the fireside she would observe his fingers clenched rigidly upon the cards, and beads of perspiration erupting on his forehead despite the bleak winter snows decorating the leaded windowpanes; then he would shiver and close his eyes while a sudden violent craving for his friend swept through him like a tornado, as if he were stricken with some terrible plague. And when they dined she further appreciated the pretence he made at consuming as much as she when the very sight of food—though appetising in every way—must have filled him with revulsion.

One could not condemn Francesca for assuming a large portion of the credit for Clarence's achievement, along with the surges of family pride which helped hold him together. After all, she was not to know the legitimate reason, namely, the topic and outcome of his quarrel with Sylvestre upon the morning the latter had absconded with such despatch from Kleine despite the elements which had raged as boisterously without as those within, and that in consequence Clarence was acutely aware that all the supplicating, bribery and sacrifice in the world would never persuade his friend to return.

For almost a month my lady revelled in her fool's paradise, convincing herself that although Clarence did not seem quite himself before long he would be over the worst and ready to begin building up his life anew. Eternally optimistic she toiled unceasingly to keep him amused and his mind off his ill-fated past, and furthered this by commanding everything in the castle even vaguely reminiscent of the Frenchman to be stored away. This included portraits, miniatures, Sylvestre's favourite books from the library, right down to the very chair in which he

151

had been wont to take his ease of an evening. All were locked inside his deserted rooms along with his other, more personal items which he had been unable to carry with him upon the journey.

The changes proved more extensive than originally planned for her ladyship went on to purchase new curtains and hangings, and all the furniture in the principal rooms was rearranged in order that nothing should look the same as before. They were to begin a new life therefore the castle must be renewed accordingly. The opportunity was also taken to lock up the bridal chamber in which, because of her own poignant memories, she could no longer bear to set foot let alone sleep. She then went out onto the battlements to fling the key as far as she could beyond the castle wall, symbolising her rejection of the past, and returned instructing the servants to prepare her a suite of rooms upon the farther side of her lord's.

But despite his lady's good intentions Clarence did not begin to pick up life anew. On the contrary, he seemed to lose interest in it altogether and now cared not whether he lived or died. He was bored with his wife's puerile attempts to entertain him and no longer made any pretence of eating. Even her ladyship was ready to admit that his excellent progress seemed to be on the wane.

Suddenly she recalled how exceedingly merry he had been upon the night of the celebrations, and as his birthday was approaching she decided to arrange a party, for what Clarence needed was company, gay lively company, to help fill the void left by Sylvestre.

And so, once again the doors were opened to the surrounding neighbours—who responded with a little more alacrity this time—including Squire Armstrong, his personable wife and high-spirited daughter; Parson Davidson and his wife; Doctor Elliott, and a spattering of tenant farmers with their good dames. The company was select but not too large lest Clarence be discouraged.

It was perhaps unfortunate that Francesca planned the *soirée* as a surprise for her husband, for had she seen fit to acquaint him with the idea she would have been left in no doubt concerning his feelings. Consequently it is small wonder that upon the crucial evening my lord obdurately refused to quit his rooms where he remained throughout the event which went off with all the ebullience of a damp squib.

Following this catastrophe the situation declined from bad to desperate. Clarence lost all will to do anything. Even the simple everyday ritual of vacating his bed and undertaking his toilet proved quite beyond his capabilities for it all seemed so meaningless to him without Sylvestre to approve or censure his dress, manners and method of applying cosmetics or styling his hair; where to place his patches and whether to powder or not. Who, at Kleine, now cared a straw whether his cravat were tied *à la Francaise* or *à l'Anglaise*; or if his toilet water permeated the fragrance of the wild rose or the piquancy of the exotic jasmin? Who would be perceptive enough to detect the most infinitesimal flaw in his attire upon those rare occasions when he must look his superlative best? But most of all who was to make the thousand and one decisions in his stead and assume the running of the estate and castle in the meticulous manner expected? Indeed, it was only now that Clarence appreciated how trying Sylvestre's life had been at Kleine, involving the demands of household, agents, tenants, and—not least of all—the owner.

Decisions! Decisions! From morn till eve it seemed to his lordship that everyone in and around Kleine plagued him interminably to decide this or that, from housekeeper to valet. Even his lady wife had joined the throng and tormented him about their forthcoming child and what it was to be named, among a host of other problems! How could he be expected to endure it when his heart and soul were slowly disintegrating in homage to his god? When would they understand that his intolerable longing for Sylvestre eclipsed all else as insignificant and worthless?

However, if Clarence thought his Viscountess was so out of sympathy with him he was equally at fault for in the depths of her heart Francesca did not blame him for fretting in the Frenchman's absence. On the contrary, though my lord would have disagreed most vociferously, she had far greater reason than he to repine and recall

Monsieur's passing, a living reason waxing within her day by day which forbad her to forget the man responsible. And when the child was finally born it would be there before her eyes every single moment of her waking life, a tangible flesh and blood reminder of Sylvestre de Villennay and her past indiscretion, always there to torment her no matter how much she might wish to forget or how many keys she discarded after locking away her bitter remembrances ... she could hardly lock away a child as easily or prevent it asking the most searching questions about its father.

Even the great castle seemed to mourn the Frenchman, if the weird moans and howls were anything to go by which resounded within its wide cavernous stone chimneys, moans akin to a human voice, like a soul in purgatory ... and Francesca became conscious, acutely conscious, of an uncomfortable sinister feeling that she was being manoeuvred not by some*one* but some*thing* for which she had hitherto held Mr Villennay responsible—but was it Mr Villennay? Was it not the castle itself? She sensed the feeling had lain dormant ever since her arrival and the nearest she had come to recognising it had been the day she had returned from riding to see the horrid gruesome head laughing at her. Had it truly been her imagination? Was it possible that Kleine Castle was a living breathing thing with a personality of its own, a power it was able to wield over its victims, to demoralize and corrupt and which mere mortal was helpless to gainsay? In short, the power to rape the human soul? And why should she sense it more poignantly now simply because one man had chosen to leave? It was eerie, chill, and dark, as upon a sunny winter's day when the sun was suddenly eclipsed by clouds. She shivered and began to feel as Sylvestre had felt, a prisoner at Kleine, to be incarcerated in the huge ugly stone fortress until she died when she would be buried beneath it in the Fennistone family crypt and left to rot there into eternity.

The climax came one day some three weeks following the abortive *soirée* when the Viscount could not be found. All main rooms and obvious places having been searched

154

to no avail it was suggested that the unlikely places be searched, but alas, this also proved fruitless. The castle grounds were about to be considered when Francesca was seized by a disturbing premonition which guided her reluctant feet to Mr Villennay's vacant rooms. Sure enough the lock upon the door had been forced and Clarence was discovered within, distraught and positively raving with grief, writhing and kicking on the bed and rending the pillows and coverlets to shreds in a frenzy of hysteria at which everyone was aghast! Moreover, his eyes were glazed and his face flushed as if he were in the throes of delirium and high fever, added to which he did not seem to recognise his wife, nor his valet who had served him faithfully for fifteen years.

Without any ado he was borne to his bedchamber and his physician summoned, who arrived from Elsdon within the hour in defiance of the crude Northumbrian elements and landscape. Upon examination the doctor too was gravely perturbed about his lordship's condition which was sorely aggravated by his loss of weight, and went on to caution all concerned that unless drastic steps were taken to ease the burden of Lord Kleine's mind—for clearly he was exceedingly anxious about *something*—and encouragement given him to eat, he, Doctor James Alexander Elliott, could not be answerable for the dire consequences—hastily appending that he had no wish to alarm her ladyship in her own delicate condition. However, as she appeared to be in excellent health, though naturally worried about her husband, it would be to the ultimate benefit of herself and child as well as his lordship if she were to indulge my lord's every whim and help disburden his mind.

If the doctor lingered over his Madeira in the faint hope that my lady might choose to confide to him the precise cause of the patient's anxiety, alas, he was doomed to disappointment. Instead, she civilly gave him to understand that she had reason to suspect what the trouble was, and assured him that everything humanly possible would be done to rectify the matter. Doctor Elliott was tolerably satisfied with this, and after donning duffle cloak, flat hat and spatterdashes took his leave, politely declining her ladyship's generous offer to partake of some repast for he had several calls to make not a few miles distant and, as things stood, would be extremely fortunate to reach home ahead of darkness. Nevertheless, before he went he felt urged to stress in an undertone that it would perhaps be circumspect if Lord Kleine were not to remain completely alone in his present state of mind for distraught persons were apt to do distraught things . . .

Francesca managed to bear up bravely before the physician but no sooner had the great doors closed upon him than she was seized with dread, for it had never occurred to her for a moment that Clarence's life might be imperilled, or that he might be driven to actually harming himself. Indeed, no one had been more horrified than she at finding him demented in Sylvestre's rooms for until then she had genuinely believed him to be overcoming his weakness. Granted, he had fretted somewhat and looked a trifle peaked but she had accepted this as perfectly natural for one suddenly robbed of a lifelong companion who had been mother, father, brother and friend to him. She had been stricken, shocked, to find that the cancer had eroded so deeply within him, and that the deterioration had reached this alarming stage.

In a turmoil of anguish she fled at once to her lord's side and was not a little relieved to find him sleeping peacefully with one hand comfortingly beneath his cheek. Never had he looked so fragile and delicate, so angelically sweet, with his auburn silken hair lightly draping the pillow and surrounding that pale ethereally beautiful face. Francesca's heart was wrung with compassion. Although she had never loved him as a man, indeed, no sister could possibly have loved a brother more than she loved Clarence, and she sadly reflected how different their lives might have been but for this evil enchantment which held him inexorably in its toils. Nevertheless, she was adamantly decided upon sending word, somehow, to Sylvestre de Villennay without delay.

It was with overwhelming eagerness that she admitted defeat and descended fleet of foot to the library where, with quill, ink and vellum to hand, she penned the vital missive in a fever of anticipation, urging Monsieur wherever he be or whatever he be doing to cast aside all past differences and come at once in the utmost haste to Kleine as his lordship's life was in deadly peril. This was scanned, sanded, wafered, and bestowed in the care of my lord's swiftest messenger who was charged to spare neither steed nor cost in getting to London and seeking out Mr Villennay whom he was to bring back to Kleine with the same breathless despatch.

The simple expedient of writing the letter had a peculiar elating effect upon Francesca, and profound relief mingled with excitement pervaded her being at the prospect of seeing once more the man endowed with the inexplicable ability to manipulate people and circumstances to his convenience, to persuade them to act in open contravention of their better judgment no matter how firm their convictions, and who—despite the explicit warning of Mr Josiah Penrose—had manipulated her more often than she cared to admit. Try as she might she could no longer reproach Clarence for becoming so addicted to Monsieur.

Five weeks elapsed before Francesca received news from her messenger during which wretched time she strove tirelessly to uplift the Viscount's shattered spirits with the assurance that Sylvestre would be at Kleine before long. But, alas, the messenger's news was anything but heartening for seemingly Mr Villennay was not to be found anywhere in London. Indeed, the servant had searched the Capital from north to south and east to west without success. Furthermore, not a living soul had seen or heard anything of him and all had sworn on oath that such a man had not set foot there. As a last resort the servant had bethought to enlist the aid of my lord's attorney, Mr Penrose, who had respectfully suggested—due to Mr Villennay being of French origin—that he might have gone to seek out his surviving family in France. This appeared to be perfectly reasonable and so upon Mr Penrose further suggesting he contact his associates in Paris and have them make the relevant enquiries, the servant

had eagerly agreed. All this was imparted in a letter in-
dited by the attorney and forwarded by the messenger
who promised to report their findings in due course and,
meanwhile, continue scouring London.

Following receipt of these rather deflating tidings her
ladyship heard no more for two long nerve-shattering
months during which she grew heavy with child and her
lord's health declined still further.

She was seated, as usual, by Clarence's bed upon the vital afternoon when a chambermaid, agog with excitement,
brought the news that the messenger was finally returned.
Clarence was desperately weak; so weak that he could not
raise his head, but his eyes brightened, which was the
only acknowledgment he could give that he had compre-
hended the news and reason for the bustle and stir. His
wife patted his hand with a reassuring smile and rose hurriedly, her heart leaping to a vibrant tattoo, to accompany
the girl from the room.

The messenger was waiting in the corridor immediately
outside the door and misgiving seized her ladyship to see
him standing conspicuously alone which would seem to
indicate his news might not be pleasant. Taking care to
close the door firmly behind her she then swung round to
confront him.

"Do you come alone?" she queried in concern. "Is not
Mr Villennay with you after all?"

"Er—no, your ladyship," confessed he, bowing as low
as his travel-weary bones would permit.

Francesca's brain was in revolt but she managed to remain calm for there could be some rational explanation
for Mr Villennay's absence. Perhaps he was following behind and would arrive before long. But when the servant
straightened up to face her she realised with a sickening
pang of dismay that his downcast expression and
drooping mien were not wholly on account of the long tiring journey, and that his news was not good. Still she did
not surrender to her qualms but instead inhaled a deep
breath and rapidly prepared herself to hear the worst as
the man stood diffidently before her, twisting his black
cocked hat agitatedly in his calloused hands, while keep-

ing his eyes humbly lowered. However, it is to be doubted whether my lady's conception of 'worst' was to come within a league of punishing fact.

"Surely you are not endeavouring to tell me . . . that Monsieur will not be . . . coming to Kleine?" she bravely faltered at length in an effort to loosen the man's tongue, for he appeared to be almost as stricken as she.

Alas, his mistress was not to know that it was not reluctance nor the disparity in their stations which bereft John Robson of speech but her condition of being with child, and the thought that she might not be able to withstand the shocking tidings it was his unhappy lot to reveal.

"I'm afraid so, ma'am," he volunteered gruffly, his eyes still fixed upon his weatherbeaten beaver.

"Well? Were Mr Penrose's French associates able to be of assistance?" she pursued anxiously, striving to bridle her impatience for her husband's life hung precariously in the balance of the man's answer.

"Yes, ma'am," he admitted forlornly. "The French authorities found Mr Villennay—"

"And do you tell me he refused to come here despite the grave situation?"

"No, ma'am. Mr Villennay did not come because—because—"

"Yes?"

"—he was . . . not able."

"Wasn't able? I don't understand you. Come, John—that is your name, is it not?" He nodded hesitantly and she went on. "You need not fear for my welfare. I do assure you, I am extremely strong and resilient, and ready to withstand your news no matter how disappointing it might be. But I simply cannot bear this silence!" she cried out in anxiety. "Why couldn't he come? What was preventing him?"

John Robson straightened up, squaring his shoulders, and doing his level best to meet her eye.

"Mr Penrose gate the French authorities all the vital information, your ladyship, and requested them most urgently to seek out Monsieur de Villennay, stressing that it was a matter of life and death which was not putting it too strong—"

"Yes, yes—and?"

"We received their reply only four days ago, ma'am, that a man named de Villennay had—had—" he broke off, deeply troubled.

"Well?" Her ladyship's anguished voice cut the harrowing silence while maid and man servants stood around in wide-eyed concern, not daring to make a sound.

"—had been found . . . dead."

Francesca shrank back, her eyes protruding from her head in abject horror.

"D-Dead!" she mouthed aghast—a cry echoed in equal horror by the staff.

"Killed in a duel, ma'am."

"No! . . . No! . . . I-It can't be! . . . I don't believe it!" she screamed aloud, her voice rent apart with her agony of soul as the man's words seared her brain, and the maids and flunkies leapt to her aid lest she collapse, as seemed very likely.

My lady could utter no more and gesticulated wildly in the direction of her apartments whither she was led by the maids, her body trembling violently and her heart choked with grief, unable and unwilling to break the news to her husband at present—if ever. Pandemonium ensued with menials running in all directions for smelling bottles, sal volatile, laudanum, and burning goose feathers, all of which were to prove wholly ineffectual in mitigating her ladyship's terrible distress.

In these dire circumstances it is hardly surprising that my Lord Viscount was banished from everyone's mind in frantic anxiety for his wife's well-being and that of her unborn child, principally because my lord was safe in his bed and could not come to any harm. After all, what humble uneducated domestic could be held responsible for failing to suspect that his lordship might conceivably be capable of rallying sufficient strength to quit his bed—indeed, super-human strength where news of his beloved Sylvestre was concerned—and eavesdrop at the door? Furthermore, that he would have secreted in a cleverly disguised cavity within one of the bedposts a silver-mounted pistol which he kept there ready primed for his personal safety?

One might have counted slowly up to twelve after her ladyship's final cry when the explosion came, devastating the atmosphere and stilling every chattering tongue. The silence which fell all around was excruciating as each paralysed brain fought to deny the obvious, to concoct some justifiable reason for the noise other than that battling for supremacy in their minds.

Lord Kleine's valet de chambre was the first person to leap to action and burst into the master bedchamber—to fall back blenching at the appalling tableau which met his gaze. There before his stricken eyes lay the master he adored, prone upon the bed, with blood seeping slowly through his beautiful golden hair from a hideous gaping hole in his right temple, while in his right hand was clasped the offending pistol from the blackened muzzle of which spiralled, tauntingly, provokingly, a thin column of smoke.

And in this same awesome stillness, as the Angel of Death hovered over Kleine, if one listened intently there might have been borne to the ear from way high above in the dilapidated stone towers of the old castle, the faint—ever so faint—echo of triumphant, ghoulish laughter, as the great fortress claimed this resounding victory not on behalf of its earthly lord, but of its infernal lord—Lucifer.

Fourteen

One would not attempt to describe the Viscountess's crucifying grief. Suffice it to say that all the suffering and humiliation she had borne over the past bitter year since her arrival at Kleine was not to be compared with the heartache which now tore her being asunder for the two men she had loved in such diverse ways; the friend she had loved as a husband, and the husband she had loved as a brother—both of whom death had brutally cheated her within the space of sixty seconds.

Hour upon wretched hour she wept into her pillows, refusing to see anyone, her arms cradled protectively round the babe in her womb as if defying God, man or the devil himself to deprive her of it also—a defiance which was ruthlessly challenged the following night when she was seized by the most body-racking pain. She screamed aloud for help which brought every servant in the castle rushing to her bedside and once again the physician, Doctor Elliott, found himself hastening to the Fennistone abode. Some hours later, at six in the morning of May 8th, her ladyship was delivered prematurely of a son, the son which Clarence had craved, yet a son who was the very epitome of all the tribulation, misery and despair at Kleine, and so pitifully thin and weak as if in protest to the months of anguish inflicted upon its mother, that it survived no more than five hours before it too departed this life.

It is reasonable to suppose that Francesca would not have grieved to any excessive degree over the loss of a child conceived beneath such ill-favoured conditions and for whom she would have been forced to act a lie for the rest of her life or own it as misbegotten and accept the consequences of being ostracised by society; moreover, have been shackled inescapably to the past she would as lief forget. But, alas, she felt the bereavement of her little son most poignantly of all for he was the only living, breathing, thing she had left, and he was the direct result of the most wonderful experience she had ever known, the most wonderful love, a love which now flooded in to take possession of her body, heart and soul; a love she had rigorously denied knowing it could bring nothing but even greater suffering to herself, for Sylvestre de Villennay had been a dangerous man, a ruthless man, who wanted only his freedom to go his lecherous ways and who had loved more women than she had consumed sweetmeats, which was a tolerable few. Besides, she had been married to Clarence, and this had been the greatest reason of all to stifle any personal feeling for Sylvestre, which she had done, beneath a profound sense of wifely duty and obedience. But now Clarence was dead. She no longer had a husband to be obedient to, and her world and values had capsized overnight! And whereas it left her free, free to confess her love for Sylvestre, what should it avail her to confess love for a man who was every whit as dead as her lawful spouse? So, she had cherished the tiny life within her, that precious part of the man she had worshipped, and which she could love for the rest of her days, had not Fate cruelly decreed otherwise and dealt her the most shattering blow of all, depriving her of the only purpose she now had for living.

Upon her ladyship's insistence the child was interred

immediately, her reason being that she could not endure the thought of the entire populace gazing upon his pathetic little form when in actual fact her concern was on account of his profusion of black hair, lest it should betray her secret.

And so, while my lady lay abovestairs devastated in mind, body and spirit not only because of her triple loss but also the aftermath of a difficult childbirth, my Lord Viscount lay in state down below in the private family chapel wherein he had been married but a few months ago. He was adorned, traditionally, in the insignia and robe of viscount, worn conventionally upon the occasion of a coronation, a robe of the finest crimson velvet complete with its precise two and a half doublets of sumptuous ermine while the corresponding coronet of silver-gilt, mounted with sixteen silver balls encircled his golden head. Thus he lay, within a huge sarcophagus sculptured in the stone of his castle, and with a tall candle as thick as a man's arm positioned at each corner, while four uniformed guards in the colours of his house stood respectfully by.

For the final time the gates of Kleine were opened to the surrounding inhabitants, squires, doctors, farmers, weavers, labourers, colliers, and innkeepers, who filed with due reverence through the small dimly lit church to pay their last respects to this strange young lord about whom little was known but much was speculated. And though some were merely curious, it surely would have done my lord's heart good to see how much respect he thus merited, and from folk concerning whose existence he had neither known nor cared.

The funeral was, for obvious reasons, an extremely private affair with a handful of mourners from outside the castle including Squire Armstrong, the beadle and bumbailiff, to add dignity to the solemn occasion. However, numbers were adequately complemented by members of the household who attended *comme toute la famille* led by valet, steward, housekeeper and Carter, the head footman.

In defiance of Doctor Elliott's instructions Francesca

struggled from her sick bed to assume her rightful place before the assembled gathering for she was determined to carry out her duty to the bitter end. What did it matter if she too perished? What reason did she now have to live?

And so she attended, though ably supported by the doctor and Martha, one upon either side. Granted, the service was a considerable ordeal but thankfully brief, and within the space of an hour Lady Kleine found herself back in her bed, with her husband duly interred alongside her son in the family vault.

Two weeks later Francesca rallied herself briefly once again, this time to acknowledge the person of Mr Penrose, come to dispose of his lordship's estate and generally sort out legal matters. As the child and Sylvestre were in no position to claim their dues the will was a mere formality, and decreed her ladyship sole beneficiary apart from one or two dispensations to my lord's doctor, valet, steward, and servants who had rendered him a particular service.

Mr Penrose was overcome with the appalling sadness of the occasion and overtured his heartfelt commiseration to Francesca that the marriage, for which he had cherished such hope, should be terminated so suddenly and so tragically. Indeed, as the lawyer had been instrument in arranging it in the first instance it is perhaps understandable that he felt largely responsible for her ladyship's present unhappy plight, though as sagacious as the gentleman was it was beyond the realism of even *his* mental capacity to appreciate in all its grim detail exactly what Francesca had endured at Kleine. Neither did she choose to enlighten him but instead assured the lawyer that it was a risk she had been quite prepared to take, and should do so again were she to be granted the choice. Mr Penrose was much inspirited that she should view the situation so philosophically, unaware that in her heart of hearts my lady blessed him for his action upon that fateful day in St James's Park because otherwise, she would never have met Sylvestre de Villennay nor known his love, a love which had been illicit and doomed yet which she would not have forgone for all the world. Being oblivious to this the attorney twisted the knife in her wound by declaring it a relief to all concerned that the villainous Monsieur de Villennay had met his just deserts and that the dubious circumstances surrounding his premature demise had not surprised himself in the least for such rogues invariably came to a bad end.

Mr Penrose expended several days at Kleine Castle, closeted with the steward and his assistant for the most part, primarily to spare her ladyship as much inconvenience as possible. However, he eventually took his leave but before doing so took the liberty of offering her ladyship some fatherly wisdom of which she stood sorely in need, and emphasized the fact that she was still young, beautiful, and extremely wealthy to boot. Before long she would be able to put all this unhappiness behind her and with this in mind he urged her to come to London as soon as could be deemed respectable. Francesca promised to give this due consideration and temporarily cast aside her aristocratic image to hug the little man warmly for he had been much more to her than a mere family lawyer. And so Mr Josiah Penrose went on his way with a tear in his eye.

Following the lawyer's departure Francesca clung to her bed for several weeks more, with the doctor in frequent attendance as the strain of losing the child had exacted a physical as well as mental toll of her strength. It was during this distressing period that she appreciated Clarence's inability to face life and his decision to opt out of it with a quick death for it demanded every grain of determination she possessed to simply continue living, to go through the monotonous motions of eating, breathing and, hopefully, sleeping.

However, with the greatest determination of all, she at last relinquished the comforting haven of her bed, realising she needs must if she was not to follow her husband and child to an early grave. Therefore, two months after the tragic day she descended the stairs upon the arm of Martha, her frail form clad in deepest mourning of unadorned black crepe and her vivid red hair respectably concealed beneath a plain black cap which contrasted harshly with her drawn ashen countenance.

The most crucial test of her courage was to simply proceed from room to room, sensing the atmosphere of each—the dining-room wherein she had sat at table with Sylvestre and Clarence, all so familiar and still very much alive with their presence; the library, the study, the music salon where she had regularly sung and played to her lord and where she felt his spirit most acutely. Thus she compelled herself to continue through every main room in the great castle, listening to the tale each had to tell of its memories, good or ill, which wrung her soul and aggravated her already intolerable burden of despair until she began to fear for her sanity. But once she had completed this painful duty and conquered the spirits of darkness by laying them to rest she felt much improved, and able to go on with her day to day living as if in this small act she had won the battle of adversity.

In this manner life was slowly resumed at Kleine as the servants followed their mistress's excellent example and went about their daily travail as if their master were still in residence and nothing had changed. However, for practical reasons part of the castle was closed off and a large number of servants discharged, but with exemplary characters from her ladyship in order to facilitate their search for new positions. Nevertheless, practicability was not the sole reason Francesca had seen fit to inhabit only the southern side of the castle, but because there were certain rooms situated on the northern side which were much too distressing to see and into which she would never have courage to venture no matter how hard she tried. These constituted her husband's private apartments and those of Mr Villennay, but in particular, the nuptial chamber; that sacred shrine with its beautiful shell-shaped bed which evoked the most soul-torturing memories of all. This she would never enter again and it would remain locked until the end of time.

And so she ordered yet another suite of rooms to be prepared in the opposite tower which looked out over the wide expanse of rolling sheep-dappled moors towards Falstone and Bellingham, with the occasional homestead of weaver or farmer, homesteads built conspicuously of stone to thwart the barbarians of bygone centuries.

Time passed during which Francesca's spiritual wounds began to heal and eventually she was able to recall Clarence with fondness in her heart instead of the pain of grief, and to gaze upon his portrait with nostalgic affection without suffering pangs of terrible remorse. But the memory of Sylvestre did not fade along with that of Clarence as she hoped it might. Instead it waxed stronger, obsessing her more and more until she could think of nothing or no one else, as if the spirit of the mortal man who had possessed her in life were seeking to possess her from beyond the grave. At night she yearned most desperately of all; wept and cried aloud for the touch of his hands, his lips, and the feel of his powerful arms around her frail trembling body—and even dreamt that he was actually there, loving her as before, to waken with a sob to find it all a cruel, cruel deception.

Francesca was understandably alarmed to find herself bathed in the same perspiration as Clarence, and shivering with ague and desire as she fell under that same enchantment, the evil enchantment which had finally proved his downfall and which would prove her own unless she undertook drastic measures to conquer it now, this moment, while she was yet in command of her senses. Three times she had changed her rooms and still the feeling haunted her. What else could it be but the castle itself? Yes! That's what it was—the castle! She would find no peace of mind until she was free of its sinister influence therefore she would move out that very day and go to live in the Dower House which looked much less noxious and really quite hospitable.

Without further ado she commanded the Dower House be made ready to receive her and within twelve hours was entering its light airy portals, not to be disappointed with what met her gaze. Although it was appreciably smaller it was nonetheless comparatively modern inside as well as out, with pillared entrance, and sash windows and wooden parquet floors throughout, which made a pleasant contrast to the cold, cold stone she had grown accustomed to within the castle. Furthermore, the windows were much larger which meant more sunlight to brighten her life and banish gloom and despondency.

My lady fell instantly in love with the place and derived considerable enjoyment from busying herself in making various improvements. Once again patterns were pored over, new curtains and hangings ordered, and Francesca found herself surprisingly content to live there—well, for a month or two anyway, after which she was not quite so certain and began to doubt if the house were not, after all, a little too close to the castle for comfort because on a clear day she could see—from a small landing window upon the western side—its blackened turrets in stark contrast with the azure skies, and suspected she could once again feel its weird influence. Moreover, having refurbished the Dower House and done everything possible to improve it short of pulling it down and completely rebuilding it stone by stone, time now hung heavily on her hands otherwise she felt sure the castle would not have bothered her in the least.

It was then that she recalled Mr Penrose's suggestion which fired her desire anew to see London; to see once more the familiar faces and places and perhaps pick up the threads of her old life, banishing for all time Kleine's mesmeric hold upon her.

To go to London was firmly decided but a few days later when a letter arrived most opportunely from her erstwhile employer, the Baroness Brindley; a letter primarily to express her deepest condolences and anxiety at Francesca's tragic loss and ill health as related by Mr Penrose, but also to invite her most fervently to sojourn a while in Clarges Street, perhaps to convalesce. The season was in full swing, being November, and whereas she appreciated Francesca was still in deep mourning and unable to partake of the gaiety society afforded, there was no reason why she should be frowned upon for making a call or two or receiving callers in return. Indeed, the Baroness was so eager in her offer that Francesca would have been hard pressed to refuse had she so wished. But she did not so wish. On the contrary she required no persuasion to accept the invitation, acknowledging the distinct advantage of staying, though temporarily, with Lady Brindley instead of at the Kleine town house in Grosvenor Street which Clarence had never used and which would need extensive preparation—and she cherished little inclination to refurbish yet *another* house at present. It also meant she was at liberty to pack up her effects and leave as soon as she had written to accept her ladyship's generous offer, which pleased her even more, for neither did she feel inclined to expend another winter marooned at Kleine by mountainous snow drifts.

As she had no way of estimating how long she would be gone from Northumberland, or indeed if she would ever return, my lady dismissed still more servants and reduced the number to the minimum although she did decide to take as many with her as she possibly could in order that they might set to work upon her house in Grosvenor Street where she must needs take up residence eventually if she elected to remain in London.

And so the Viscountess turned her back upon Kleine and set out *en grande tenue* upon her journey to the Capital, a journey deemed by many to be extremely hazardous, laborious, and nerve-racking yet which she anticipated with some degree of enthusiasm for she had been long cloistered in her fortress home. Nevertheless, after five long tiring days upon the rutted muddy roads of England her enthusiasm was on the wane and giving way to apprehension as she gradually drew nearer to the City and the prospect of reuniting with Lady Brindley, for she herself had changed during the last eighteen catastrophic months, even if her former employer had not.

However, upon arrival in Clarges Street Francesca's qualms were put to instant flight by the Baroness who was even more fervent in her personal welcome than in her written invitation. Tears rolled unashamedly down the cheeks of both women as they embraced each other for, though their separation had not been of outstanding duration, both were conscious that so much had happened to transform their relationship which had been one of aunt and niece, but which was now more akin to mother and daughter.

Well might one imagine the animated conversation which ensued outvying the tinkle of delicate china and intermittent mouthfuls of ginger cake as Francesca related as much as she dared and thought proper concerning the past episode of her life to her hostess who 'ah'd, oo'd' and wept in keeping with her guest's diary of events. Francesca made no mention of Mr Villennay, bethinking it unnecessary, and persuaded Lady Brindley to assume that the child had naturally been her husband's, which in turn gave excellent reason for his taking his life if she distorted the fact slightly and pronounced it to have been prompted by the loss of his son.

Lady Brindley, meanwhile, was shocked at the change in her former companion but endeavoured not to show it and remarked with genuine admiration upon her slender figure and tiny waist instead of admitting how washed-out and wasted she looked. And what was become of the sparkle in her green eyes, and that happy vibrant spirit which on more that one occasion had caused her (the Baroness) to burst her whalebones with laughter?

Without further debate the venerable lady determined that Francesca's mind was to be diverted from her tragic past at all cost and though she herself was rather advanced in years to undertake this formidable duty (for the girl seemed to be hopelessly abandoned to her misery and despair) she nurtured suspicions of someone who might prove more than equal to the task, someone to whom she was sure her guest would not be averse and who had been a most persistent caller for news of the erstwhile Miss Northwood, news which she had declined to give for her companion was then a very respectable married woman; and so the caller had grown discouraged and his calls had dwindled to a halt. Indeed, the young man had been most diligent in his soliciting and vowed ardently that he simply wished to assure himself that Miss Northwood was happy and content in her chosen life. And although her ladyship believed him to be sincere and trustworthy, yet had she withheld the information concerning Francesca's whereabout and whom she had married lest he jeopardise her marriage and future well-being.

It was now some months since the beau had called leaving the direction of his lodgings in the Haymarket, and Lady Brindley doubted whether he would still be there. Nevertheless, she sent a servant round the very next day with an invitation for the young man to sup with her that evening at eight, stressing the fact that if he did so he would learn something to his great advantage.

Yes, Lord Tristram Fortescue was still lodging in the Haymarket, and did not require a second summons from my Lady Brindley. Moreover, he was established upon the steps of eleven Clarges Street fully fifteen minutes before the appointed hour, duly prinked out in his fashionable best coat of delphinium blue corded silk edged with gold braid. This was complemented by a blinding waistcoat of cream figured loretto picked out with brilliants; and a black beaver hat in a moorfields cock, sporting a blue cockade, sat upon his curls at a rakish angle. His hair powder and lace ruffles were toned to a subtle blue shade to complete the effect, while a full complement of seals, rings and keys jangled merrily at his waist and three black silk patches of a decidedly astral flavour graced forehead, cheek and chin.

Far from being disconcerted by my lord's impetuosity Lady Brindley was somewhat relieved for with Francesca still at her toilette it granted herself the vital opportunity to draw the young lord into the intimate confines of the small drawing-room and discreetly impart to him the confidential and most delicate details of Francesca's disastrous marriage, and caution him to guard his tongue and actions lest he unwittingly cause offence at a time when he might least wish so to do; also to help him understand and be prepared to excuse the young widow's reticence to converse and her occasional lapse of attention. Lord Tristram was horrified at the sad tale and assured his hostess most zealously that she could rely upon him wholeheartedly to do and say all that was right and proper and not to put a foot wrong.

However, although Lady Brindley had prepared his

lordship concerning Francesca's recent past she had not bethought to prepare him for the transformation in the girl herself; consequently, it required all his self control to stifle the gasp of consternation when he was brought face to face with her. She was dressed in the essential black, a voluminous sacque spread over a large fan hoop which seemed to emphasize her emaciated frame and fragility, giving her an ethereal quality, as if she might blow away on a light breeze. Her black French cap was modestly frilled beneath which her beautiful hair was neatly, if severely, coiled.

Unaware that she was being observed she descended the stairs with caution, as if uncertain whether her legs would support her all the way to the bottom, and carried a black lace fan in one hand while the other gripped the wrought iron balustrade to maintain her balance. On she came slowly, steadily, with but five more steps to negotiate when her eyes alighted upon his lordship and she smiled wanly but with genuine pleasure.

"Why, Tristram!" she exclaimed as he hurriedly recovered himself and sprang up the remaining steps to assist her. "What a wonderful surprise!"

Yes, that was it precisely; a wonderful surprise, no more, no less. But what had he expected in the terrible circumstances? She could scarcely have thrown herself into his arms and shouted aloud that she loved him as she would have done years ago.

Lord Tristram bowed low over her black-mittened hand, hardly daring to touch it lest it crumble in his grasp, and as he straightened he glanced up into those green lack-lustre eyes, searching in vain for a flash of the old sparkle, the impish gleam he had loved so well. And the girlish dimples which had played about her lips when she laughed—usually about silly, frivolous things—were gone; gone for all time from those same sweet lips which now seemed as if they would never laugh again. No, this wasn't the Francesca he had known! This proud stately aloof viscountess wasn't *his* Fran!

'Oh Fran! Fran! What have they done to you up in the

God-forsaken North?' he longed to cry out, but held his peace.

Bearing Lady Brindley's explicit warnings in mind his lordship allowed Francesca to lead the conversation through the simple but tasteful meal, of which she ate conspicuously little though managed to prolong it an unconscionable length of time. However, he lost not a single opportunity to pierce her guard and catch a glimpse of the old Fran beneath the cold dignity of the viscountess but alas, to no avail for she continually channelled the discourse along lines of informal small-talk and topics common to them all, giving only the occasional very brief allusion to their former intimacy. Furthermore, my lord discovered very early in the proceedings that the last eighteen month period of her life was sacrosanct and she would suffer no one to touch upon it no matter how artfully or discreetly they contrived.

Not surprisingly by the end of the evening Lord Tristram was feeling more than a trifle mortified for he had made no progress whatsoever with Francesca, a feeling more poignantly felt when, upon taking his leave, she merely bestowed upon him her hand and a forced smile such as she might have deigned to offer any ordinary mortal. What was more, she had offered him not the slightest encouragement throughout the entire night, nor had a solitary spark of the old affection manifested itself. But then my lord soundly rebuked his impulsiveness, telling himself that his dearest Francesca had suffered much and that it would demand every grain of patience and understanding he could muster if he would win her back to his arms.

Evidently he did not conceal his despondency as well as he might for before he was ushered out of the door into his waiting sedan Lady Brindley once again took him aside to try to raise his spirits by breathing a word or two of motherly advice into his dejected ear, primarily echoing his very own sentiments on the matter; to exercise infinite patience with Francesca who was not the same Francesca she herself had known either. The girl had been hurt more deeply than anyone could possibly imagine and it would require a deal of time and tender nurturing to heal her wounds and restore her to the old Francesca they both had known and loved. The Baroness went on to state, however, that she did not doubt if he and she rallied together in this common cause, before long they would meet with success; and to this end she invited him to call again on the morrow to take tea.

Following his pitiful reception that evening Lord Tristram wished he might share his hostess's optimism but, even so, found his sense of chivalry asserting itself and with it his enthusiasm and hopes for the future. And when her ladyship stressed the fact that he—apart from herself and Mr Josiah Penrose—was the only friend Francesca had in the whole of the great City to turn to and care about her well-being, his lordship went on his way rejoicing for who was better able to undertake this important task than he himself, the man who loved her and had her interests at heart?

Fifteen

Upon arrival in Clarges Street the following afternoon Lord Tristram was overjoyed to see Lady Brindley's prediction proved true and Francesca ready and awaiting him in the small drawing-room, in which their hostess deemed it cosier and more intimate for three persons to partake of tea; and whereas Francesca was perhaps not as pleased to see him as he could have wished, he had to admit that she was a sight better pleased than she had been the day previous.

Far be it from anyone's deliberate intent to term Lady Brindley's motive suspect in selecting the most intimate room in the house, because the cosy tea party passed off in much the same manner as supper had the night before, with conversation centred upon the commonplace; and nothing untoward occurred, that is, until the Baroness was overcome by a sudden urge to procure more seed cake in spite of the fact that they had a plentiful supply already to hand, not to mention a plentiful supply of servants to undertake the errand. It is feasible, of course, that Lady Brindley nurtured a latent addiction to seed cake for she was absent from the room such an inordinate length of time that one was tempted to wonder if she had not consumed a morsel more than was prudent.

Granted, Lord Tristram had no way of determining exactly how long his hostess would be gone but even so was not going to let slip idly by this golden opportunity to further his interest for it was the first time in nigh on twenty-four hours he had been privileged to be thus alone with his Francesca, and to say he had much burdening his conscience would be putting it mild indeed. Therefore the door had barely closed upon his hostess's stout back when he cast himself down upon his satin-breeched knees by his lady's chair.

"Francesca! My own, my adored one! Forgive me, I beseech you!" he supplicated brokenly at her feet, his hands clasped dramatically aloft. "I crave forgiveness—see here, on bended knee—"

"Forgiveness, my lord?" prompted she guilelessly, a frown of perplexity marring her brow as if she were gazing down upon an utter stranger. "Forgiveness for what?"

His lordship gaped at her, stunned, unable to credit that she could have possibly forgotten.

"Why, for the way I did shamefully spurn you for another. Surely you recall that calamitous day in the park?"

"Oh that . . ." she mused awhile, a strange enigmatic smile playing about her lips as if she savoured a private jest. "Yes, I forgive you, Tristram."

My lord sprang to his feet, affronted. "You smile! Damme, you smile, Francesca! What is there to smile about? Confound it, I stretch my wit the length o' the Thames to make you laugh and you sit with a face as hangdog as Jack Ketch! And when I would be deuced serious, rot me, you smile! Don't you regret what happened that day?"

She met his gaze unflinchingly. "No, Tristram."

"No!" he ejaculated, flabbergasted. "Fran, what's wrong with you? What has happened to you over the past months?"

Francesca hesitated, and my lord endeavoured to becalm himself with the knowledge that it had been a marriage *à la mode*, for convenience's sake—she could scarcely have loved the man!—therefore there was no reason why they should not resume their courtship amicably enough, and anon wed as originally planned for he loved her more than ever and was quite confident that deep down beneath all the heartbreak and tragedy she still loved him.

My lady heaved a sigh, as if trying to rid herself of the oppressive burden she still bore.

"A great deal happened, Tristram . . . more than you or anyone could possibly imagine," she murmured half to herself, in a kind of reverie. "Yes, I've suffered . . . I've certainly suffered . . . but I do not regret a single moment of my life at Kleine. Does that sound odd?"

She looked up at him questioningly and his lordship was taken further aback to see a strange light burning in the depths of her heavy dark-ringed eyes, a light harbouring some mysterious secret and which he would swear on oath had never burned for *him*.

"Fran," he began again, taking her hand in his and gently caressing it, "do I hope in vain? Is there, perchance, someone else?"

Something like a sob reverberated through her frail body.

"There was s-someone . . . but he is gone . . . perished."

His lordship clasped her hand tighter and pressed it feverishly to his lips. She did not resist the passionate overture, nor choose to correct his assumption that the man she loved had been her lawful wedded spouse.

"B' gad, you cannot conceive how my heart leapt when I heard you were a free woman again," he breathed ardently if a trifle unsympathetically.

"You did not wed the Lady Georgina after all?" Was that a note of irony in her voice?

"Nay—would you believe it?" He tried to make light of the heinous insult with a forced smile. "I had a run of substantial wins at the tables which granted me a fortuitous reprieve."

"Most fortuitous."

My lord laughed again, a little more convincingly this time, but upon his lady's lips there was not the vestige of a smile, and his heart sank to the depths of despair.

'Oh Fran!' he groaned inwardly, 'have you left your soul forever in the outlandish North? Am I never to hear again that infectious giggle which did nought but irritate me all those long months ago?'

"I searched everywhere for you, Fran," he gushed on. "I turned the whole o' London inside out but no one knew where you'd gone. Forsooth, I was heartbroken!"

"So was I, my lord, when you did cruelly jilt me," she parried in monotone.

His fair head drooped in abject remorse. "I-I'm sorry, Fran. Won't you forgive me? You must see I had no choice."

"Yes, Tristram. I have already forgiven you."

"And everything will be as before?" he enthused, hardly daring to hope, implanting another kiss on the hand he still clung to. "W-We will resume our courtship?"

She sighed again and nodded.

My lord almost fainted away with excitement. "Y-You mean, you'll wed me—when you cast off your weeds?"

"If you so wish, Tristram," she replied in the same expressionless voice.

'Why not,' thought she, for if she did not accept Tristram, who at least loved her in his own capricious way and cherished good intentions even if they seldom matured, what would her existence otherwise be? What was the lamentable alternative? She had loved him once before and could see no logical reason why she should not do so again when her heart had been given time to heal.

It was all too much! Lord Tristram could contain himself no longer and threw his arms about her to embrace and kiss her just as he had done two years ago. Francesca tried hard to reciprocate and recapture the old feeling— she had to! This was Tristram loving her, Tristram!—for whom she had yearned at Kleine, but in particular upon the night of her bitter sacrifice as she had awaited Sylvestre in the bridal chamber. Well, what more did she want? Here he was bestowing his light six-second kisses upon her hands and face, and embracing her as if she might break in two but oh, how different from Sylvestre! Sylvestre, who had treated her not as a porcelain figurine but as a woman! a full-blooded mature woman who was crying out to be loved. Loved!—Not petted and fondled like a lap dog! No man was to be compared with Sylvestre, her god, on whose altar she had been sacrificed most heinously—yet would she willingly give everything she possessed, even her life, to be so sacrificed again.

Fortunately for Francesca, though not so for her zealous swain, Lady Brindley chose this untimely moment to return, bearing a silver salver, not of the requisitioned seed cake, but of sugar-plums and comfits. There was a jink of china and a scuffle as his lordship, cursing volubly beneath his breath, made haste to resume his seat, a manoeuvre his tactful hostess pretended not to notice.

These initial visits of Lord Tristram to Clarges Street were but a prelude to many. Indeed, his lordship was there so often that the Baroness was tempted to suggest he take up permanent residence. Nevertheless she was delighted to be able to further Cupid's cause and encourage the young couple in every way she could, for it did her heart good to see them so idyllically happy—well, his lordship anyway, for although time went by Francesca's depression showed no evidence of lifting.

However, to be fair, she had made some effort to socialise on a modest scale by strolling about town, in the parks, visiting exhibitions and museums, and regularly attending church each Sunday in company with the Baroness and his lordship. Eventually it was seemly for her to graduate to second mourning and cast aside her weeds. This enabled her to wear gowns of grey or white, in silk, brocade or satin, if she so wished, and which served in some small measure to dispel her dismals. Along with her weeds she tried to cast aside the past and a further attempt was made to please Tristram, or at least be grateful for the manner in which he strove unstintingly to please her. Once again she tried to respond to his ardour, suffering him to kiss and embrace her as often as he desired for she wanted desperately to love him as she had done before, and just as desperately prayed every night for God's help to forget Kleine and all its bitter memories, to let her enjoy life once more and let everything be as it had been two years ago. All she wanted was to be allowed to forget ... forget ...

Lord Tristram was to be admired for the way in which he tolerated Francesca's unpredictable humours, but eventually her whole attitude towards him, their future, and indeed life itself began to pall. Granted, she did not repulse his advances but her kisses and touch were wholly devoid of warmth and spontaneity, almost as if her spirit had died alongside her husband and child, and there were nothing left for him but the pathetic remains of this once breathtakingly beautiful vital young woman, the empty lifeless shell of the Francesca Northwood he had loved.

Poor Tristram! How was he to know his Francesca had lain in the arms of one of the world's most accomplished lovers—a master of the art who had instilled in her heart, mind and body, desires which no other mortal was able to fulfil? Or that each time he took her in his arms she was not kissing him but Sylvestre, a Sylvestre who fell far short of the original? How on earth was he to begin competing with this paragon he knew not of?

"Fran! What the deuce is the matter with you?" he was finally heard to remonstrate one day. "You shrink from me as if I were the devil incarnate! Plague on't, you couldn't have known the man all that long and he's been gone out of your life for a year now. Dammit girl, you can't languish over him forever!"

Francesca's temper frayed before his accusation though admittedly it was just.

"Had not you cruelly rejected me in the first place, my lord, we would not now be in this unhappy predicament!" she retorted in turn.

"Be reasonable, Fran. I've explained all that and you forgave me. Besides, you professed love for me devilish longer than a year—six years in all—yet I'll warrant you didn't repine my loss half as much."

His words stung deeply yet Francesca could make no rebuttal for they were perfectly true and she could not bring herself to hurt Tristram, provoking as he was, by confessing so. Instead, she simply swallowed her pride and apologised, vowing to make a concerted effort to put the past behind her once and for all. Meanwhile, she continued to suffer his lordship's six-second kisses in the fervent but forlorn hope that one day they would perhaps thrill her as wildly as Sylvestre's had done.

Sixteen

The stalemate situation rose to an unexpected climax some three weeks later at the Bedford's grand end-of-season ball which anyone aspiring to any social standing made it their business to attend, for the Bedfords were the richest family in England, had powerful influence at court, and were therefore the very last persons one could afford to offend.

Of course Francesca must go to the ball, Lady Brindley was heard to declare in no uncertain manner. There should not be the slightest cause for gossip as long as she donned her most decorous gown and went merely to observe and not take active part in the festivities.

It was here discovered that the Baroness had more influence in the lofty realism of society than Francesca had given her credit for as an invitation was immediately procured for Lord Tristram too, who would escort them both to Bedford House on the evening in question. Thus, before Francesca could voice an objection, Lady Brindley had already replied to their Graces in the affirmative on behalf of all three, primarily because in her own opinion the Bedfords' ball was just the thing to shake the girl out of her apathy, an opinion, one need hardly state, heartily endorsed by Lord Tristram.

However, to her companions' surprise it was found that Francesca had no intention of refusing the Bedfords' kind invitation, and following her initial somewhat feeble protest about whether or not it would be fitting for her to attend, she grew almost excited at the prospect, or at least as near to registering emotion as the Baroness and his lordship had witnessed since her arrival in London, amply testified by the fact that throughout the preceding week to the gala occasion not once was the word 'Kleine' heard to escape her lips.

Even so, she conducted her toilette with the essential decorum and ultimately emerged from her dressing closet modestly though exquisitely gowned in a trained sacque of silver grey lustring, plain and unadorned except for a minimal trimming of white lace upon the sleeves and respectably-low décolletage. Her red hair, unpowdered and glinting like polished copper, was discreetly concealed beneath a fetching white lace cap but for a wayward ringlet which hung down onto her left breast; meanwhile the only jewelry she wore were her wedding and betrothal rings, and her face was devoid of cosmetics.

Lord Tristram arrived in Clarges Street at the appropriate hour dressed as always in the pink of ton, his slender figure tastefully yet colourfully arrayed in a coat of flowered satin, with yellow satin waistcoat sprigged with gold and styled in the new double-breated fashion sporting lapels. His hair was liberally powdered and arranged in a bag à *la pigeon*, secured with a rosette instead of the customary bow, to match the rosettes adorning his red-heeled shoes, while the purest white lace flounced at chin and wrists, and a silver fringed cocked beaver sat his curls at the precise angle.

Thus it was that Francesca found herself entering the grand portals of Bedford House which dominated Bloomsbury Square, with Lord Tristram on her left and Lady Brindley—her full-blown figure appositely clad in amber brocade, and thinning hair duly frizzed and powdered—upon her right. Having entered, the three followed the continuous stream of illustrious guests through to the glittering ballroom where the dancing was already underway, if the stately strains of a minuet were anything to go by.

Lady Kleine fought bravely to smother her gasps in awe of the splendours which met her vision for it was considered shockingly provincial to register surprise at *anything*, and the most unforgivable *faux pas* to be heard actually gasping. Nevertheless, it did not prevent her eyes deviating from right to left in order not to miss a single item—at the tall Corinthian columns, blinding crystal chandeliers, rich embroidered hangings, and flunkeys clad in the orange livery of the Bedford household who seemed to be everywhere at once.

Upon being presented to their Graces Francesca bestowed her lowest and most dignified curtsy, first to the rather stern faced Duchess, then to the plump gout-ridden Duke who, though lacking in height, looked every inch the Lord High Constable of England which he was recently become. Next to their Graces stood their son and heir, the ill-fated Francis, Marquess of Tavistock, and next to him was his enchanting sister, Caroline, the new Duchess of Marlborough, accompanied by her Duke.

Having duly paid her respects Francesca suffered herself to be led to one of the many purple plush upholstered chairs circuiting the walls of the magnificent ballroom, where she apprehensively established herself, her eyes still darting hither and thither at the impressive gathering for she had never in all her years attended anything quite so grand, even in company with her dear departed parents for then she had been too young. Had she spared a thought for herself at this moment she might have experienced a degree of embarrassment arrayed thus in her plain gray against such a lavish background; but it was this very simplicity coupled with her extraordinary beauty which made a refreshing contrast to the overdressed, overpainted and patched guests, all fittingly bespangled as the occasion warranted, and adorned in every hue from variegated purple to cloth of pure gold.

As dancing was out of social bounds to my Lady Kleine and Lady Brindley should have found it a physical impossibility, there seemed little else to do but remain seated as they were and partake of the refreshment which Lord Tristram procured with clockwork regularity while the Baroness kept the young girl's interest nicely simmering by indicating to her eager eye various persons of importance, for example, Lords March, Eglinton, Edgecumbe and Palmerstone; the Queensberrys, Hydes, Northumberlands, and the Graftons, not to mention the incorrigible 'Jemmy Twitcher' and the infamous Sir Francis Dashwood, together with a handsome proportion of French aristocracy who had crossed the Channel to swell the ranks.

Francesca's eye suddenly alighted upon the Macaroni set and she emitted a peal of laughter at their ludicrous apparel, laughter which delighted the Baroness. Yes, Lord Tristram was also delighted to hear his lady laugh again, though not as delighted as he might have been for her laugh was empty, mirthless, as if it were merely a cheerful veneer for the benefit of her companions, a veneer she would discard upon quitting Bedford House. Moreover, her eyes remained lack-lustre and hollow, which served only to confirm his suspicions, and until that essential sparkle lit up her beautiful green eyes he could not own her truly happy.

"Good gracious, my dear! Just look yonder at my Lady Telford," exclaimed the Baroness in censorious tone, tapping Francesca's arm with her filigree fan to claim her attention. "How positively outrageous of her to squeeze her great bulk into a gown *that* size. I do declare if she were to sneeze she'd be out of the garment altogether!"

Lady Kleine strove to stifle her giggles. "I protest, your ladyship," chuckled she in turn, "that Miss Lavinia Kinghorn looks every whit as ridiculous." Attention now revolved to the left where the young damsel in question tripped gaily down the line of dance unaware that she was the source of considerable amusement. "I vow if her fashionable rainbow petticoats were any shorter and the neck of her gown any lower she'd be clad in nothing but a sash."

As the merriment abated Lord Tristram chose to comment, while he dispensed the fourth supply of cordial to the ladies then seated himself upon Francesca's nether side. "Aha, I spy some late arrivals."

"Late indeed!" seconded the Baroness with a disparaging glance at the party of four poised upon the threshold. "Fortunately the Prince has not yet arrived otherwise the fat would certainly have been in the fire."

"Two gentlemen of some consequence, and their ladies," my lord saw fit to enlighten them amiably, as if the Baroness and Francesca did not have the ability to see for themselves. "I believe the one in puce is my Lord Shackleton—er—not certain about the other . . ." he pondered, sipping his Burgundy with due deliberation.

"Bah! Gentlemen serve no purpose accompanied by ladies," grumbled the Baroness as if she had half a mind to seize one of the gentlemen for herself. "We've females in abundance already!"

"Hm, very fetching females all the same, ma'am, if I may say so," approved his lordship subjecting the damsels in question to a long dedicated scrutiny through his silver framed eye-glass—to ejaculate of a sudden: "Good gad! Stap me if it ain't the Lady Fanny Birthwaite! Well, may I be eternally—"

Precisely what his lordship was destined to be, alas, will never be known for at that moment the major-domo thudded his gold-knobbed staff to command order and enunciate in stentorian tones:

"The Most Honourable the Marquis of Shackleton and the Marchioness of Shackleton." A further thud, thud, resounded to present: "The Comte de Roqueleux and the Lady Frances Birthwaite."

"Roqueleux?" No, apparently the Baroness did not know the name either and was about to solicit particulars of the striking French Comte from the wizened dowager on her left when Francesca's glass fell from her bewildered grasp to shatter into fragments upon the floor,

187

claiming her companions' attention to the exclusion of all else, even handsome French counts.

"Francesca, child! What's amiss?" exclaimed the Baroness in concern, as a lackey hastened to remove the broken glass and pool of cordial at their feet. "Good heavens! You look as if you've seen a ghost!"

Precisely how near the truth she had struck the Baroness had no way of knowing as Francesca sat petrified, her eyes protruding, riveted to the group in the doorway while her lips worked pitifully to make utterance but to little effect, and her bosom heaved as if she were choking to death.

"Fran, what is it? What's wrong?" burst out Lord Tristram, his anxiety waxing amain with Lady Brindley's.

"S-Syl . . . vestre . . ." gasped she, almost inaudibly.

"Who?" prompted his lordship wondering if he had heard correctly. "Sylvestre? Sylvestre who?"

But Lady Kleine was incapable of further sound. In her present state of health it was demanding all her strength and physical resources to fight the emotional conflict raging within for her entire body seemed to be running out of control. Suddenly the blood was pounding furiously through her veins, head, and heart, until everything spun madly, as if the whole world had shot off its axis.

However, no one privileged to be at Bedford House that night would have thought it particularly strange that she should gape thus at the French Comte, for many were doing the same. Indeed, the man stood out in marked contrast against the gay butterfly colours of the gathering, with his powder-free raven black hair and full skirted coat of sumptuous black Genoa velvet, relieved only by the silver embroidery upon the pockets and huge cuffs, and the finest white lace ruffles. Granted, he was French; nevertheless, he was tall, fashionably dark, and handsome in a sinister way. But above all he was a mystery, and there was nothing society adored half as much.

No, it couldn't be Sylvestre—he was dead! Dead! As dead as Clarence! Gone, lost to her forever!—Francesca continued reiterating to herself, defying the mortal evidence confronting her. Yet there he was in the flesh, bowing, smiling and complimenting the ladies as if he had languished at court all his life—*her* Sylvestre; the man whose child she had borne, for whom Clarence had fretted and died, and for whom she had suffered the agonies of hell—there he was before her eyes, dancing attendance upon this Lady Fanny with all the audacity and nonchalance of the practised seducer he was.

Lord Tristram also gaped, not at the Frenchman but at Francesca who was coming to life beneath his gaze; the *real* Francesca; the Francesca he had known and loved all those many months ago was now materialising. It was not a forced reaction in any way but one so natural that she was quite oblivious to it, yet her heart was palpitating like a war-drum and her green eyes were suddenly alight with that inner radiance he had long sought to no purpose. And she was trembling violently with the confused emotions of shock, disbelief, joy, horror, but dominating over all he sensed a vital yearning which was not, apparently, directed at himself. At whom then?—this Frenchman?

The Baroness was every whit as confounded as my lord with whom she exchanged extremely worried looks before reverting her attention to the Comte de Roqueleux, at present bowing graciously over his hostess's multi-ringed fingers, while the alluring Lady Fanny hovered close by his side as if daring anyone to challenge her claim to his affections. However, she was not permitted to hover long as her hand was committed to Lord Tavistock for the gavotte about to commence, commitment she could scarcely refuse which left the Comte conveniently to his own devices alongside the Marquis and his lady.

Meanwhile, Francesca sat with bated breath, her fingers rigid upon the arms of her chair while her eyes remained fixed just as rigidly on that tall sinister figure in black, her being consumed with a mixture of dread and desire; dread, lest he take just one step towards her at this crucial time before she could recover her faculties and strength, for it would require every ounce of spirit and ingenuity she could muster to confront Monsieur in this painfully unprecedented situation; and desire, a desire as insane and unprecedented as the situation, a desire which burst into a flaming passion, flames which leapt inside her, higher and higher, until her whole being was engulfed with a blazing longing, a longing only he could appease.

He was alive! Thanks be to heaven, he was alive!—her heart rejoiced, while the resplendent gathering, Lord Tristram and Lady Brindley all faded into obscurity, leaving only herself and Sylvestre, the ruler of her fate.

And so she sat motionless as the group of three lingered awhile to survey the throng besporting themselves in time to the music.

Here, Lord Tristram eased his restricting lace cravat and stammered agitatedly: "I-I'll—er—procure more refreshment, I think,"—and took himself off while Lady Brindley said nothing but kept her eye as assiduously trained upon Francesca, as Francesca's was upon the Comte.

The group eventually moved away from the entrance, and although Fate did not guide Monsieur's elegant feet directly across the ballroom to Francesca's side it was nevertheless with an uncanny accuracy that the Comte began sauntering round the perimeter of the room in my lady's direction, his eye idly combing the gathering and still to alight upon her, a manoeuvre which threw Lady Kleine into a state of panic. What ought she to do? Swoon? Conceal herself behind the Baroness and trust to good fortune? Or concoct some excuse to beat a swift retreat? No, her legs wouldn't support her from the room! What then? She had to think quickly—he was only a matter of yards away!

The three paused, and she breathed more easily as Lord Shackleton gestured in the direction of the card room on the farther side; but the Comte declined and sauntered on, while Francesca's heart beat more wildly than ever as he drew even nearer, his face fortuitously towards the dancers. Only ten feet . . . eight . . . six— when he turned to overture some comment to his companions. It may have been her austere attire, or the glint of the overhead chandelier upon that long vibrant red ringlet which suddenly arrested his eye and brought him to an abrupt halt; so abrupt in fact that two guests collided with him from behind.

While Monsieur le Comte stared at her in stark stupefaction Lady Kleine braced herself and tried to stare just as fixedly back, doing her level best to rally herself for the confrontation which seemed inescapably imminent and wishing with all her being that she might evaporate into the damask-hung wall behind.

It seemed almost a lifetime that the two stared thus each at the other, insensible to their companions and the surrounding revelry, she marvelling how he came to be miraculously resurrected from the dead, while he wondered what she was doing there at Bedford House besporting herself. The fact that he was able to make utterance before she, did not indicate his astonishment was any the less, but that his ability to discipline his emotions was the stronger.

"Lady Kleine!" he exclaimed, the astonishment pervading his voice. "What do you here?"

Francesca swallowed hard and forced herself by sheer strength of will up onto her feet. When she spoke, however, her voice emerged weak and tremulous though she was surprised it emerged at all.

"M-Monsieur . . . I may well . . . ask you the s-same—" She broke off, raising a feeble hand to her head as if about to faint in all earnest, but before she could do so he stepped swiftly forward and took her arm.

"Come, a breath of air is needed—this room is stifling."

And so saying he guided the Viscountess away with a brief murmured excuse to Lady Brindley whose highest indignation was clearly reflected in her countenance, but before she could voice her disapproval the two were gone.

Francesca suffered Sylvestre to lead her where he would as she had no desire for Lady Brindley, or anyone else, to overhear the intimacies about to be revealed. He led her away from the boisterous ballroom along a wide corridor, neither pausing nor speaking until the noise had receded into the distance, when he drew to a standstill by a velvet upholstered settee upon which he invited her to be seated.

"You have been ill, your ladyship?" he queried rather than stated—somewhat curtly thought she, though his face harboured concern.

"Surely that is not surprising, monsieur," she began when he cut in hastily.

"Ah, the child . . . yes—er—of course."

He fell silent as if debating how to follow this up while bitterness welled inside Francesca at his arrogance and shameful treatment not only of herself and his child, but Clarence! Clarence who had loved him, worshipped him with every sense of his being throughout his entire life which he had finally sacrificed for him; Clarence, who had lain with his precious blood dripping on the floor while he, Monsieur le Comte, was enjoying himself; revelling in his licentiousness with his Lady Fanny Birthwaite! And what of the tribulations she herself had endured? The loss of her son for which she had almost given her own life; and the long torturous months of mourning him dead. Dead! Yet here he was standing before her dressed like the King of France, as if the whole world were exactly the same as he had purportedly left it.

"Where's Clarence?"

The question struck her like a thunderbolt. "Clarence?" she faltered stupidly.

"Madam, you gape at me as if I were a Hottentot! I repeat, where is my Lord Viscount? Why do you court scandal and gossip by coming here alone?"

Despite his objection my lady could not contain her amazement. Surely he wasn't . . . he couldn't be in complete ignorance of the ghastly events?

"I-I beg your pardon, Monsieur le Comte, but Clarence is—is—"

A pained expression crossed his face. "*Sacré diables*, I trust you have not deserted him, Francesca," he appealed to her with a sigh, relaxing a little and becoming more human. "I appreciate more than anyone how trying he can be but—"

"Sylvestre," she broke in when able, "Clarence is . . . dead."

The Comte stared at her, stunned, as if he had gazed upon the Gorgon and turned to granite, while her calamitous words slowly penetrated his brain, to sear it like branding irons.

"He was interred in the family vault little over a year ago," she clarified with due reticence at perceiving the drastic effect of her disastrous news.

Still he stood stricken with revulsion and disbelief, before he gasped at length: "*C'est impossible!* He can't be dead! He was young, virile, and despite his affliction was the epitome of health!"

"I'm afraid he did not die of natural causes, monsieur."

"An accident?"

"No—he took his life."

The Comte unleashed a groan and closed his eyes as Francesca burst out, unable to hold back any longer.

"Oh Sylvestre! Where on earth have you been all this while? Where were you when he was ill? Why, why didn't you come when he needed you most?"

"He killed himself on *my* account?" he recoiled in abject horror.

Francesca cursed her careless tongue for she would have spared him this despite all. Having blundered into the trap there seemed nothing else for it but to confess the whole sordid truth as sympathetically as possible.

"We were informed of your death, sir, that you had been slain in a duel, and which is why I continue to gape at you in astonishment for I cannot . . . credit that . . ."

"Dear heaven!" He turned away with a blistering oath, unable to face her at this crippling blow. "Spare me the rest, ma'am, I entreat you! I begin to under . . . stand."

But the Comte did not suffer alone. The most racking anguish lacerated Francesca's heart to see the Frenchman, always the quintessence of self-assurance, so stricken down with grief; the man she loved, adored, with every fibre of her being! Oh how she longed to weep for him, console him, in this his blackest hour when he stood alone, bowed over a huge ornate marble-topped side-table, his face averted as he gripped the table with his long white fingers.

Thus Sylvestre laboured beneath the emotional tide, for although he had endured much over the years on Clarence's behalf he had never endured anything as devastating as this excruciating agony which battled fiercely to control him and overthrow his own ruthless self-imposed standard of discipline. Never in his life had he come so perilously close to betraying himself before a lady, and the experience was far from pleasant.

"I'm profoundly . . . sorry, Sylvestre," she endeavoured to convey her sympathy. "I should not have broken the news so bluntly, but I thought you knew . . . that you had perhaps read—"

"What do you take me for, madam?" he rounded on her furiously. "Do you presume for one moment I should have stayed away from Kleine—knowing *this*?"

In the dire circumstances Francesca forgave him the brutal rebuff as soon as it left his lips.

"Monsieur, the whole tragic incident might have been avoided had not my lord's attorney, Mr Penrose, informed us quite emphatically that a man named Villennay had perished by the sword in an affair of honour. Do you tell me he was in error?"

He shook his head helplessly. "No, he was not mistaken," he confessed at length. "A Villennay did depart this life in like manner . . . my elder brother, Raoul. Hence my unexpected elevation to the title."

My lady was at a loss whether to congratulate or commiserate with him for clearly Clarence's martyrdom was set at nought. It was tragic enough for him to have died for a cause in the first place but for that cause to been no more than a cruel quirk of Fate was tragedy indeed.

"We searched the length and breadth of England and France, monsieur, to no avail," she informed him, trying to quell the bitterness in her voice. "Would you be good enough to tell me where you were?"

The question asserted him and he drew himself up to his full height, shook out the Mechlin lace beneath his chin and swung round to confront her with a swish of whaleboned skirts—the old arrogant Sylvestre de Villennay once more in evidence.

"Aye, ma'am, I'll tell you where I was," he flung back with blistering disdain.

"With your family in France?"

"No—fettered in the Fleet!"

She gasped aloud.

"Well might you gasp, mistress," he mocked derisively.

"Y-You were arrested, for debt?"

"*Vraiment*! Incongruous is't not, that it should be a debt which Clarance himself had refused to pay?"

"But he did not have his son, monsieur," she challenged swiftly, leaping to Clarance's support not because she thought he had been in the right of it but because of the way Mr Villennay had stormed out of Kleine and deserted them both, the remembrance of which would persecute her till her dying day.

The habitual sneer curled his lip. "You no doubt appreciate, ma'am, that a son specifically is something even *I* could not guarantee. Apart from which, Clarance was given ample warning that I should quit Kleine the instant it was established you were with child—and he agreed; undoubtedly because he had no intention of keeping his promise, then or ever! I swear on sacred oath, he refused to pay my debts for one reason only—to keep me at Kleine; so I defied him and left. And make no mistake, mistress, he knew well enough what my fate would be when he watched me ride away—yes, he who loved me, worshippped me and vowed he'd give his life for me adamantly refused *his* aid when *I* needed it most."

"Am I to assume from this, sir, that you did not wish to be found? That your personal animosity superseded all else—even my lord's life?"

The Comte reined in his temper with commendable effort. "No, your ladyship! I would scarce knock on the door of the Fleet and demand hospitality! Ye gods! Do you have any conception of life inside that abominable rat-infested hole if one has not the wherewithal to buy privileges, and if one has the added misfortune of being French? How one is reduced from the status of human to that of animal—stripped of pride, self-respect, even one's very clothes?"

Francesca choked back her revulsion.

"Fear not, ma'am," he appended with scathing condescension. "I shall gallantly spare you the more lurid details."

"What of your creditors? Surely they knew of your whereabouts?"

"Pray, why should they help me escape from a prison they had long striven to put me in?" he countered sardonically. "I was every kind of fool for setting foot in London in the first place but I had with me several thousand I anticipated might keep the duns at bay a month or two, anyway, until I had recouped my losses at the tables. But I anticipated wrong. Ha! My miserable pittance barely settled the interest. And all those long agonizing months Clarence lay pining for me, ma'am, he might have ransomed me from my dark dank prison cell any time he chose and had me at Kleine within the week."

The most harrowing doubt began to circulate within Francesca at his words in which there was more than an element of truth. Was not it possible that Clarence had known yet had chosen to suffer simply because his insufferable pride would not allow him to admit defeat and grovel? Moreover, had he taken his life, not for love of Sylvestre, but because the terrible guilt obsessing his conscience would not allow him to live?

"And were you ultimately released, monsieur?" she asked, greatly subdued, gazing down forlornly at the ivory fan in her hands.

"No. I effected an escape along with other poor wretches, and fled to France where I discovered I was become Comte with wealth to command. *Il est trés ironique, n'est ce pas?*"

"But did not the French authorities inform Mr Penrose—that you were at least alive?"

He shrugged indifferently. "To what avail, ma'am? Wouldn't it have been all too pitifully late?"

She bit her lip to prevent herself crying out that it would not have been too pitifully late to have spared her the unbearable grief which had been her tragic lot, believing him dead. Instead, she fired a shot at the root of her suffering.

"Monsieur, would you tell me the reason, the true reason, why you felt obliged to leave Kleine so abruptly?"

His eyes wavered and fell, veiled by the sweeping black lashes.

"You already have my reason," he murmured.

"But surely you could have stayed to see the fruit of your labours and your child duly born?"

"Twenty-five years at Kleine is more than enough for any man."

"Nevertheless, sir, a further six months or so could not have made a deal of difference," she challenged doggedly, driving him to confessing the reason she had long painfully suspected. "By which time Clarence might have been more amenable and ready to come to terms for he would have had his son."

A piercing silence greeted this, before he prompted hesitantly: "You had a . . . son?"

"Yes."

He seemed embarrassed. Odd indeed, for Sylvestre de Villennay and embarrassment were strange bedfellows.

"I did not wish to see the child. Moreover, there *was* another reason—you are right—something more personal. I had to go when I did. It was imperative."

"A reason which directly concerned me, monsieur, did it not?"

"In what way precisely, ma'am?"

"Do not gammon me, sir!" she accused hotly, all the suffering and bitter resentment of the past two years flaring up within her, bringing her to her feet. "Admit truthfully that you left in such haste because I was beginning to repel you!"

One thick black eyebrow shot up in question. "*You* repel *me*?"

"Yes! Confess, Monsieur le Comte, how you did find the task for which you were hired most distasteful, that in comparison with your Lady Fanny Birthwaite I was but poor entertainment!" And having thus fired her Parthian

197

shot she stood with head upflung and bosom rising and falling tumultuously in evidence of the storm brewing anew within.

But her emotional storm brewed no fiercer than that of Monsieur le Comte whose black eyes flared in twin orbs of living fire, and the set of his jaw grew murderous as he stepped forward. Francesca froze in sudden fear as the storm rose to its height ready to burst from him.

However, burst it did not for there appeared most opportunely an irate intruder in the form of Lord Tristram Fortescue who had waited, cordial in hand, a veritable age for his lady to return, and now spying her in company with the dubious Frenchman whose very expression and stance totalled malicious intent in his lordship's reckoning, his sense of outrage knew no bounds.

"Hold, sirrah!" cried he, arresting the Comte with bumptious air. "What d'you think you're about, damme?" He then jerked round to face his lady whose countenance was sufficient to confirm his worst fears and enrage him the more. "Francesca, what goes on here? Rot me, the fellow looked about to assault you!"

"I-I vow you are quite mistaken, Tristram," she laughed tremulously, in an effort to reassure him that despite the evidence before his eyes all was well, and hopefully avert further hostility. "The Comte is a very old and valued friend."

The words almost choked her and sounded so, which did little to ameliorate my lord's rampaging suspicions as he exchanged strained civilities with the Comte.

"Lord Tristram Fortescue, brother o' the Marquess o' Wrixborough—er—somewhere in Staffordshire, I believe," he completed on a deflating note for he visited the family seat but rarely.

He straightened up to find himself thrown at a disadvantage with a stranger confronting him, for the Comte had undergone a startling transformation. The storm had vanished and before my lord stood the nonchalant exquisite he had seen arriving half an hour ago, and who was indolently surveying him through insolent black eyes while an equally insolent smile flitted about his lips.

"Ah, Lord Tristram Fortescue," he rolled the name round his tongue, his voice complementing his new humour. "My lady's current diversion, if I interpret it right."

"Devil take ye, sir!" Lord Tristram took heated umbrage at this derogatory inference. "I'll have you know that Lady Kleine has done me the unprecedented honour of accepting my hand in marriage."

The Comte stiffened and his eyes narrowed so imperceptibly that it might have been an illusion.

"My felicitations, young sir," he drawled, his demeanour bordering on insult as he flung Francesca a contemptuous glance. "My Lady Kleine does not allow the grass to grow beneath her dainty feet."

"Take care, Monsieur le Comte," cautioned his lordship, averse to the other's tone and manner. " 'Pon rep, your remarks grow offensive. Her ladyship has been gravely ill and I'll suffer no one to disquiet her. It so chanced that I was on hand to proffer consolation when she needed it, which is more than be said in *your* favour, old friend or no!"

"Methinks I stand rebuked," smiled the Comte, unruffled, turning to incline his head in condescension to Francesca. "Permit me to volunteer my profoundest condolences upon your tragic loss, ma'am, though I am persuaded in the circumstances it could be nought but a blessed release."

"You are very cruel, monsieur," she murmured, wounded to the core.

"Faith, at least we are agreed upon that, my lady. I declare, inflicting torment upon my fellow mortals has been my sole fulfilment in life. However, it may gratify you to know that I am to pay due retribution for my sins, for as Comte 'tis also my unhappy lot to tread the nuptial path and beget an heir. *Parbleu*, 'twould appear I'm doomed to expend my entire life begetting heirs—would it not, your ladyship?"

Francesca crumbled within as one by one he rammed each shaft home with punishing accuracy though why he should choose to wound her so she could not begin to reason, unless he held her responsible in part for

Clarence's death. Or was it simply that the traumatic news was cauterizing his soul, forcing him to seek a scapegoat? And she was the most convenient goat to hand.

Meanwhile Lord Tristram could do little but swivel his powdered head between his lady and the Comte, equally dubious concerning the latter's motives yet finding nothing he could quite put his finger on when the fellow beguiled his speech with ambiguities and smothered it beneath sangfroid and apparent *bonhomie*. In consequence he was in some dilemma concerning the part he ought to play or rather whether he really ought to play any as he cherished little inclination to meet Monsieur le Comte in the cold grey mists of dawn at Lincoln's Inn Fields, for if the scoundrel manipulated a sword as deftly as he did a snuff-box there was no question who would come off worst.

But salvation descended in the ravishing person of my Lady Fanny who in a flurry of spangles, silk petticoats, fluttering hands and pinked pride burst upon the group at this vital moment.

"Sylvestre, darling!" she cried in high dudgeon, seizing the Comte's left arm possessively as if she were already his Countess. "Come! His Royal Highness is about to arrive."

A fanfare of trumpets sounding at this point would seem to indicate that Prince Edward had already done so.

"I shall come directly, Fanny," he responded dryly, his sinister regard not deflecting from Francesca.

"But His Royal H-High . . . ness . . . ?" Lady Fanny's indignant cry gradually tailed off as she sensed her darling Sylvestre was taken by a strange humour and was not to be provoked.

Nevertheless, she refused to abandon him to a female almost as ravishing as she herself—even if the attire were woefully drab and unbecoming—and so she clung to his velvet clad arm all the tighter while pouting petulantly at the company like a spoilt child threatened to be deprived of its favourite toy, her haughty gaze dwelling disparagingly upon her rival on whose behalf she was not going to be ignored.

"Your son, ma'am," the Comte then resumed from Lord Tristram's intrusion. "How does the child?"

"He does not do at all, monsieur," she rejoined with all the asperity she could muster, for the vainglorious Lady Fanny with her flagrantly exposed bosom was not going to be granted the satisfaction of seeing her weaken. "He lived but five hours."

Monsieur seemed to pause an interminable time during which Francesca could feel his gaze focused upon her as if willing her to look at him but she fought the impulse and kept her eyes discreetly lowered upon the hem of her gown, while my Lady Fanny and Lord Tristram stood mutely by in a mixture of confusion and suspicion as the discourse drifted meaninglessly over their fashionable coiffures.

"Dare I say it, my lady?" ventured the Count anon. "That it must also have been *une bonne délivrance*?"

This was the cruellest shaft of all. She had loved her son and had wept unconsolably over his tiny lifeless body, a body which had been but a poor return for the abundance of passion his father had donated to his conception. She could endure no more of his barbs. Her vision began to grow misty but still she steeled herself, determined not to break down and weep before him and his paramour.

"How, sir?" she cried out, battling to control her voice. "When I wanted the child more than anything in the world?"

"*Pourquoi, madame*?" he parried blandly. "So that he might succeed as tenth Viscount Kleine?"

If Francesca could endure the Comte's blighting rebuffs Lord Tristram certainly could not.

"Guard your infernal speech, Frenchman!" he sprang forward to charge him, hand clenched upon bejewelled sword-hilt. "I will not stand idly by while you sharpen your vip'rish tongue on my lady!"

"No, Tristram!" Francesca stayed him with an anxious hand as Lady Fanny emitted a scream and sought refuge behind the Comte. "Nothing will be achieved by violence—"

"You loved your son yet you would have had him survive to be raised at Kleine?" The Comte's voice cut through the commotion like a knife, silencing everyone. "You would have sacrificed the child limb by limb, bone by bone to that accursed place? You would have raised him within its satanic walls, thriving upon its evil aura until he became another Clarence Fennistone? No, madam, your son is better dead for was not he conceived in hatred, under the influence of the devil himself?"

"No, Monsieur le Comte!" she hurled at him, tears now running freely down her face. "He was conceived in love, for I loved his father as I did him—with all my heart!"

For the third time that evening Monsieur le Comte was stricken with incredulity, but it was the very first time in his entire life that he found himself utterly bereft of words and unable to summon any apt response. He alone was able to appreciate the full literal meaning behind this declaration which merely followed the rest of the discourse over the powdered heads of the gullible onlookers, a discourse which for the most part remained incomprehensible to them for indeed, what reason had my Lord Tristram and my Lady Fanny to suspect that the ill-fated child of Lady Kleine had been begot by a man other than her erstwhile spouse? Least of all that that same man should be the very French nobleman standing brazenly by their sides?

Needless to say, one greatly doubts if they would have stood by quite so calmly, glancing with no more than a modicum of concern and curiosity between the two leading characters in the drama, before Francesca uplifted her petticoats and with a body-rending sob fled the scene with a bewildered Lord Tristram hastening on her heels.

Seventeen

It is doubtful if even the refugees from the Great Fire of 1666 abandoned London more quickly than did Francesca that same night despite the witching hour and its accompanying darkness.

Lord Tristram, suspecting his lady might resort to impetuous action, had dogged her sedan all the way back to Clarges Street where he whined in piteous accents outside her boudoir door while she applied herself within, changing her apparel for the road, and the maids packed her trunks and valises with feverish haste. Her coach and six had already been requisitioned and was due to be at the door within the half-hour by which time it was expected Lady Brindley would be returned, and she would duly express her profound regrets to her friend for such a sudden departure, together with her overwhelming gratitude for having her stay.

Not surprisingly, when Francesca eventually emerged from her room to bravely face her swain there ensued a scene much akin to that at the beginning but with the roles conspicuously reversed and she confessing in all contrition that she found herself unable to wed his lordship, after all, while his lordship fretted, fumed and pleaded as volubly as *she* had done two years ago for further consideration, pronouncing her upset, distraught, unaware of what she was saying, doing, and after a week or so would see things differently. But, alas, my lord's supplications were as ineffective as Francesca's had been upon that momentous day in the park for she had but one objective—to return to Kleine with all possible speed and seek the solace and seclusion it had to offer in the rugged grandeur of its environment and for which she suddenly longed with an all-consuming desperation. This, despite the implementation of every wile and dodge my lord boasted in his repertoire, was the only reason she would volunteer for her abrupt departure and firmly declined to say whether or not she would ever return to London.

Kleine was invincible! She had fought the battle and lost. She had fled from chamber to chamber, castle to Dower House, and Dower House to London, a distance of three hundred miles yet there was no escape. She could flee to the other side of the world but she would never conquer the spell of Kleine which hung over her like a curse, drawing her irresistibly, refusing to let her go or forget; compelling her to admit defeat and return to perish beneath its battle-scarred walls and grotesque overhanging towers, just as Clarence had. Even now she could feel the castle's fatal charm drawing her more powerfully than ever before, a force she was too weak to gainsay any longer and which she must finally own victorious. No longer did she care if she met her doom, nor languished cursed beneath its ruined towers in bitterness and heartache for the rest of her days, repining her loss and dreaming of what might have been.

Why, oh why, couldn't Fate have allowed her to remain content in her grief and ignorance? Why had Sylvestre to be at Bedford House on this particular night simply to prove he was just as unattainable as if he had been slain, and that he despised her just as intensely? But the man she had encountered at Bedford House wasn't Sylvestre, not *her* Sylvestre. No, he was merely moulded in his likeness, for the real Sylvestre was at Kleine—Kleine! The two were inseparable. The castle exuded every facet of his personality as if he had breathed his life into it until every crude roughened stone and turret were impregnated with his being. Long after he had gone she had continued to sense his presence, dominating over all as if he had never left; and it was this very spirit of the bygone Sylvestre, the Sylvestre she had known and loved, which was calling her back—a call she must obey.

As foreseen, the Baroness was not long to follow the two to Clarges Street where she was desolate upon finding Francesca so adamantly set upon leaving. Lady Brindley did not doubt that Monsieur le Comte was largely instrumental—upon Lord Tristram relating all that had transpired in the corridor at the Bedfords' ball—and concerning whom she may have put one or two pertinent questions to the Viscountess had not good manners forbidden her so to do. Indeed, the Baroness and Lord Tristram were not too kindly disposed towards the Count for, in one brief hour, undoing all their good work and ruining their cherished plans for Francesca's future.

Right up till the final hour when his lady's coach and retinue rumbled off down the cobbled street his lordship toiled unceasingly in his efforts to assure her that what she was about was quite alien to the course of nature and true love. Lady Brindley, on the other hand, was eventually able to accept the sad news with good grace, possibly because she was older than my lord and her entire future happiness was not at stake, and stated that whereas she would sorely miss her former companion, she understood her need to be alone awhile but hoped most earnestly that she would see her in Clarges Street the following season; a wish fervently seconded by his lordship though he was naturally loth to wait so long. Thus the Viscountess departed, leaving a thunderstruck Lord Tristram Fortescue gaping after her coach and six, unable to believe she had actually gone.

Francesca could not afterwards recall the journey back to her Northumberland home except that it seemed to endure forever and was exactly like the journey thence apart from her change in spirit from anticipation and excitement to bitter disillusionment. Nevertheless, she considered herself fortunate that she should compass the three hundred miles and sustain nothing more grievous than a raging headache, to arrive at the Dower House upon the evening of the fifth day whereupon an extraordinary feeling of welcome assailed her, as if she were back where she truly belonged; and she felt almost happy, the nearest she had been to experiencing that elusive emotion for some tolerable while.

Throughout the journey she had sensed the challenge of the castle growing stronger until upon arrival she sensed it with overwhelming force, a force she continued to struggle against for the sun was setting and darkness would be upon them within the hour.

She supped then adjourned to her bedchamber, but did not retire; and when Martha attended her to help her undress she dismissed the girl only to question her action afterwards, namely, why she should do so when she was so exceedingly tired and the bed so inviting. Instead she wandered restlessly about her chamber, tensed, irritable, nervous, unable—or unwilling—to say why though deep, deep down she knew she was deceiving no one, and that if she retired to the haven of her bed she would suffer no peace of mind unless she first of all proved that the castle was not the source of her discontent. It would do no harm to but take a look.

Off she sped, quickly and quietly, not pausing until she reached the west wing, and rushing up the stairs to the small landing window, flung wide the casement, then gasped!

The sky was ablaze with fire fading to a molten gold upon the horizon as the sun sank to rest, and there starkly silhouetted stood Kleine Castle in all its gruesome glory, its three unscarred towers jutting to the north, south and east, piercing the vivid skyline like weird fingers uplifted to the heavens and beckoning to her—yes, it was beckoning! She could see it with her own spellbound eyes, sense it in every tingling nerve, and almost hear it calling, coaxing, commanding!

Thus she stood electrified, riveted to the spot, oblivious to the sombre hills on the right and the dark rolling moors on the left, oblivious to everything but the ruin before her which held her inexorably in its power. Everything seemed to stop including her very heart; even time itself. One brief glimpse was all she had wanted; but one brief glimpse was all that was needed for the castle to do its work and seize her in its merciless grip. Even as she gazed upon it she was slowly succumbing. One by one the warnings became manifest; the overwhelming weakness, the trembling, the perspiration upon forehead and neck, followed by an insane desire as her resistance crumbled to Kleine's superior will—drawing, compelling her to come. And as darkness deepened the stronger it grew, and stronger grew her longing for Sylvestre de Villennay for she could still sense his presence there—but suddenly with a terrifying force!

In frenzied haste she returned to her room, not pausing to change from the white sultane in which she had completed the journey for its hoopless petticoats would not impede her progress, and throwing a cloak about her shoulders she crept soundlessly off, procuring a lanthorn and set of duplicate keys to the castle, as she had no wish to disturb Mr Willis the lodge-keeper, and his good dame.

It was almost ten o'clock when Francesca stealthily approached the castle, her heart beating in unison with her quickening breaths and steps as her strained vision outlined in the gathering gloom every rough stone-hewn battlement and turret which really ought to have repelled her when she recalled the horrors which had been enacted within. Soon it loomed over her, a gigantic black grotesque spectre with arms extended eagerly to embrace her and which consumed her with a petrifying fear, dread and nausea, yet which she strove in vain to conquer.

Apprehensively, she pushed open the old weather-beaten side door which groaned a welcome enough to daunt the stoutest spirit; but if Francesca nurtured any intention of evacuating the scene at this stage she was given no choice as a peculiar force seemed to urge her from behind, compelling her through the door into the all-engulfing blackness beyond.

She entered then shivered for it was intensely cold inside despite the time of year, and she drew her cloak more securely about her shoulders. Holding the lanthorn aloft she glanced about her and shivered again, this time not solely on account of the cold. Yes, she knew exactly where she was, and with cautious steps she set off along the narrow passage, picking her way by the dim light which cast all manner of phantom shadows cavorting in her wake. The intense silence was perhaps the most petrifying of all, broken by nothing but the sound of her own breathing, her deafening heartbeat, and the soft swish of her petticoats.

As if by instinct she proceeded from room to room, just as she had done upon Clarence's death, reliving moments of extreme pain and pleasure and in so doing fulfilling a latent masochistic need to suffer the slings and arrows of outrageous—no, not fortune, but love.

Following simply whither her feet would lead she came to the Plantagenet Chamber where she paused a while longer for here the atmosphere was pregnant with the past. Bygone days, spirits and memories swirled about her in a kind of hypnotic dance until she began to believe she could see and hear Clarence and Sylvestre laughing and chatting by the great stone fireplace, and she hastened across to caress its elaborate sculptured surface, as if seeking to reassure herself that it was real and not merely a ghost like the gentlemen; that she was actually there in the flesh and not a ghost too. Suddenly there was a loud thunderous rumble and she leapt back in fright! A deathly quiet followed, and when courage permitted she gingerly raised the lanthorn to illuminate the scene and gasped in astonishment at sight of a huge gaping orifice in the wall to the left of the fireplace, wherein a flight of narrow worn steps wound upwards into an even denser blackness.

Francesca trembled and clutched frantically to the comforting light for it was the only friend she had. Even so, her inherent curiosity urged her forward into the cavity and up the secret stairway. Up and up, round and round she went, clasping her petticoats about her knees lest she trip and fall, until the stairs ended abruptly with a door which could not have been more than four feet high. At the second thrust of her body the door gave way and she stumbled into a room; which room precisely she had no way of telling until she held aloft her lanthorn upon the scene. Something scuffled to the right, like a mouse scurrying to its hole, as an inarticulate cry escaped her for where should she be standing but in that very chamber which evoked the most crucifying yet fondest memories of all, that sacred shrine—the bridal chamber. This was how Sylvestre had gained access to the room without falling prey to her traps and locked doors!

With a gasp of ecstasy—or was it agony?—she all but threw herself across the room towards the bed, the black shadowy phantoms frolicking relentlessly behind. Yes, there it was, the beautiful shell-shaped bed, evocative of those rapturous nights with the man she loved; there it stood, still draped with its love-knots and silver bells, exactly as she recalled it. An asphyxiating sob erupted from her and she swept a tress of hair from her cheek to find her hand emerge wet for she was weeping without even realising it as she gazed upon this familiar scene—oh, so dearly familiar! Here she had learnt what it truly meant to love, to live; her life had been borne anew in the arms of her master. And though many naive women must have fallen victim to his devastating charm, surely none had been more naive than she?

Suddenly overcome by the terrible nostalgia, she extinguished the light and fell prostrate upon the bed in the sympathetic darkness to relinquish herself to her grief, remembrances, and soul-torturing desire; to live again in her demented brain those wondrous moments with de Villennay, the man with whom her fate was so inextricably bound yet who was soon to be inextricably bound to another; to rest her head where his had rested, and lay her body where his had lain. Nowhere on earth did she feel closer to him than here, in this room; and as she lay the castle gradually eroded her will . . . her will to leave . . . and finally, her will to live.

Again she heard a sound and her flesh began to creep as she sensed someone in the room just as she had upon the night Sylvestre had left.

She sat bolt upright in the bed. "I-Is anyone . . . there?" she called out in a pitiful voice, but there was no response.

Why should there be? How could anyone be there? Was her mind finally beginning to crumble beneath the strain of Kleine and all she had suffered? Did she imagine in her sick brain it was Sylvestre coming to love her as he had done all those long, long months ago?

"Fran . . . cesca," came a sudden gasp, like someone exhaling their last breath.

"Who's . . . th-there?" she cried in panic, leaping from the bed and making haste to relight the lanthorn, her fingers shaking and fumbling so much that she wanted to scream.

"Please . . . don't light the candles," groaned the voice—*his* voice?

No, it couldn't be, he was in London! Moreover, it was a voice broken with anguish and despair. In sheer fright she sprang back to the wall in the opposite direction to the sound, her hand clasped over her mouth lest a cry escape her and it further betray her position. Could it be Sylvestre's spirit?—or perhaps the ghost of Clarence come to claim retribution?

"Francesca?" came the voice again, just as tired but a little more urgently, to which, as before, the dire fear and fantasies devouring her being forbad her to respond. "Damnation! She's fainted."

No! No! It couldn't be he! She had finally lost her senses and gone raving mad! All the same, it was very like *his* voice.

"S-Sylvestre?" she probed tremulously. "I-Is it . . . you?"

"Of course it's me, Francesca!" Yes, that was more like him. "Are you all right? I'm sorry if I startled you—I thought you were living at the Dower House—"

"It can't be! I've gone mad!" she reiterated to herself the while. "He's in London and loves another."

"What are you gabbling—catechisms? Good heavens, girl! You can't think I mean to harm you?"

"N-No . . . I can't believe it! I shouldn't have come! I-It's the castle . . . it's haunted . . . you're in London . . . I *must* be mad!"

"No, Francesca, I assure you I am here in the flesh— but only barely." He unburdened a great sigh. "I've ridden long and hard, and *je suis très, très, fatigué* . . ."

Yes, he certainly sounded tired.

"Why? Why? You detest Kleine and couldn't escape from it quick enough. Why should you want to come back?" she cried out hysterically.

"I came to pay my respects to Clarence—"

"Clarence?" she exclaimed with a wild laugh, as if she had never heard the name before. "Of course, Clarence! How silly of me to forget."

He paused, puzzled by her strange reaction, then went on: "—also to recapture the experiences we shared, here, in this room . . . and to . . . to . . ."

"Yes?"

". . . to question your parting statement in London."

Francesca was bereft of words. "Y-You mean, you've ridden all this way simply to ask if I love you?"

"For one grain of your affection, madam, I'd have galloped to the ends of the very earth."

A vibrant thrill shot through her frail body, snatching her breath with it.

"Are you telling me . . . you l-love me . . . in return?" she managed to stammer anon.

"Aye, my lady—and an unholy botch I'm making of it!"

It was too much! It was sheer madness! Her shattered constitution could not stand it! Her poor brain had not yet grown accustomed to the idea that the man was alive and here he was not twenty feet away offering his heart—a scene she had envisaged day and night throughout the last twelve ghastly months until her head reeled with the impact of it. How then was she to know she was not simply dreaming again? How could she trust her mind, a mind which saw castles and doors with laughing ghoulish faces?

And all the madness, terror and hysteria she had battled the while to suppress suddenly burst from her in a fit of frenzied blood-curdling laughter.

"I believed it! Can you imagine? I actually believed it!" she giggled wildly. "And it's all a trick! A horrid fiendish trick of my distempered brain. He's not here after all! There's no one here—no one at all!"

The laughter rose to screaming pitch to stop short on a peculiar choking sound before she fell into a paroxysm of weeping, her body racked with the most heart-rending sobs it had ever been his misfortune to hear from any woman let alone the woman he loved.

"Francesca! Dammit, where are you?" he swore in desperation to reach her, falling foul of footstools, daybeds, and chairs in his path before he reached the windows and heaved with all his might at the thick velvet curtains which descended to the floor, allowing the moonlight to flood into the room and illuminate her pathetic figure huddled down by the bed, while the misery and anguish burdening her soul took savage toll of her mind and body.

In three huge strides he was at her side, sweeping her into his arms, arms strong, powerful and unyielding as the castle itself and which cherished her body to his with a yearning as violent as her own; to strain her to him as if seeking to merge them both into one; craving her with a passion almost savage in its intensity, a passion which blazed in his veins, his hands, his gaze. And with this passion he devoured her lips, her cheeks, her eyes, and finally her lips again, to breathe it into her very blood and pervade her with new life.

"Francesca—dear heart, dear life, I implore you not to weep so!" he besought her at length. "You have nothing to fear . . . I'm here to protect you, to love you—by the death, how I love you!"

Again he sought her lips, trying to convince her that this was reality. Great sobs continued to shiver through her feeble frame but her tears now ceased as her whole being leapt to the master's call, responding instinctively to his familiar touch and abandoning herself utterly to his volcanic desire, his demands, his love. Oh yes! Yes! This

212

was Sylvestre—*her* Sylvestre! No spirit or figment of her imagination could love like this. Those hands, that touch for which her flesh had hungered and her heart had bled; those lips, tenderly nurturing hers one moment and consuming them with a Bohemian, almost brutal, desire the next—oh, how could she doubt for an instant when that precious adored body was pressed to her own as it had been many times before, and that same electrifying thrill was spiralling up and down her spine as his mouth scorched her neck and shoulders.

"Francesca—my dearest, forgive me, I beseech you!" he gasped, choked with passion. "I swear I didn't mean to insult you in London—I can't think what possessed me. Your broadside caught me unawares . . . I was distrait, wild with jealousy that all and sundry should know before I myself. It was inconceivable that you and Clarence, the two people I loved most in all the world and would have lain down my very life for had suffered so heinously because of me and I wasn't even aware of it. I had no idea—I never thought—by Satan, I daren't say what I thought!"

Cloak and cap fell to the floor and pins scattered in every direction as he ploughed his fingers into her beautiful hair to uplift her face and crush her lips beneath his more fiercely than before, as if his passion would never be assuaged—desperately, fervidly, leaving her gasping for air and frenzied with longing for the antidote which he alone was able to administer yet which he significantly chose to deny her, though it racked his self-discipline to unprecedented lengths when the very bed in which he had initiated her in the rites of love stood invitingly behind, and the whole atmosphere of this, the nuptial chamber, was redolent with erotic memories of the past.

"Francesca . . . Francesca . . . how could any man fail to love you?" he breathed amorously in her ear. "Despite the rumours about my supernatural powers, I am but human. Gad! I've been a fool—an unmitigated fool! I should have warned you from the outset. Damn it, I should never have summoned you to Kleine!"

"P-Please . . . don't say such a dreadful thing, Sylvestre," she faltered into his shoulder. "Had I not come to Kleine I should never have known you nor your love."

"Would that have been so tragic?"

"Yes! Yes! I'd never have known what it was to live! Nor what a wonderful place the world could be," she protested passionately, her eyes glistening with adoration and unspent tears as she gazed up into his drawn handsome face. "I swear on all I hold dear, I don't regret a single moment of my life here. The beautiful experiences we shared more than compensate for the suffering I've borne. Even that might not have been so bad if . . . if I'd only known . . . you w-were alive."

Tears threatened once more and he bent his head to still the trembling of her lips with his, to kiss her long and with infinite tenderness—proof that her words had affected him very deeply.

"Nevertheless, Francesca, your life here cannot have been easy," he added at length.

"Not when you'd gone, I must confess," she sighed. "Clarence's strange humours I might have endured, but not the terrible heartache and longing. Oh, how I wanted you, Sylvestre. I really couldn't bring myself to reproach Clarence for fretting the way he did."

" 'S death, child," he groaned into her dishevelled hair. "How could you have longed for one whose soul is branded by the devil, and who thwarted you from the day you arrived? How could your heart and body crave for one guilty of defiling your sweet innocence, who desecrated the sacred shrine of your honour? Above all, how can you love one who has used you so abominably?"

"If you hadn't, Sylvestre, someone else undoubtedly would have done," she parried softly.

The very conception was a dagger in his breast. "I could never have borne it," he gasped in anguish, his arms involuntarily tightening round her as if challenging the castle and all its spirits of evil to do their worst and wrest her from his grasp. "None had greater right than I, not even Clarence. None loved you as I loved you, revered you for the goddess you are. None other could have sensed your tenderest feelings, your reticence, your hopes, fears, and indulged them accordingly. But most of all, my darling, no one was able to appreciate more than I the cost to you in pride and humiliation at being compelled to sacrifice your most priceless gift to a man you openly despised."

She laid her head on his shoulder with her face averted, deriving overwhelming comfort from the feel of his muscular strength beneath her cheek. Never had she known such bliss, such unspeakable contentment.

"Did you love me then, Sylvestre, so long ago?" she murmured wistfully. "Is that why you felt obliged to leave in such haste, without recompense or farewell?"

"Aye, I loved you. Though at first, I confess, 'twas a selfish love. You were a challenge, Francesca! No woman breathing had ever denied me and the more you rebelled the more it whetted my appetite, my desire, until I began to anticipate my ultimate conquest with relish. But I wanted you willingly, to sacrifice yourself on the altar of my arrogance." He winced at the recollection. "I finally cornered you, brought you to your knees, and claimed a resounding victory, alas, the fruits of which were anything but sweet. Yes, it was then I realised I loved you; loved you with every inch of my flesh, every breath of my body, but you were another man's wife—you belonged to Clarence." He heaved a sigh and cherished her still closer to his heart. "It was increasingly difficult by the hour to conceal my true feelings from Clarence. He had me well marked and was observing me closely, suspiciously, calculating how often I looked at you, smiled at you—even the number of words I spoke. He noted the tone of my voice, my expressions, gestures, until I was obliged to be almost uncivil to you in order to convince him that there was no intrigue between us."

Her eyes waxed like full moons. "Was he so *very* jealous of me?"

"So much so, my love, that had I betrayed an inkling of my genuine feeling I believe he would have put period to your existence without the slightest compunction."

His lady shivered in horror and deemed the moment

215

opportune to relate the incident with the whip, appreciating only now how close her end had indeed been.

"I'm sorry, Francesca," he murmured, drawing her over to the window to gaze out upon the hushed moonlit vista where not a soul stirred. "I realised Clarence might seek to heap recrimination for my leaving upon your sweet head but it was a risk I had to take which, even so, was not as great as the risk had I stayed."

He fell silent, uncomfortably silent, for a prolonged while as if reflecting upon his friend's short lamentable life, and when he resumed his voice was strained and barely audible.

"He appeared to develop an affinity with you . . . an affinity he had shared with no one but me . . . I was pleased and felt you might both fare better without me. Alas, little did . . . I realise . . ."

"Poor Clarence," she repined sadly. "He fought most desperately to conquer his weakness, Sylvestre, right to the very last."

Francesca too fell silent as they stood by the narrow latticed window, and at length she thought the topic banished from his mind when a warm tear splashed onto her arm and she realised with a pang of remorse that his suffering ran much deeper than he would have her believe. Oh, how terribly, terribly, wrong Mr Josiah Penrose had been!

"In spite of all, you loved him a great deal . . . did you not, Sylvestre?"

"Yes," His voice was hoarse with emotion and the words seemed to be wrung from him. "I loved him more than is humanly possible for one man to love another . . . but all I could offer was a good wholesome affection which wasn't what he wanted . . . it did not satisfy his physical craving." He too shivered, and glanced up all about the room. "Strange, but I sense his presence devilishly, as if he were still here . . . some . . . where . . ."

Francesca snuggled deeper into the comfort of his embrace and the sudden movement broke the enchantment, drawing his vision from the exquisite artistry of Ricci high upon the ceiling to the eager upturned face of the woman beside him, to gaze upon it rapt in wonder and admiration, bethinking she had never looked more breathtakingly beautiful than at that moment in the half light with the moon's beams glinting in her glorious fiery hair . . . except, perhaps, upon that first crucial night when he had come to fulfil her husband's command and he had found her standing thus in this exact spot; but though she had looked every whit as beautiful there had not been that radiance shining in her eyes, that smile of welcome upon her lips, nor that passionate warmth exuding from every pore of her sensuous flesh.

It was a magic moment, when the feeling stirring deep within them both was conveyed with the senses instead of mere words, and she raised a trembling hand to gently trace the outline of his face, the features she now knew and loved so well and which, significantly, still bore the scars of the emotion he had been giving licence to prior to her intrusion.

"I would not have had you see me in this lamentable state," he whispered as if divining her thoughts. "I intended presenting myself in all my finery at the Dower House tomorrow."

"After spending the night here?"

"Alone," he appended, his tone laden with meaning as he raised her fingers to his lips. "Francesca," he continued softly, preserving the beatific tranquillity, "would you marry me?"

"Yes, Sylvestre," she replied without hesitation, her very heart in her voice and the radiance in her eyes flaring to a wondrous brightness.

"Though I come to you corrupt, my armour tarnished with sin and decadence?"

"Yes! Yes! I care not about the past—only the future."

"Will you wed me now? Tonight?"

Her delectable mouth fell ajar in astonishment. "Tonight? How can we possibly wed tonight, Sylvestre? We have no parson, no licence—"

"You forget, dear one, that Kleine boasts a most advantageous position," he enlightened her with an enigmatic smile.

"I don't understand . . ."

"Look yonder, and tell me what you see," he invited, indicating with a languid wave the magnificent view from the window.

Francesca duly looked but still could not comprehend his meaning. "I see only the Cheviot Hills."

"And beyond?"

"Scotland!" she cried excitedly, her spirit of adventure and romance leaping to the fore as she envisaged galloping in the moonlight to Gretna Green with the man she loved. "Oh Sylvestre! What a wonderful idea! Do you think we really could?"

"I don't see why not. But what about my Lord Tristram?" he rallied her.

"And what of my Lady Fanny?" parried she with beguiling innocence.

He threw her a sidelong glance of utter unconcern with not a flicker of conscience.

"I would have wed her for one reason only, ma'am, a reason which is no longer à *propos.*"

"You speak in riddles, Monsieur le Comte," she rebuked him coquettishly.

He returned a whimsical smile. "Does it not strike you as a most singular coincidence, ma'am, that my erstwhile bride did bear the name Frances, was an outstanding beauty, and sported the longest, reddest hair ever beheld upon a female?—er—other than your own, o'course."

"Sylvestre . . . y-you mean, you would have wed her simply because she looked like me?"

"Aye, though I'm loth to say my Lady Fanny falls far short of her ideal for she can neither sing in key nor ride to hounds. And her conversation bores one absolutely rigid."

"Poor Fanny," chuckled Francesca.

"Poor Tristram," seconded he with like indifference. "I trust one might duly find consolation with the other. Come, my love, let us away—er—if you feel you can survive the journey. 'Tis all of thirty miles and it's not to be forgotten that you have been gravely ill—"

"Nor that you have ridden long and hard all the way

from London, monsieur, and are *très très fatigué*," she bantered him shamefully with an impish giggle which he repaid with a contemptuous raised eyebrow.

"Mock me if you will, saucy chit, but if it's a challenge you want, a challenge you shall have. Procure yourself a horse and I'll race you there!" he declared roundly, setting off towards the door and snatching up his plumed beaver which he clapped on his head.

"For what prize, sir?" she arrested him coyly.

"Prize? Er—choice of bedchamber," he invented on the spur of the moment.

"That choice is already made," she informed him, striving to keep her countenance as she glanced significantly in the direction of the nuptial bed.

"Here!" he ejaculated aghast. "Francesca, why? What the devil for?"

"Please don't goggle at me like that, Sylvestre. You are the *last* person who needs to be told precisely what couples do in a bedchamber when they have just been wed."

"Aye, but here?" He glanced all round with a grimace. "Where the very air is alive with the most excruciatingly painful memories."

"Indeed, so excruciatingly painful, Monsieur le Comte, that I would have you remind me most poignantly once again, omitting not a single sordid detail."

The disarming smile she loved so well hovered around his lips.

"Am I to understand, ma'am, that t'was not excruciatingly painful after all? Mayhap, even enjoyable?"

"Mayhap it was," she countered mischievously.

Her heart missed a beat as the old wicked gleam flared in his dark eyes which suddenly held hers captive just as they had upon their first calamitous encounter in the round drawing-room.

"Do not overlook the fact that you were then Clarence's wife, sweetheart, and as such I had vowed not to take nor bestow more than was necessary to accomplish our aim. This time you may not be spared. This time you will be *my* wife and I shall be at liberty to demand all I wish." The gleam intensified and her heart dissolved beneath the intoxication of his black devouring gaze. "In fact, I make bold to prophesy, Francesca, that before cock-crow you might find yourself begging for mercy."

"Oh, that I might die such rapturous death, Sylvestre," she whispered, as he sealed his threat with a kiss.

"So be it," he despatched the matter. "We will come here for one night, and one night only. Agreed? I dare not risk my heir being begot in this infernal clime."

He released her to retrieve the cloak which he draped about her shoulders as she cleared her throat, apprehensively.

"Er—Sylvestre?"

"Madam?"

"Could I . . . I-I mean, would you guarantee me a son . . . the same as the one I l-lost?—with raven black hair . . . a son exactly like you?"

His lips twitched irrepressibly. "My lady, I guarantee you not only a son the living replica of myself, but that there will be the very devil to pay if he's not. Moreover, he will be born on my native soil, at the Château de Roqueleux in the heart of the Loire Valley."

"Another castle, monsieur?"

He drew himself up to the pinnacle of arrogance and flung her a look of withering disdain.

"*Vraiment, madame*! I trust you have not the unmitigated impudence to liken it to this confounded place."

His lady was commensurately subdued. "Your castle is very beautiful, Sylvestre?"

His arrogance ceded to deep affection. "You won't be disappointed, *ma petite*," was all he replied ambiguously with a knowing wink before guiding her across to the door in preparation to be gone when he paused and cocked his head to one side as if listening intently for something.

Instinctively Francesca listened too and way above in the old ruined towers she heard ever so faintly, not satanic laughter as before, but a gentle sigh as of a balmy breeze, a sigh of utter contentment which might have echoed from her heart. Apparently Sylvestre had heard it too, to comment:

"I sense a wind of change in the place, Francesca, as if the evil spirits had flown. Do you feel it?"

She nodded in agreement as his arm progressed around her shoulders to draw her to him protectively.

"It can't be all bad, I suppose," he opined, more to himself. "I languished here not two hours ago yearning for you as no man has ever yearned for a woman before, praying desperately for you to come to me, willing you to come with all the crucifying ache and longing in my tortured soul, *et voila*, my darling . . . you came."

Francesca looked up into his face and smiled a smile of mutual understanding.

"Yes, Sylvestre . . . I think the castle has forgiven us . . . we have exorcised its evil with our love."

And at length, as the two rode off into the starlit night over the Cheviots, my lady besought her Frenchman to pause a while, to glance back at Kleine Castle basking in the moonlight before it passed from view, and whereas it still resembled a demon's head it no longer seemed evil or frightening. Likewise, along the battlements were arrayed the same rows of grinning teeth as if the castle were laughing; and Francesca laughed too, for the castle was no longer laughing *at* her . . . but laughing *with* her.

About the author

Before she started writing Freda Michel worked as a secretary though her ambition was to become a concert pianist. She holds nine certificates and three diplomas for piano, including the coveted performer's licentiate of Trinity College, London, and several trophies.

Quest for Lord Quayle is Mrs. Michel's fifth novel. Her first novel, *The Price of Vengeance,* won the R.N.A.'s award for a first, unpublished novel in 1975.

Born and educated in Newcastle, Mrs. Michel now lives with her husband and their three sons in Leeds.

Let COVENTRY Give You
A Little Old-Fashioned Romance

DAWN   50049 $1.75
by Tania Langley

LOVE'S DUET   50050 $1.75
by Patricia Veryan

ENDURE MY HEART   50051 $1.75
by Joan Smith

DARK ENCHANTRESS   50052 $1.75
by Sylvia Thorpe

LADY MARGERY'S INTRIGUE   50053 $1.75
by Marian Chesney

THE MASQUER   50054 $1.75
by Denice Greenlea

Let COVENTRY Give You
A Little Old-Fashioned Romance